DARK INDISCRETIONS
SEER DESTINED

SHAKUITA JOHNSON

Dark Indiscretions: Seer Destined
By Shakuita Johnson
Copyright © 2015 by Shakuita Johnson

eBook Edition, License Notes

This eBook is licensed for your personal enjoyment only. This eBook may not be re-sold or given away to other people. If you would like to share this book with another person, please purchase an additional copy for each recipient. If you're reading this book and did not purchase it, or it was not purchased for your use only, then please return to your favorite e-book retailer and purchase your own copy. Thank you for respecting the hard work of this author.
This book is a work of fiction. Names, characters, places, and incidents either are the product of the author's imagination or are used fictitiously. Any resemblance to actual, locations or persons, living or dead, is entirely coincidental.

All rights reserved. Except as permitted under the U.S. Copyright Act of 1976, no part of this publication may be reproduced, distributed, or transmitted in any form or by any means, or stored in a database or retrieval system, without the prior express, written consent of the author.

This book is intended for mature audiences only. It is not suitable for anyone under the age of 18.

ISBN-10: 1508641617
ISBN-13: 978-1508641612

Cover design by Daria Brennan
Editing by Peter Gaskin
Proofreading by Silla Webb
Formatting by Shakuita Johnson
Published by Shakuita Johnson

To my soulmate…may we meet in this life soon.

CONTENTS

Acknowledgments	VII
Word Meanings	VIII
Prologue	Pg # 1
Chapter 1	Pg # 3
Chapter 2	Pg #7
Chapter 3	Pg #15
Chapter 4	Pg #21
Chapter 5	Pg #27
Chapter 6	Pg #33
Chapter 7	Pg #39
Chapter 8	Pg #43
Chapter 9	Pg #51
Chapter 10	Pg #59
Chapter 11	Pg #71
Chapter 12	Pg #75
Chapter 13	Pg #81
Chapter 14	Pg #87
Chapter 15	Pg #91
Chapter 16	Pg #97
Chapter 17	Pg #103

Chapter 18	Pg #111
Chapter 19	Pg #123
Chapter 20	Pg #129
Chapter 21	Pg #135
Chapter 22	Pg #141
Chapter 23	Pg #147
Chapter 24	Pg #153
Chapter 25	Pg #159
Chapter 26	Pg #165
Chapter 27	Pg #169
Chapter 28	Pg #175
Chapter 29	Pg #179
Chapter 30	Pg #183
Chapter 31	Pg #191
Chapter 32	Pg #197
Chapter 33	Pg #203
Chapter 34	Pg #207
Chapter 35	Pg #211
Chapter 36	Pg #217
Chapter 37	Pg #221
Chapter 38	Pg #225
Chapter 39	Pg #229

Chapter 40	Pg #233
Chapter 41	Pg #241
Epilogue	Pg #245
Other Works by This Author	Pg #251
Rumspringa	Pg #253
About the Author	Pg #259

ACKNOWLEDGMENTS

I'll never be able to thank my AMAZING cover artist, Daria Brennan enough. You have once again blown me away with your ability to give me just want I want in a book cover. If you would like to see more of her work, visit her website at http://thebookcoverdesign.tumblr.com/.

To my beta readers, Amber, Jess, and Julie thank you for your continued interest in my work and your suggestions and comments. Your feedback means the world to me.

To my kickass street team <3. Keep doing what you're doing.

To my PAs, Ebony and Heaven thank you! I know I ask a lot but you get the job done.

To my readers, you continue to make Dark Indiscretions what it is. Thank you for sticking it out on this journey with me and demanding the next book in the series.

To my editor, Peter, you rock and thank you!

To the many bloggers, authors, friends, supports, and everything in between that I've met on this amazing writing journey, thank you!

Thank you to everyone who's shared my page, tweets, posts, links, covers, and just anything to do with my books. You are truly appreciated more than you know.

To my family, I love you all! Your support means the world.

And, as always, to my heart Gavin for being you at all times.

WORD MEANINGS

Mystic - part vampyra, part shape-shifting witch

Nyhiya - soulmate, one true love

Dylia - shape-shifting wolves

The Tarnished - name for all supernatural beings, coined by the Mooyer Society

Mooyers - Society whose singular goal is to exterminate the supernatural forces from the world of man

Hyjia – human-cat hybrids

Venefica - witches that control the four basic elements of fire, earth, air, and water

Adducere - the name given to the lead element that a Venefica wields better than the others

One moment can change your life forever
Once moment can make or break you
One moment was all it took to bring together, face-to-face, three people who couldn't have been more different
Secrets, lies, betrayals, and centuries-old curses, three lives on a collision course to destruction

PART ONE

ISOBELLE

PROLOGUE

MASSACHUSETTS, 1972-1986

Bethany Spears met the love of her life at twelve-years-old. Her crush had just moved to Massachusetts with his family, and he was the cutest boy she had ever seen. His name was Cassidy Mina. As soon as she looked into his hazel eyes, she knew right then that she was going to marry him. He was tall for his age, lanky, and had a nest of black, messy hair on his head. It didn't hurt that his smile cut the cutest dimples into his cheeks. She loved to see him smile. She had wavy, dark brown hair and cocoa eyes that lit up every time she saw him.

Lucky for her, his family had moved next door to hers the summer before they were both scheduled to start the sixth grade. That summer they spent every moment together and were inseparable forever afterward. After graduating high school, they both went to Salem State University together and stayed on for grad school, too. As soon as they both had their Master's degrees, Cassidy took her to a very romantic dinner, not only to celebrate but also to ask for her hand in marriage. He had come a long way from that tall, lanky boy, to a six-feet even man with lean muscles and expert-styled hair into a fauxhawk. She also couldn't forget those damn dimples. Of course she said yes and their parents were ecstatic.

The whole year they were engaged went by in a blur. They had both found jobs in their chosen professions, and the wedding planning went from simple and elegant to a huge gala-like affair. Cassidy was happy as long as Bethany was, and Bethany was ecstatic.

They didn't want to wait to have children, so they tried right away. Starting with their honeymoon. They tried for months to no avail. Once they had been married six months without any luck, they went to a fertility specialist.

They saw the specialist for months, also to no avail. Next thing they knew it was a year into their marriage and still no baby. Cassidy started working later and later every night for the entire month after their first wedding anniversary, leaving Bethany alone at home. It didn't take long for her to grow depressed, lonely. One evening, she decided she needed to get out, so she called up her friends and they took her to their old hangouts.

On her night out, Bethany met a man. His name was Derrick Casey. It didn't take long for them to hook up, and soon they were meeting regularly in the city, from one hotel to the next. Thus began their two-month long affair. Bethany wasn't sleeping with Derrick for love. She wanted a baby and since her husband's sperm count was low, she had decided to find a stranger to impregnate her. Derrick was handsome, with chestnut brown hair, baby blue eyes, six-feet two inches, and roughly about one hundred and eighty pounds, and lucky for her, had fathered two sons and a daughter already. She told him she was on the pill so he wouldn't suspect a thing. Low blow? Absolutely. Did she care? Not one fucking bit. Desperate times and all. Maybe one day she would regret her actions, but today wasn't that day.

She made sure to sleep with her husband often, so once she was pregnant there would be no doubt in his mind. By the end of the second month after meeting Derrick, Bethany had gotten pregnant. She ended things with him right away, telling him she had decided to work on her marriage. He didn't seem to care at all. She never told anyone about her betrayals. Not even her diary.

CHAPTER 1

1987

"Cassidy, I think it's time. The babies are coming," Bethany panted.

Damn, those contractions hurt like a son of a bitch. She wasn't ready. She didn't think she would ever be ready. Twins! She had never expected... never thought she would be carrying identical twins. It was a miracle. They didn't know the sex yet. They wanted to be surprised. When she came home and told her husband that she was pregnant, he was so happy he had cried. He stopped working late and had been very attentive ever since. She couldn't have been happier.

"Honey, are you sure this time? We have at least two more weeks," Cassidy replied.

"Of course I'm sure, because I've either peed myself, or my water just broke!" Bethany barked.

Cassidy held his hands up in surrender.

"Okay, okay. No need to get snippy. Remember our birthing plan. I'll just get the hospital bag and meet you at the car."

"Please hurry."

There. She could play nice, for now. She had a feeling all bets were off once push came to shove. She wobbled her way to the car and maneuvered her way in. She was huge and had to turn completely sideways to slide—or, rather, dump herself in the car. By the time she had finally managed to get in, Cassidy was coming out the door with the hospital bag. He put the bag in the back and got into the driver's seat.

"I would have helped you get in, honey. I just wanted you to walk outside, not try to stuff yourself in the car like a burrito," he said.

"Just drive," she snipped.

"I hope you're yourself again after the twins," he deadpanned.

She just looked at him out of the corner of her eye. What she really wanted to do was punch him in the face, but that would mean he would be delayed in getting the car to the damn hospital. She couldn't wait to meet her little babies.

"Push, baby! Push!" Cassidy yelled. "That's it... just a few more pushes and we get to meet one of our babies."

"I HATE YOU!" Bethany cried. "This is your fault."

"I know, baby, I know."

"Bethany, you're doing good, honey. Just one more push and one of your babies is here," the doctor said.

Bethany felt like she was dying. Why the hell didn't she take the epidural when she had the chance? It was too late for it now. The babies were coming. She wasn't ready. She needed more time to prepare. She had no idea what she was doing. What if Cassidy could tell the babies weren't his? She couldn't lose him, but she also couldn't ever tell him what she'd done. It would kill him, and she couldn't be responsible for that. Bethany prayed for forgiveness for what felt like the thousandth time since her transgression. It wasn't getting any easier to keep this secret, but it was one she had to take to her grave.

"I'm sorry, Cas. I don't hate you. I'm just in a lot of pain," Bethany said.

She was feeling guilty for yelling at him. He wasn't even the reason she felt like her insides were being ripped apart. She needed to calm down and stop acting like a lunatic. She was just ready for her babies to be born. After everything she'd gone through to bring them into this world, she was just in a hurry to see them.

"Come on, Bethany, just one more big push and baby number one will be here," the doctor said.

Beth pushed with everything she had and finally heard the high-pitched wails of her firstborn. She watched anxiously as the nurse took the baby away to be cleaned after Cassidy had cut the cord. She had one more, and she was done.

"You're doing great, babe," Cassidy said, smiling. "Just a few more minutes and our second baby will be here, too."

Bethany heard the doctor tell her to push again, and she used the last of her failing strength to bring her youngest into the world. Once it was done, she listened for the screams, but none came. Why wasn't the baby crying? Maybe this one was just a really calm baby.

"Excuse me a moment," the doctor said before taking the baby to a little cart.

"What's going on? Cas, why isn't the baby crying?" Bethany asked.

But no one was answering her. The delivery room had gone quiet, and the only sounds that could be heard were the whirs and beeps of the machines hooked up to her. Beth watched the doctor shake her head from behind the delivery room window, then look up to the ceiling in defeat. Why wasn't anyone talking to her?

"Mr. and Mrs. Mina, I'm sorry... but your second little girl didn't make it. I'm not sure what happened. I know it's not what you want to hear, but she was fine moments before her birth. I don't know what could have gone wrong. It's like her little heart just stopped beating," the doctor said.

Bethany couldn't think, couldn't move, couldn't breathe. Her girl was gone. That's all she could hear besides the ringing in her ears and that little devil voice in the back of her mind that was telling her this was all her fault. She was being punished for her infidelity. She had no one to blame but herself. How could she have been so selfish? She had paid the ultimate price for her betrayal—with one of her daughter's lives.

CHAPTER 2

1992

Five years later and the pain was still fresh. Every day Bethany woke up and it felt like tiny daggers were being plunged into her heart. Most days she didn't even want to get out of bed, but Bethany still had one daughter that needed taking care of so she forced herself to get up and pretend as if her life were perfect. When in fact it was slowly falling apart.

"Mommy, what's taking so long? I'm hungry!" Isobelle screamed.

She was always screaming. It was as if the girl had only one volume: loud. Most days Beth could handle it, but today, her daughter's birthday, wasn't one of those days. Where was Cassidy? She couldn't do this today. She knew it wasn't fair to him or Isobelle, but this was the worst day of the year for her. It would probably always be. They had agreed never to tell Isobelle about her sister. No need for her to miss her if she never knew about her. It would get harder to hide behind a mask the older Isobelle grew, but for now she was still hopelessly clueless to her mother's moods.

"Dear girl, Mommy has a headache. Do you think you could lower the volume on your excitement a bit?" Bethany asked.

"Okay, Mommy," Isobelle said in a loud whisper.

Bethany couldn't help but laugh at her poor, clueless daughter. They would have to work on her inside voice. For now, Bethany didn't have the heart to correct her; it was her special day even if all Beth wanted to do on this day was cry.

"What do you want for breakfast, birthday girl?"
"Ice cream!"
"Try again."
"Cake!"
"One more time."
"Pancakes!"
"Now we're getting somewhere."

Bethany went to the kitchen with her new five-year-old behind her, talking about she only knew what. She had to have one of the weirdest children on the planet. Always talking to herself and seeing things that no one else could see. Half the time, Bethany was freaked out and the other, she didn't even know. Isobelle would say something and days later it would happen. Cassidy thought it was amusing and would try to get lottery numbers from her, but Bethany was afraid. Hopefully it was a phase, and Isobelle would soon grow out of it. Didn't make it any less creepy, though, whenever she was right about someone dying or knowing where things that were lost could be found.

Beth shook herself out of her wanderings and concentrated on cooking Isobelle's birthday breakfast. She vaguely heard a door open but knew it was her husband as soon as Isobelle screeched and took off out of the room. She was going to need a hearing aid if Isobelle didn't learn how to speak in a normal tone of voice soon.

"Ddddaaaadddddddyyyyy!"

Oh my god! Beth was going to put a muzzle on that girl.

"There's daddy's little girl," Cassidy laughed. "Happy birthday, baby! Let's go find your mama."

"She's in the kitchen making pancakes!" Isobelle yelled.

Beth was a few seconds from shaking that girl. She needed to invest in some earplugs.

"Could you please tell your daughter to stop all the screaming? She's going to wake the dead," Beth said in greeting.

"It's her birthday, and she's excited is all. Stop being such a grouch."

"Whatever, here's breakfast. I'm going back to bed."

Cassidy was trying really hard to give Bethany the benefit of the doubt, but his patience was wearing thin. She wasn't the only one who'd lost a child.

"Here, baby, sit and eat your breakfast. I'm going to go talk to Mommy for a bit, then we'll get your birthday started right," Cassidy said.

"Okay, Daddy!"

Cassidy was barely holding on to his temper. He wanted to scream at Beth, but he didn't want to upset Isobelle on her birthday. Still, he'd had enough of Bethany's selfishness, and she would either get over it or he was taking his daughter and they were leaving.

"Have you lost your mind?" Cassidy asked, his anger boiling just below the surface.

"Excuse me?" Bethany asked.

"Cut the shit, Beth."

"You don't talk to me like that."

"I'll talk to you any way I want as long as you keep treating our daughter like crap. She's a child and it's her birthday, so of course she's excited. You should be as well, seeing as we could have easily lost her, too. So get your ass up, clean yourself up, and get downstairs and get excited for your daughter turning five fucking years old!"

"My daughter is dead," Bethany said in a harsh whisper.

"So is mine, but you don't see me acting like an asshole. Now either get yourself together or Isobelle and I are leaving and we're not coming back. Do you understand me?"

"You don't have the balls."

"Try me."

Cassidy turned his back on Bethany and took a little detour on his way back downstairs to have breakfast with his birthday girl. He wasn't going to let Bethany ruin another one of her birthdays by being petty. He understood her pain, but Isobelle needed them, and he was living for the child he still had, not the one he'd lost. After getting his temper under control he went to find Isobelle still in the kitchen.

"Are you eating all the bacon?" Cassidy asked with a smile.

"No," Isobelle mumbled around a mouthful of bacon.

"Guess I'll have to just cook some more," Bethany said.

She was looking better. At least she had clothes on and not that damn robe. It was progress. She'd also combed her hair, but more importantly she believed Cassidy was serious about leaving. Cassidy looked over at Isobelle to tease her some more but she had a blank, faraway look on her face.

"Isobelle, honey, what's wrong?" Cassidy asked.

She didn't respond. It was like she couldn't hear him.

"Isobelle?" Bethany tried. "Cas, what's wrong with her? Should we take her to the hospital?"

"Pawpaw's dead," Isobelle suddenly said.

"What are you talking about, sweetie? Pawpaw is fine. We're going to see him in a little bit," Cassidy said.

"No we won't. He's dead."

Cassidy watched Isobelle's eyes carefully, confused. In an instant, Isobelle went back to stuffing bacon in her mouth. What the hell was that about? He was about to ask her when the phone rang.

"I'll get it," Cassidy said. "Hello. Mom? What's wrong. Slow down. Why are you crying? Let me talk to Dad. Gone? What do you mean Dad's gone?"

Cassidy looked over at his daughter and a chill ran down his back. How had she known? His father was dead, and Isobelle had known.

Cassidy was trying really hard to give Bethany the benefit of the doubt, but his patience was wearing thin. She wasn't the only one who'd lost a child.

"Here baby, sit and eat your breakfast. I'm going to go talk to Mommy for a bit, then we'll get your birthday started right," Cassidy said.

"Okay, Daddy!"

Cassidy was barely holding on to his temper. He wanted to scream at Beth but he didn't want to upset Isobelle on her birthday. Still, he'd had enough of Bethany's selfishness and she would either get over it or he was taking his daughter and they were leaving.

"Have you lost your mind?" Cassidy asked, his anger boiling just below the surface.

"Excuse me?" Bethany asked.

"Cut the shit, Beth."

"You don't talk to me like that."

"I'll talk to you any way I want as long as you keep treating our daughter like crap. She's a child and it's her birthday, so of course she's excited. You should be as well, seeing as we could have easily lost her, too. So get your ass up, clean yourself up, and get downstairs and get excited for your daughter turning five fucking years old!"

"My daughter is dead," Bethany said in a harsh whisper.

"So is mine, but you don't see me acting like an asshole. Now either get yourself together or Isobelle and I are leaving and we're not coming back. Do you understand me?"

"You don't have the balls."

"Try me."

Cassidy turned his back on Bethany and took a little detour on his way back downstairs to have breakfast with his birthday girl. He wasn't going to let Bethany ruin another one of her birthdays by being petty. He understood her pain but Isobelle needed them and he was living for the child he still had, not the one he'd lost. After getting his temper under control he went to find Isobelle still in the kitchen.

"Are you eating all the bacon?" Cassidy asked with a smile.

"No," Isobelle mumbled around a mouthful of bacon.

"Guess I'll have to just cook some more," Bethany said.

She was looking better. At least she had clothes on and not that damn robe. It was progress. She'd also combed her hair, but more importantly she believed Cassidy was serious about leaving. Cassidy looked over at Isobelle to tease her some more but she had a blank, faraway look on her face.

"Isobelle, honey, what's wrong?" Cassidy asked.

She didn't respond. It was like she couldn't hear him.

"Isobelle?" Bethany tried. "Cas, what's wrong with her? Should we take her to the hospital?"

"Pawpaw's dead," Isobelle suddenly said.

"What are you talking about, sweetie? Pawpaw is fine. We're going to see him in a little bit," Cassidy said.

"No we won't. He's dead."

Cassidy watched Isobelle's eyes carefully, confused. In an instant, Isobelle went back to stuffing bacon in her mouth. What the hell was that about? He was about to ask her when the phone rang.

"I'll get it," Cassidy said. "Hello. Mom? What's wrong. Slow down. Why are you crying? Let me talk to Dad. Gone? What do you mean Dad's gone?"

Cassidy looked over at his daughter and a chill ran down his back. How had she known? His father was dead and Isobelle had known.

1997

"Isobelle, your parents are very worried about you. They say you know things before they happen, and you're seeing things. Is this true?" the therapist asked.

"I don't know, maybe," Isobelle said.

"Can you tell me what kinds of things you know before they happen?"

"I guess. I knew about my pawpaw dying before my dad got the call from his mom."

"How did you know that?"

"I don't know. I was five. I don't really remember."

"I think you do. You're in a safe place, Isobelle. I can't help you if you're not honest with me."

"I don't remember."

"Okay, tell me about some of the things you do remember."

Isobelle was confused. She wanted to talk to someone about the things she saw but she knew it was scaring her family, and every doctor she tried to talk to thought she was crazy. She just wanted to go home. She didn't want to play these stupid games anymore. She didn't know how she knew the things she did when she wasn't supposed to. It just happened, and she had made the mistake of telling her parents about every one of them. At first it wasn't that big of a deal. They brushed the weirdness off, but when it grew more frequent and more specific they had started to freak out—hence, the reason she was in this stuffy old office talking to this ancient man about her "abilities." She felt like a freak, and the kids at school were starting to treat her like one as well. She had to do something before things got out of hand.

"I want to leave now. Where are my parents?"

"We still have twenty more minutes together."

"No! I want to leave. NOW!" Isobelle screamed.

She screamed so loud her parents came rushing in the door, frantic.

"Isobelle, what's happened?" Bethany asked.

"Take me home, please. I don't want to do this anymore."

"Isobelle needs to face her issues head on," the therapist said.

"Mom, Dad, please. I don't like this. I want to go home," Isobelle cried.

"Of course, sweetie. Let's go. Doc, we'll call you," Cassidy said.

"You're making a mistake. She is hiding something."

"She's ten years old. What exactly could she be hiding?" Bethany asked.

The doctor's eyes grew wide. They also started to look a little glossy, almost crazy. The Mina family took a step back.

"We need to run more tests. I need to run more tests. Something is going on, and I want answers."

"I think we're going to get a second opinion," Cassidy said carefully.

"You're making a mistake, a huge mistake! Isobelle needs extensive therapy."

"We have to go," Cassidy said, now practically racing his family from that maniac's office. What the hell was that about? The doctor had seemed so sane their first few family sessions together. No wonder he was so affordable. He wasn't only certified—he was certifiable.

"I'm so sorry, Isobelle. I didn't know he was so… unstable."

"I don't want to see any more doctors. I'm fine now. The episodes are gone. I just want to be normal."

"Sweetie, there is nothing wrong with you. We will start fresh. A new city, new school, new jobs. We will be fine. Isn't that right, Cas?"

"Exactly. Let's go home and start looking for new places."

Isobelle had to ignore whatever was happening with her. She didn't want to end up in an institution for the rest of her life. She could ignore the visions. It would be easy. From now on she was normal Isobelle, not the weird girl who saw things and knew things she wasn't supposed to. She could do this. She had to do this. It was her only shot.

CHAPTER 3

2002

"Isobelle, come on! Let's go. We're going to be late for class," Skylar Grace said.

Skylar had been Isobelle's best friend since she moved after the therapist debacle. They had been joined at the hip ever since that first day of school. Isobelle wasn't sure how she'd functioned without the girl before then. Isobelle looked up from her locker to reply to Skylar when a rare vision overtook her. She didn't have them as often as she used to since she'd been ignoring them, but the occasional one slipped through every now and again. Apparently, today was one of those days and what she saw caused her to drop all of her books.

It couldn't be real. She was just imagining things, right? In her heart she knew better. She saw death, Skylar's death, in a car crash. But she didn't know when. It could be today, tomorrow, or a few months from now. That was one of the downsides from ignoring her "gift" all these years. Her visions were no longer as accurate as they once had been. She could tell down to the minute before, where now the window was much bigger. Isobelle didn't know what to do. If she told Sky to stay away from cars, Sky would just look at her strangely. So Isobelle did what she always did these days and ignored it. Maybe it wasn't true. She'd also gotten a few things wrong since she wasn't actively interested in the visions anymore. They were sometimes hit or miss. Maybe this was one of those times. Even still, Isobelle couldn't shake the sense of dread in the pit of her stomach.

"Oh my god! Isobelle, are you okay?" Skylar said. "You're extra clumsy today. We are going to be late for last period. We need to hurry. Here, let me help you."

"Yeah, thanks. I don't know what's wrong with me."

But she knew. She just didn't know exactly when.

"Okay, let's go. We don't want to be late," Isobelle said.

Isobelle couldn't concentrate on anything the teacher was saying. The vision kept replaying in her head. She really hoped it didn't come true. She didn't know what she would do with herself if it did.

TWO WEEKS LATER

"Belle, honey, what time did you say that Sky was supposed to be here? We're going to be late for the fundraiser," Bethany said.

Isobelle looked at the clock. Sky was supposed to be here about thirty minutes ago. Where was she? Maybe they ran into some traffic, but that didn't sound right either.

"She should have been here by now, Mom. Let's give it a few more minutes then I'll call her house to see if they have left yet."

Ten minutes later and Sky was still a no show. Isobelle went to the living room and dialed Sky's number.

"Grace Residence," said a shaky voice.

"Hello, this is Isobelle. Is Skylar still at home? She was supposed to be here about forty minutes ago."

"I'm sorry, sweetie," the voice said, clearly in distress. "This is Skylar's aunt. Sky and her mom were in a car accident, and Skylar didn't make it. We just found out not too long ago. Her father was going to call you to explain. I'm so sorry."

"I—I'm so sorry. I have to go."

Isobelle couldn't breathe. This couldn't be happening. This wasn't real. She picked up the phone, ripped it out of its socket, and threw it across the room. She was vaguely aware of the screaming. It was the only thing she remembered before everything went dark.

2005

"Honey, we're going to be late. We still need to make sure there are enough seats for the family," Bethany said.

"The auditorium is huge," Cassidy said. "I'm sure we will have more than enough space. Besides, everyone RSVP'd so it's not like there won't be room for everyone."

"That may be, but we want to be sure we all sit together and not spread all over the place. The sooner we get to the school, the better chance we will have to get seats together."

"Whatever you say, dear."

Bethany rushed all her family and friends out the door. Today was the big day: Isobelle was graduating from high school. The last three years had been hard for Isobelle since Skylar died, but hopefully she would be too busy preparing for her first year at Harvard to be so sad. Bethany's fingers were crossed. She was hoping for a distraction. Not the healthiest way to deal with the death of a friend, but she just wanted her happy little girl back.

With the heavy flow of traffic, they made it to the school in just under an hour. They should have left earlier, but it was hard as hell to move so many people at one time. Just when you thought you had them all rounded up, someone else deviated from the trail. Didn't matter—they were here now. Finally. Beth even managed to find seats for all of them in the same area. It was perfect for when picture time came. Good thing Isobelle had to be there earlier or they might have still been home waiting for her to get ready. The girl was slow, especially when trying to look fancy. She always got hung up on her eyes and making sure her makeup didn't clash. Beth always told Isobelle she was ridiculous, but her daughter was always such a girlie girl. It didn't help that the girl had worn red highlights for the last two years, so it was even harder to match colors correctly.

"What are you thinking about so hard over here?" Cassidy asked.

"Isobelle. I'm worried about her. She hasn't been the same since Sky's death," Bethany said.

"Everyone grieves differently. Just give her time and make

yourself available to her. You should take her on a mother-daughter spa weekend in a few weeks. Help her to relax. She's been knee-deep in school since the funeral and hasn't really come up for air. Besides, it could be worse. She could have decided to stay out all night, drink alcohol and do drugs, and end up pregnant."

"You're not funny."

"I'm a little bit funny."

"Only to yourself," Bethany said with a smirk.

"Whatever. Why do you hurt me so?"

"You're such a dork."

"I'm pretty sure it's why you fell for me."

"It was your money."

Cassidy's reply was cut short by the movement on the stage. Everyone was getting into place and the excited graduates could be heard shuffling behind the double doors as they waited for their cue to walk to their chairs for the ceremony.

"We will finish this conversation later tonight," Cassidy promised.

Bethany could see the smile in his eyes, and she couldn't help but laugh at his lameness. It was times like these she remembered why she'd wanted him all those years ago. He could always make her smile, even when all she wanted to do was give up. He had never given up on her, and he kicked her in the ass when needed. He was the best man she knew, and she was so lucky to have him. He was also an amazing father. The best she could ever hope for. She no longer regretted her actions or blamed herself for their daughter's death. She'd made peace with her past.

Bethany continued to enjoy the ceremony as the doors were opened and the students marched to their places. She listened to the valedictorian's speech, the one that Isobelle should have been giving, with an open mind and found that it spoke to her on levels she never knew she possessed. There was something so pure and new about graduating from high school. Their entire lives were ready to be claimed, and the choices they made from here on out would continue to mold them into the people they would become. Only now without the unwanted guidance from their parents. Although some students were still under the strict guidelines of their parent's failed dreams. Beth was glad that she and Cassidy weren't pressuring Isobelle to follow in their footsteps. They encouraged her to pave her own path and let the wind take her where it willed.

Bethany waited patiently for her daughter's name to be called.

"Isobelle Catherina Mina."

The Mina family and friends erupted with applause and catcalls louder than any other section. It seemed like Isobelle was well represented today for her accomplishments, even if she didn't want to be named valedictorian. Bethany still didn't understand that one, but she supported her daughter's decision to not be made a spectacle of. As long as the title would still be on her transcripts, Beth and Cassidy hadn't made a big deal about it. The rest of the ceremony went by with little fanfare, and before long she was hugging her baby girl and snapping as many photos as her camera could hold.

"We are so proud of you, sweetie," Bethany cried. "You're growing up so fast. Before long, you won't come home for school breaks and then we might only see you on Thanksgiving and Christmas."

Beth watched as Isobelle rolled her eyes at having to hear the same speech for the last year now. It still didn't stop her from telling it over and over again though.

"Oh, leave her alone, Beth," Cassidy said." I'm sure we will see her as much as she's able to."

Bethany just gave him the look, the one that said, "If you don't shut up, you'll be sleeping on the couch."

As they spoke, Bethany noticed an older man from the crowd approach their group. He turned to Beth and said, "Excuse me, Mrs. Mina, I know this is probably a bad time, but I would love to talk with you for a moment about a fundraiser I'd like you to help set up. I heard you were the best. And, Isobelle, sweetie, congratulations on your graduation. I'm sure your family is very proud of your accomplishments. Although I'm sad you didn't give the valedictorian speech."

Bethany watched as the stranger hugged her daughter like he'd known her all his life. She found it very strange.

"Thank you, sir. Mom, go ahead, we will wait for you outside. It's getting extremely crowded in here," Isobelle said.

Bethany watched her family make their way out of the auditorium and then turned to the stranger that seemed so familiar with her family.

"I'm sorry, how do you know me again?" Bethany asked.

"If you'll follow me to a place a little quieter I will tell you all about it."

Bethany reluctantly followed the stranger to a back corner where they could speak in private. She felt relief in the fact that her family knew she was with this man and had seen what he looked like. Once they were safely tucked away from prying eyes, the smile slid from the man's face and was replaced with a scowl.

"I know the secret you carry. Did you really think I wouldn't know my own flesh and blood? I know everything my son does and every child he's fathered, and even still her eyes are a dead giveaway."

Bethany's eyes widened in fear, and sweat had started to bead across her upper lip.

"Who the hell are you? I have no idea what you're talking about."

"So that's the game we are going to play? Very well. My name is Derrick Casey, Senior. I believe you know my son."

Bethany couldn't breathe. She could barely string coherent thoughts together.

"Wha—"

Bethany cleared her throat and swallowed a few times to moisten her increasingly dry mouth.

"What do you want?"

"I just want you to know that I know the truth. I will be watching her, and there isn't a damn thing you can do about it. She is my blood, and one day I will know her and she will know the other side of her family and the lies you've told her. I also know about her sister."

"Please, I'm begging you."

"You should have thought about that before you used my son. I would say I'd be in touch but that would be a lie. Have a good day, Mrs. Mina, and if I were you, I'd make the best out of the time you have with Isobelle. Because once she finds out the secret you've been hiding from her she might hate you. You've robbed her of so many things, and you've made a very powerful enemy in the process."

Bethany was left clutching at her chest. Her world was falling apart and the worst part was that she was powerless to stop it.

CHAPTER 4

2009

This was it. She would be graduating with her Bachelor's in Criminal Justice tomorrow, and she was accepted into Harvard Law for the following school year. Everything was going according to plan for Isobelle. Her parents would be getting in later tonight, and she couldn't wait to see them. It had been months since she'd last seen them. She would be very busy in the next couple of years, and her visits with her parents probably wouldn't be as frequent. So she was going to seriously enjoy this visit. She was hoping to also introduce them to her mentor, Derrick Casey. The man was like a godsend. He understood her in a way her parents never had. He'd helped her more than he would ever know these last four years. It also didn't hurt that he was a predominant figure in the community, him and a lot of his friends. Initially, his interests surprised Isobelle. She'd remembered him from her high school graduation after seeing him at a campus event a few months after her freshmen year.

After that, he'd made it his mission to help her in any way he could, since she didn't have family in the area. She didn't know why she'd kept their friendship a secret from her parents, but she was excited to tell them now. Too bad the fundraiser idea he'd wanted to talk to her mom about that day didn't work out. It would have been a big hit. Honestly, he was a big part of the reason she'd been accepted to Harvard Law. His recommendation went a long way with the committee, and Isobelle learned that a lot of his colleagues had attended the university. Isobelle was ecstatic, and she was already getting job offers. She had her pick of the litter, and it was all thanks to her unexpected guardian angel.

When she could, she accepted dinner invitations at Derrick's home with his wife. They were like an extra set of grandparents for her, and she had grown to love them both. Isobelle sometimes didn't know how she'd managed to live without them. They were the first people who didn't question her visions. She'd had a rare occurrence at their house one day and after her reluctance to tell them, she'd found once she did they'd understood. Derrick had cautioned her to never tell anyone else, though. He'd said not everyone would be as understanding and he didn't want to see her in a padded room. She'd confessed to him everything, and for the first time in her life, she didn't feel like a freak. She only wished her parents had reacted that way, instead of sending her to that whack job therapist. Didn't matter now, she had someone she could discuss things with when she was struck with something she couldn't explain.

Isobelle's trip down memory lane was cut short by a knocking on her door. She'd gotten the apartment a year ago as a gift from Derrick and Kalliope, his wife. She'd refused but they wouldn't hear of it. They insisted she needed a quiet space to study outside of the school's ever-loud dorms. She hadn't told her parents how she'd gotten the apartment either, and they hadn't asked too many questions, thankfully.

"Mom, Dad, how was the drive? Was traffic bad?"

"I just don't understand why driving around in New England takes forever," Bethany said.

"It's not like she did any driving," Cassidy said.

"Of course not. That's what I have you for," Bethany said.

"You guys are insane. Do you want to rest for a while then get some food?" Isobelle asked.

"That sounds lovely. Where should we put our bags?" Cassidy asked.

"Here, I'll take them to the bedroom. You guys sit down and make yourselves comfortable. Do you want some water or something?" Isobelle asked.

"I'll get it. I see the kitchen," Bethany said.

Isobelle placed her parents' bags in her bedroom, then joined them in the living room.

"So I was thinking we could have dinner with my mentor, Derrick Casey, tonight. He's been really helpful since I started school here," Isobelle said.

Bethany barely managed to stop herself from spitting the water out of her mouth. This was not possible. What kinds of games was the old man playing with her daughter? Beth had finally convinced herself that he was bluffing the night of Isobelle's high school graduation. Instead, he'd been brainwashing her daughter for the past four years.

"No," Bethany said.

"What, why?" Isobelle asked.

"Because I said no."

"Oh and that's supposed to work on me. I'm not a child anymore, and to be honest I'm not sure what your problem is. Just because you didn't get to run that fundraiser event is no need to be rude."

"My decision is final."

Bethany's face flamed red at the sound of Isobelle's bitter laughter. She would understand later that it was for her own good, that her mother was only trying to protect her.

"You know what? You're both capable of finding your way around town, so I'll leave you to it. I'll see you tomorrow at graduation."

With those words, Isobelle grabbed her keys, purse, and cell phone, and walked out the door without a backward glance to her parents.

"What the hell is wrong with you, Bethany?" Cassidy asked. "We don't control her life anymore. She's twenty-two and capable of making her own decisions. Telling her 'Because I said so' doesn't do anything but piss her off."

"I'm her mother, and I know what's best."

"No. What you're doing is pushing her away. She already barely comes home, and this Derrick person is obviously important to her."

"If he was so important, she would have mentioned him before."

"She has. She just never mentioned his name. I'm going to go pick up some food."

Bethany didn't care about her family being angry with her. She had to protect them from the secret she carried. She would do whatever it took to make sure they never found out her secret.

Isobelle decided a walk in the park was just what she needed in order to clear her head. She couldn't believe her mother was still trying to dictate things to her like she was a child. She was unjustly judging the Caseys before she even really sat down and got to know them. The decision to go with another chair for the fundraiser was a business decision and not a personal one. The committee had decided to go in another direction, and it wasn't like her mother to hold grudges. At least Isobelle had never thought it was in her nature before now.

Isobelle was tempted to call Derrick and have him pick her up, but she thought it best to work through her frustrations alone. She needed a clear head to deal with her mother, then maybe she could make her see reason and they could sit down to a nice dinner. She should be celebrating for goodness sake, and she couldn't think of a better way than with her family and the people who'd been like a second family to her since her arrival at Harvard. The relative quiet was doing much to soothe Isobelle's rattled nerves. Soon she would be calm enough to make the trip back to her apartment, but an eerie feeling up the length of her spine stopped her dead in her tracks.

Something was wrong, but she couldn't quite put her finger on it. She strained her eyes to hear even the slightest disturbance but there was nothing. Her mind was obviously playing a trick on her, but just when she was about to dismiss her cause for concern she heard a slight hissing noise from the park's tall grass. Perhaps a stray cat was roaming around the park as well. She'd always had a strange relationship with cats; it was like they had an exaggerated hatred for her. She'd never understood it, and the one time her parents had gotten her a kitten, it attacked her unprovoked. She tried to stay away from them ever since.

Maybe it was time to go home after all. She turned to retrace her steps but was knocked down from behind as a huge weight was pressed against her.

"Catch it before it gets away again," a voice called out.

Catch it. Catch what, exactly? Isobelle tried to regain her footing when she was snatched up by whatever had almost mowed her over.

"Come any closer and I'll rip her fucking throat out!"

Isobelle didn't mean to but she laughed. Loudly. She wasn't some helpless little girl who needed a hero to save her. Cassidy Mina had made sure his only child could take care of herself. Isobelle allowed her body to become dead weight, throwing her captor off balance. She spun from his grasp and landed a kick to his stomach. It wasn't her best work, but it got the job done. She jumped back so he couldn't grab her again but when he looked up into her face, what she saw gave her pause. He wasn't fucking human!

"Get the hell out of the way, you idiot!" the voice Isobelle had heard earlier yelled out.

Isobelle jumped to her left just before a bullet whizzed past her head and into the creature's heart. She couldn't believe what she'd seen. He'd looked almost cat-like in his appearance. What the hell was going on?

"Chain it, quickly, while I call for a cleanup crew," the man said.

"You mean the police!" Isobelle screeched. "What the hell is that thing?"

"Shut the hell up!"

"I'm calling the police."

"You'll be eating a bullet before you even get your phone out of your pocket."

"Kill me and you'll wish you were never born. I know people. Powerful people."

"Really? Like who?" he smirked.

"Derrick Casey."

Isobelle took satisfaction in watching the smirk fall off that smug asshole's face. That's right, she knew people. She watched as he took his phone out and dialed a number.

"Sir, we have a problem. You need to get down to the park immediately. There is a girl here who says she knows you and she saw some things she shouldn't have. Of course, sir. We'll see you soon."

"You know Derrick? How do you know him?"

"You can ask him yourself when he gets here. Stay there."

Isobelle wanted answers. It was the only reason she was staying. She stood silently as the man made another phone call, and about ten minutes later two vans pulled up. She was in utter fascination as they loaded the creature into one and drove away, while the other cleaned around the area. Derrick wasn't too far behind.

"Derrick, what is going on?" Isobelle asked.

"Get in the car, Isobelle. We have much to discuss tonight, and your decision in this matter will be the hardest one you've ever had to face."

The only thoughts Isobelle could come up with so shortly were what had she gotten herself into, and if she was ever going to see her parents again.

CHAPTER 5

2011

"Isobelle, you've made amazing progress since you've joined The Society, and Alexander and I believe it's time to move forward in your training. There is someone we would both like you to meet. Come by the house tonight for dinner."

Isobelle graciously accepted Derrick's offer and assured him she wouldn't miss dinner for anything. It had been two years since her eyes had been opened to what was happening every day in the world right before her. She couldn't believe she'd been blind to the supernatural creatures living silently among humans for centuries. What she'd gotten caught in the middle of that night was The Mooyer Society eliminating one of the evil bastards. The Society hunted these beasts and made sure to keep them from human knowledge, while also protecting those who knew nothing about them. The Society had been hunting them for centuries because the beast had dared to kill one of the founding members' twelve sons. Isobelle couldn't even begin to imagine the pain that man must have felt. It was unthinkable to find all your sons in pieces.

It was definitely one hell of a way to find out those creatures existed. Isobelle's choices were few that night: death, commitment to an insane asylum, or join the cause. What The Society was doing was noble, and Isobelle had jumped at the chance to contribute. She was close to becoming an investigator and she was rapidly moving through the ranks of even Legacy members. Derrick had been thrilled at her progress, and she couldn't help but think he was a big part of the reason why she was doing so well. He was still mentoring her, even now.

She still had no clue why her mother didn't want her around him, but Isobelle had refused. So that made their relationship strained. She still talked to her dad a lot, though, even though her mother tried to get him to agree to her outrage. She told herself it didn't matter, but it still hurt. Isobelle shook her head to dispel the negative thoughts and concentrated on who the mystery guest could be.

"What should I wear? I want to make a good impression, but I don't want to overdo it. Maybe I should purchase something new entirely," Isobelle said to herself.

One of the perks of the job was a stellar pay and a nicer place. Not to say the apartment wasn't nice; it just wasn't hers permanently. She could afford almost anything she wanted now. It wasn't like her parents didn't have money, but nothing beat having your own that you worked hard for. And work hard she did. The training program for The Society was insane, but it had to be when dealing with the ferocity of these supernatural creatures. Isobelle had seen the tapes and some of the bastards were ridiculously fast. So that meant they had to be faster, which meant training regimens tougher than any military unit. Regardless of gender and skill. To make it in The Society you had to be able to hold your own and not just in the field. Intelligence was a big part, as well. After reading from The Society's archives, Isobelle understood why. There had been a lot of mistakes over the centuries in dealing with the problem, but The Society was better at its job now, more efficient.

"I think a shopping trip is just what I need."

"So you think this outsider is ready to be trained by my boy?" Alexander asked.

"Isobelle is my granddaughter. It's her birthright," Derrick said.

"When were you going to tell me?" Alexander growled.

The veins were popping out of Alexander's neck in his effort to keep his voice civil. It was quite amusing for Derrick, really. It was rare these days to catch the great Alexander Carvanis, Senior, current head of The Society, off guard. So if he relished the moments more than he should, well no one could really blame him. The man had a stick forever lodged up his ass.

"When the time was right? When you started to question her place among us or in my life. You've wanted to say something for years, Alexander. I'm surprised it took you as long as it has."

"I'm in charge, or have you forgotten?"

"And do tell, exactly what laws have been broken?"

When all Alexander could do was spit and sputter, Derrick knew that Isobelle's place in The Society would be safe. The old man was just mad that Derrick wasn't trying to kiss his ass like some of the other family heads. Fuck that, Derrick was a Legacy in his own right and the head of his own family. Alexander didn't own him, and he certainly couldn't tell him how to handle his own family members.

"What makes you think she's ready to train with Alexander? She wasn't raised into the family business. She's progressing faster than some of the other non-Legacy and even some of the Legacy members, but she's still not on Alexander's level."

"Precisely why I want her to start training with him now. She will be a great asset to our cause, and who better to train her than the best that we have."

"He won't like it," Alexander smirked.

"And when have you ever cared what your youngest son liked? He will do it, and he won't hold back. Which is what she needs to be properly nurtured into the killer we need her to be. It's time we finished what your ancestor started."

"Fine, but if she fucks up, she's your problem. Oh, and let me guess, this is another one of Derrick Jr.'s mistakes, yes?"

When the glass hit the wall besides the son of a bitch, his only reaction was to laugh. Damn him and damn his foolish man-whore of a son.

Isobelle was so nervous that she ended up thirty minutes early to the Caseys' home. She paced in front of her car for several minutes before she heard the front door open. When she looked up, Derrick was coming down the porch steps with a small smile on his face.

"Isobelle, sweetie, what are you doing outside? Why didn't you come up and ring the bell?" Derrick asked.

"Just clearing my head a bit and making sure I don't embarrass myself," Isobelle said with a little laugh.

She needed to get her shit together. She was in an exclusive, mostly male-dominated club, and she was being foolish. Thank goodness none of the other members were there to see her weakness. Her hard-earned reputation would be ruined.

"No need for that. Come on, let's go inside."

Isobelle allowed Derrick to lead her to the house. She waited as he shut the door behind them, and then led her to the study to introduce her to everyone.

"Isobelle, you've met my wife many times and Alexander but this is his youngest son, Alexander Jr. and his fiancé, and my granddaughter, Nicole Casey."

Just as Isobelle was going to speak, her words were caught in her throat for two reasons. The first being the girl before her could have passed for her twin, and the second being that Alexander caused her to have one of her rare visions. The last time one came to her was over a year ago, and now it came like a punch in the gut. She grew lightheaded, and it was getting harder to breath. Her palms were sweating, and a ringing echoed in her ears. She could feel herself moving, but she couldn't tell if it was forward or backward, upward or downward. Then there was nothing.

PART TWO

ALEXANDER

CHAPTER 6

1984

"Alexander, I'm pregnant again," Cassandra said.

"Yes, that's exactly what we need—another child this close to my appointment as head of The Society," Alexander said. "Very well, hopefully it's a boy. At least then it would be of use. Isn't Derrick Jr.'s wife pregnant as well? If they have a girl and we have a boy they will be married. I will talk with his father to ensure it. He's the head of the Casey family."

"Of course, dear. Whatever you believe is best."

"What's best is not having any more children. We already have nine, which is plenty."

"Of course, it won't happen again."

"Good, see that it doesn't."

Fucking idiots surrounded him; didn't Cassandra understand he didn't need these sorts of distractions this close to taking over The Society? No, of course not. The bitch only thought of herself, as usual. She was all looks and no damn brain, but a nice body and pretty face only got you so far in life. She wasn't getting any younger, and her looks were starting to fade. Her once perky body was starting to sag a bit and her once thick, jet-black hair was starting to gray and dry out like a bird's nest. Alexander wasn't a spring chicken himself, but he still looked good, and he wasn't dumb as hell. If it weren't for duty and honor, he wouldn't even be stuck with Cassandra, but arranged marriages still existed in his world. Had he gotten his way, he'd have married her sister. She was smarter and had a drive that matched his own. No need in dwelling on it now, he supposed; he couldn't change the past, and sadly Cassandra's sister was married to his brother anyway. Alexander was just glad he was being appointed head of the family rather than his older brother, or he would have killed someone.

"So have you come up with a guest list and menu for the party yet, or are you going to wait until the last minute like you do everything else?" Alexander asked.

"I haven't decided yet on the menu, and I'm waiting on the guest list from you because I know how particular you are," Cassandra said.

"Very well. I'll have a list for you tomorrow. The ceremony is two weeks away. Will you have everything ready a few days before so that I may look over it?"

"Yes."

"Good. And could you have the children come see me in my study, please?"

"I'll send them right up."

Now that Alexander was going to be in charge of the Carvanis family, he needed to ensure that his children were the best of the best. They had to outshine and outclass everyone else in the family. Failure and embarrassment weren't options for any of them. Not before and definitely not now. There would be no second chances. Every hair was expected to be in place at all times, even in the middle of the night. He would take to teaching them himself. He couldn't afford for someone else to teach them what he needed them to know. Not anymore. All his children resembled him in one way or another. They either had his looks or his mannerisms. The girls started to favor their mother more as they grew, but anyone looking at them would know Alexander was their father.

He looked up to find all nine of his children in order from age, starting with the five-year-old and ending with the thirteen-year-old. They all lined up in synchronized military step without making a sound. Perfect. Just what he liked to see: his little soldiers ready for their next assignments. His four boys and five girls were dressed in the finest garments Alexander's money could buy. Say what you wanted about his wife, but the woman had the best taste in clothing, and she made sure their children dressed according to their station in life.

"I've called you all here tonight to share some news and rules. First thing's first: your mother is pregnant again. Hopefully it's a boy, but regardless, this will be the last child we have. Secondly, I will be appointed the new head of the family in two weeks, and from then on I will be watching to see which of you will take my place. So I suggest you make sure to impress me. Finally, I will take over the majority of your lessons and oversee your combat training as many times as I can. Our family will be in the spotlight once I take my place, and we cannot afford to have people question the validity of that choice. Am I understood?" Alexander asked.

"Yes, sir!" barked the children.

"Any questions at this time?"

Alexander scanned each child's face for any flicker of movement. He gave his children time to think of questions and determine if they should ask them. He was patient and didn't rush them. It was one of the first lessons he taught them: to think before they spoke because once they started they couldn't take anything they'd said back.

"What categories will we be tested in to be qualified for the next head of this family?" Misha, the oldest, asked.

Alexander's eyes sparkled with pride. Leave it to his boy to ask a question worth asking.

"I'll have something written up for you in the next few days. I'll officially start looking once I'm appointed, so in the meantime get yourselves ready for the challenge. I'll be a bit easier on the younger ones but not by much. If that's the only question, you are all dismissed."

Alexander watched as his children exited his office in a single-file line. He had the best children, and he wasn't worried about picking the next leader. He would have fierce competition once the time came.

TWO WEEKS LATER

The ceremony was set to begin in just a few short hours, and Alexander was frantic. Everything that could possibly go wrong, had. The caterer had messed up the menu. Instead of roast beef, mashed potatoes, steamed vegetables, and red velvet cake, they'd brought chicken, macaroni and cheese, green beans, and cheesecake. Alexander was livid, but there was nothing to do on such short notice. He did, however, make clear that he would not be paying for a single thing and might never use the company again for future events.

Then the decorator had the color scheme as black and red, when it should have been white and gold. Alexander was ready to strangle someone, and Cassandra was no help at all. Due to the pregnancy, she had to take measures not to get too stressed, so he'd had to deal with everything himself. He blamed her for everything. Had she not gotten pregnant to begin with she would be handling these disasters, not him. Didn't matter now, as soon as he had a spare moment he was getting a vasectomy. He should have done so years ago, but he trusted Cassandra to take care of her birth control. That was a mistake on his part, and one he planned to rectify at the first chance.

Alexander just wanted this day to be over with. What was supposed to be the most important day of his life was turning into a nightmare. He would be the laughingstock of his family and an embarrassment to his father. Alexander went upstairs to prepare for the ceremony to distract himself from the fiasco taking place in his home. After a nice, relaxing soak in his Jacuzzi, dressing in his best suit, and some minor preparations, he was ready to face the coming crowd. It didn't take long for the doorbell to start ringing. His oldest son and daughter were playing ushers to the arriving guests, taking turns escorting The Society's many families to the ballroom where the ceremony was taking place. Forty-five minutes later, everyone was in place and Alexander's father made his way to the podium from his seat of honor on the makeshift stage.

"Thank you all for gathering to recognize my son, Alexander, as the new head of the Carvanis family," Thomas Carvanis announced. "This was one of the hardest decisions I've ever had to make, and I trust that Alexander will do that decision proud. Of all my children, Alexander always went the extra mile to stand out of the crowd and ensure his place as my successor. Without further delay, I present the next head of the Carvanis family and newest member of the inner council."

Alexander approached the podium, shook his father's hand, and accepted the responsibility that was now his. Now all he had left to do was recite the Mooyer Motto.

"I, Alexander Carvanis, promise to uphold our motto which reads: 'That which creeps and stalks the night, you aren't forever from our sight, once we have you in our grasp, you will be taken right to task, with several bullets and a gun, we will eliminate you all one by one.'"

The applause was deafening while also humbling. This was it. He had done it. Now he was in charge, and he couldn't have been happier.

SIX MONTHS LATER

"It's time. The baby is coming!" Cassandra yelled.

Alexander leaned back in his office chair and sighed. He had a shit ton of work to do today. He didn't have time to be in a delivery room for god only knew how long. Yes, she'd had nine babies before this one, but he had a feeling that their latest little bastard would be on his or her own time. He didn't know how he knew, he just knew. This one was different, whether it was a good or bad, different was yet to be seen.

"Very well. Where is your bag and Misha?" Alexander asked.

"My bag is in the living room closet, and Misha is training with his siblings in the basement."

"Meet me in the living room. I'll go inform Misha that he is in charge until we return, and to call my father to check in on them later."

Alexander headed down the basement steps to let his children know they would be leaving shortly. He paused at the last step and watched as Misha and the older siblings led the younger ones through a series of drills. Good, they were taking their training seriously. Alexander cleared his throat to get their attention.

"Your mother has gone into labor. We will be leaving for the hospital. Misha, you are in charge until we return. Call your grandfather and tell him to check in on you in a few hours. Make sure you all eat and finish your studies as well. No slacking off because I won't be around to watch you. I'll call in for an update later tonight."

"Yes, Father, I will take care of it," Misha said.

"Good, carry on."

Alexander ascended the stairs, grabbed Cassandra's bag, helped her into the car, and made his way to the hospital to get this over and done with. Hopefully he would be able to return home in a few hours. He really had a million things to take care of. The drive to the hospital went by quickly, and before he knew it, they had Cassandra all checked in and in the delivery room. The rest was up to when their child decided to formally enter into their lives. Luckily, Alexander had his travel laptop in the car and he could get some things done while they waited for Cassandra's contractions to increase in frequency.

Half a damn day later and it was time to push. Alexander couldn't believe the little asshole held out for twelve whole hours. Not long now before the little demon came screaming into the world.

"Okay, Cassandra, get ready to push for me, okay?" the doctor said. "On the count of three: one, two, three!"

Cassandra's screams could be heard for miles. Alexander would have thought by now she'd be used to the pain. He guessed he was mistaken. Three more pushes and then... silence. Alexander's mouth immediately formed a hard, thin line. He let go of his wife's hand and took a peek at their child. It was a boy and his eyes were wide open and his tiny fists were stuck in his mouth. Alexander was transfixed. For a minute he'd assumed the worst because the boy never made a sound. It just looked around like it hadn't just shoved its way violently into the world.

"What's going on, Alexander? Is the baby okay?" Cassandra's distressed voice cried out.

"He's fine. He seems ignorant to the fact that he just scared five years off each of our lives with his silence," Alexander said.

"Would you like to cut the cord, Mr. Carvanis?" the doctor asked.

Alexander took the shears he was handed and snipped where the doctor pointed. The nurses took the baby to clean him, but it wasn't long before he was resting safely in Alexander's arms. Yes, this one was particularly different from the rest, and at the moment, Alexander's namesake.

CHAPTER 7

1989

"Alexander, it's time for you to start training with your brothers and sisters officially. I know you've been attempting in the last year, but now it's time to take things up a notch," Alexander Sr. said.

"Yes, Father. I'm ready," Alexander Jr. replied with a level of confidence.

"Good. Find your brother, Misha and have him train you and tell you the rules that you must follow."

"Of course, Father. I won't let you down."

Little Alexander went down to the basement where his siblings were already training. He had nine in all, and their names from order of oldest to youngest were: Misha, Rebecca, Kyle, Samantha, Daniel, Veronica, Cameron, Monica, and Caroline. They were all in competition with each other, each one hoping to be their father's successor, but Alexander had no time for such nonsense. Time spent fighting with his siblings was a waste of energy. He kept himself distanced from them and was only around them when completely necessary, like now, for training. The fact that he didn't resemble any of them in the slightest may have also played a role in his discretion. Anyone of the outside looking in would swear Alexander was adopted, but he shared the same mother and father as his siblings. Didn't matter: he planned to outshine them all regardless of the whispers heard behind his back about his parentage. He wasted no time in getting Misha's attention.

"Misha, Father says it's time to properly train me and explain the rules," Alexander said.

Misha stopped sparring with Cameron and told Kyle to take over.

"Come to the other side of the basement so we can discuss this in relative silence," Misha said.

Misha was eighteen now. A man for all intents and purposes, but to Alexander he was a stepping stone to his future. Once this training with his siblings was over, Alexander knew the real fun would begin.

"Now, first things first, you must never show weakness or cry. If you do, Father might have you beaten or, worse, killed. He does not tolerate failure, although for your age he may give you a chance or two before he takes any action."

"I'm not weak, and I've never been a crier."

"No, you haven't. That will serve you well because I won't hold back in our training much. I'll go a bit slow in the beginning, but in the next six months I'll be coming at you in full force."

"What's first? Let's get this over with so we can move on."

Misha raised an eyebrow like their father sometimes did. Alexander returned his brother's look with one of his own. His blank face, the one that annoyed most of his siblings because it told them he found them boring and lacking.

"Don't get too cocky, little brother. Today is your official day of training. What you've been doing for the last year is nothing compared to what's to come."

"I can handle it."

"Very well."

"For starters, you will hold two books in each hand with your arms spread out in front of you. You will do that for ten-minute increments for an hour every day for two weeks. Then we will move to twenty minutes and increase that by ten minutes every two weeks until you get to an hour."

"Understood. Then what?"

"We will run. Not very long, about ten minutes a day for two weeks, then increase that by ten minutes every two weeks until you are going two hours straight. You might never know when you have to chase someone down or run for your life."

"What else?"

"You will conduct research by watching old videotapes of hunting, capturing, killing, and sometimes questioning the creatures. I hope you don't have a weak stomach because vomiting is not allowed either. Then, once you've mastered these things, the second phase of your training will begin."

"I'm ready."

For the next five years Alexander went through rigorous training. Some days were better than others, but he didn't dare complain. Sometimes his father could be seen watching in the shadows with his notebook, judging them. Expecting some to fail and bringing down the wrath of the gods upon whoever dared to not meet his expectations. Already, the three siblings before Alexander had been deemed unworthy to ever become the head of the family. It was all they could do to not be executed by their father. They may not be in the running for head of family, but it was still their duty to hunt and kill "The Tarnished", and it was a mission their father never let them forget.

Sometimes their father would spar with them or teach them a lesson or two, but mostly he left that to the older siblings. He would have rather overseen their training himself, but his duties as the family head kept him busier than he'd thought. While training, they barely broke to eat or sleep. They lived and breathed The Society and its teachings. Every day was like the one before it. They had a strict schedule that was never altered. Alexander couldn't wait until his second phase of training when he could practice his skills against those besides his siblings. He needed bigger challenges, and he was ready to face them head on.

CHAPTER 8

1994

Alexander was up earlier than usual today, probably because he was finally starting the second stage of his training: hand-to-hand combat. He'd been waiting for this day for what felt like forever, and to a ten-year-old, five years was indeed forever. Today also was his birthday, and he wondered if he would get that knife he'd been eyeing every time his father took him to a sporting goods store. It was a rare treat to go into town with his father, and one all his siblings enjoyed when he'd bring them. Most were old enough to go themselves and didn't need special permission anymore. Six of his siblings were over eighteen now, so they came and went as they pleased.

Misha still made time for Alexander, though; he still sparred with him when he was home from a hunt and taught him things he'd learned from experience out in the field. Alexander couldn't wait to be in the field, so he rushed downstairs to whip up a quick breakfast. His mother rarely cooked, and even if she did, she was never up this early anyway. So Alexander was left to fend for himself. Being the baby of the family sometimes had its perks, and most of his siblings suspected that he was their father's favorite. Alexander didn't worry himself with such trivial things and thought they were just trying to throw him off his game. He would be his father's successor if it were the last thing he'd do.

"Alexander, son, what are you doing up so early? You should be resting. You have a big day today," Alexander Sr. said.

"I couldn't sleep... too much excitement. So I figured I'd make myself a bit of breakfast. Are you hungry, Father?" Alexander Jr. asked.

"Well, if you're already cooking. So how is your training going? Are you ready for hand-to-hand combat with your cousins?"

"The history of it all is fascinating, the videos are very informative. My cousins aren't as good at fighting as Misha, Kyle, or even Rebecca, and I'm sure the more advanced hand-to-hand combat will be even less challenging with them. Hopefully I can convince one of my older siblings to practice with me on one of their hunting breaks."

Alexander Sr.'s laugh almost startled Alexander. His father was rarely in a joking mood and most thought he lacked a sense of humor. But he was more laid back with Alexander, and he would slip a smile or occasional laugh.

"I'll make you a deal," Alexander's father said. "After your lessons, come find me and we'll practice a bit together. I'm still in fighting shape and I'll fix whatever your cousins mess up. Can't have you being taught by incompetent idiots."

"Thanks, Father. Here's your plate. I'll get you some orange juice."

"Thank you and happy birthday, Alexander."

Alexander smiled to himself. His father never forgot his birthday, even though the younger siblings liked to tell him how upset their father had been with their mother for getting pregnant again. Although Alexander was sure it was true, he knew his father loved all his children in his own way. Alexander poured juice for his father and himself and sat down to eat his breakfast. He had a big day today, and he was going to need his strength.

After cleaning up the dishes and talking with his father a bit more, Alexander went upstairs to shower and dress for his first advanced lessons in fighting. He knew a bit from sessions with Misha, but his brother had warned him that it was nothing compared to what was to come. Alexander felt confident that he was ready for whatever came his way, but he wasn't stupid enough to believe he should walk into the training room cocky. His uncle, David, was in charge of this class, and the man hated all of his brother's children because they were the next in line as head of the family. Rebecca had told him that their uncle was harder on them than any other students. So Alexander had to be on his A-game.

"Alexander, you're early. Good, promptness is encouraged. There will be five other students joining us, two of your cousins, a Casey, a Connelly, and a Singer. If you'd like, we can go through a few warm-up drills that I'm sure your brother has already taught you," David said.

"Yes, Uncle, that would be great," Alexander said.

For the next twenty-five minutes, Alexander went through a set of warm-up exercises with his uncle while they waited on the rest of the class to begin their training. Although his uncle was being nice to him at the moment, Alexander didn't let that fool him. He was not about to let his guard down. Kyle had warned him that his uncle would try this route and Alexander was ready. Then, just as he'd thought, his uncle kicked out. Alexander had been anticipating the move, and he fell back and rolled into a crouch.

"Very impressive. I see your siblings have been telling you all my secrets. Good, I'll just have to come up with new material. Until next time, though, my boy. The other students are arriving."

Alexander got up and went to his spot on the mat as the other students came in. His cousins sneered at him, and Alexander ignored them both. Amateurs, the both of them. The Casey boy just gave him a lopsided grin, the Connelly boy just grunted at him, while the Singer boy didn't even glance his way. Alexander was ready to get this over with so he could practice his skills with a worthy opponent—his father. But he had to endure a few hours of this nonsense before he could get to the real work.

"Good morning, second-phasers," David said. "At this point in your training everything is going to get harder not easier, so I do hope you're up for the challenge. Every day, our teams are taking out "The Tarnished" abominations, and still they keep coming. Some days it seems this war is never-ending, but for us to come out victorious we have to train the next generation of hunters, and that would be you. So pay attention, and you might just learn something. For those of you who may not know me, my name is David Carvanis. Now, partner up and let's begin," David said.

Alexander watched as his idiot cousins paired off together, and the Singer and Connelly boy did the same. So that left the Casey boy and him. Didn't matter, he was either pretty good and would provide a bit of a challenge for Alexander, or he wasn't and Alexander would wipe the floor with him.

"I guess it's you and me, kid. Name's Samuel but I usually go by Sam," Sam Casey said.

"Alexander Carvanis."

"As in the head of the Carvanis family? Alexander Carvanis?"

"He's my father."

"Cool… my grandpa is Derrick Casey Sr., so it don't bother me none."

"Nice accent you have going there."

"Mm, raised in the South by my mama until I was five, then my father came and got me. Apparently, I'm a love child," Sam said with a smile.

"So it's a nice way of saying you're a bastard."

"Yep. And my brothers and sisters like to remind me every chance they get. I don't mind, though. I kinda feel bad for them. While my mama's sweet as pie, theirs is the devil. I can see why our father was drawn to my mama in the first place."

"Your father's drawn to a lot of people's mamas."

"Touché."

Alexander couldn't help but like Sam. He wasn't a pureblood Legacy, but it didn't matter. He turned out to be a decent partner, too, and Alexander had the feeling that they were going to be good friends. By the time class was over, Alexander was sweating something awful, and he'd been put on his ass a time or two by Sam. His uncle went around fixing their stance and offering corrections when needed. Alexander hoped he wasn't too tired to practice with his father when he got home.

"Hey, Sam, I'm going to practice a bit more with my father, want to come?"

"Sure. I'll call my pa from your house."

Alexander and Sam made their way to Alexander's house and went to find his father. On the way, Sam called his dad to let him know where he was. They found Alexander's dad in his study. Alexander lightly knocked on the door and waited.

"Enter."

Alexander opened the door and entered the room, with Sam trailing behind him.

"Father, this is Samuel Casey. He's my sparring partner and

actually not that bad. I figured he may be a great partner for me one day and was wondering if it was okay for him to practice with us."

"Great thinking, son. You're one of Derrick Jr.'s boys?"

"Yes, sir. Found out five years ago from my mama, and then Pa came and picked me up when she got sick," Sam said.

"She's doing okay now, though?"

"Yes, sir. Thank you for asking."

"Good. Now show me what that idiot brother of mine taught you today, and then I'll teach you the right way."

Alexander and Sam showed Alexander Sr. the new moves they had learned. Every few minutes he could be heard grunting and cursing under his breath. If Alexander wasn't trying to concentrate he would have laughed. After a few more minutes his father stopped them.

"I guess David didn't do a completely shitty job of it. You're both off to a good start, and, Samuel, you have a nice form. You and Alexander would complement each other as partners very nicely. It also seems you're comfortable with each other and trust each other, which is a good thing to have in a partnership. Now let me show you a few things that will help you in class. We'll do this once a week."

They practiced with Alexander for another hour, and then Derrick came to pick Samuel up. Alexander did a bit of homework after he cleaned up and ate dinner. In the morning he got up and went to class the same time as the day before. That was his routine for the next two years.

1996

"So what the hell is phase three exactly?" Sam asked.

"Weapons," Alexander said.

If it wasn't for all those years spent learning to contain himself, Alexander would have been jumping up and down at the thought of finally being able to use weapons. It was a dream come true.

"Like hunting rifles?"

"Better."

"What's better than hunting rifles? Ain't nothing better than hunting rifles, boy!"

Alexander rolled his eyes. He swore Sam's accent got thicker at times just to annoy the hell out of him. He did it on purpose to sound as ignorant as some of the other legacies thought he was, but Alexander knew better. Sam was smarter than Alexander, and Alexander was a genius.

"You're an idiot."

"Yep, and you still love me. Who's teaching us these weapons you're so excited about?"

Alexander gave Sam a rare smile.

"My father and your grandfather."

"Don't do that shit! I hate when you get that creepy smile on your face. It's borderline psychotic."

"And I hate when you sound like Hillbilly Bob, but you do it anyway to annoy me."

"Truer words ain't never been spoken."

"Let's go, Bob."

Alexander and Samuel rushed to the shooting range on the hundreds of acres of land owned by The Society. Most of the Legacy families also had houses on the land, but there was also cool stuff like the gym and this range. They were early as usual, but Alexander's father and Sam's grandfather were already there as well.

"Well, someone's eager for weapons training," Derrick said.

Sam pointed his finger at Alexander, and Alexander slapped it away.

"I just like to be early to things," Alexander Jr. said.

"Like your father that way," Derrick said.

"I learn from the best," Alexander Jr. said.

"Flattery won't soften me up, son," Alexander Sr. said.

Sam snickered in the background.

"I can still beat you up," Alexander Jr. said.

"I've been practicing with my brother," Sam said, raising his chin.

Alexander smiled when his father and Derrick started laughing at Sam and his bickering. Apparently they had the same relationship as he and Sam and were partners as well. Still were in some things, although they didn't go on hunts as much as they used to.

"So since you're both here early," Derrick said, "come have a look at the knives we'll be teaching with today. They're commanders and are pretty new to the knife family. We got a shipment in not too long ago, and this will be the first knife you master. Go ahead and take one. It's yours."

"Hot damn!" Sam exclaimed.

Alexander was no less excited, but he was better at holding it in.

"So when do we learn how to shoot?" Alexander Jr. asked.

He watched the smirk on his father's face morph into a grin.

"Soon, once you master the knives," Alexander said. "Then we'll move on to the guns. So I suggest you boys pay close attention. And since you're now in phase three, you are assigned personal instructors—Derrick and myself. So let's move to our area of the range and get to work."

"So we don't have to wait on the others?" Sam asked.

"No, it's just the four of us, and we can set our own pace," Derrick said.

At that, Alexander was ecstatic. Sam and he would be shooting guns in about a month, maybe more. He was liking phase three more and more every day.

CHAPTER 9

1999

Alexander doubled-checked his gear for the third time. He wanted to make sure he had everything necessary for his first official trip with Misha and their father. This was what he had been working toward for years, and he was finally ready. Only thing missing was Sam, but he was going on his own hunt with his older brother and father in another state. Alexander had never been outside Massachusetts, but he was looking forward to going to Missouri and hunting his first supernatural creature. He was going to have to be on his p's and q's because he didn't want to disappoint his father or embarrass himself in front of his older brother.

Once he was sure he had everything he was going to need, Alexander picked up his pack and made his way to the living room where his father and brother were waiting for him.

"Finally!" Misha snapped. "What were you packing up there? Your entire room?"

"Shut up, Misha! I needed to make sure I didn't forget anything important," Alexander said.

"Like what? We're going hunting, not on a nature trip!"

Alexander ignored his brother's whining and marched to the car. They were all going to be stuck in the same damn car for twenty hours. Alexander thanked whoever was listening that he'd remembered to pack his headphones and mp3 player. Alexander placed his bigger bag in the trunk and kept a backpack with him full of books. His knife from his third phase of training was in his pocket, and he was ready to get this show on the road.

After another ten minutes the three men were pulling out of the driveway in no time. His father was driving first, and that was Alexander's cue to put his music on and fall asleep. He didn't want to listen to his brother's bitching and moaning about their late start. Alexander was sure the abomination was still terrorizing the streets and would be there for them to take out regardless of being an hour behind schedule.

Alexander awoke when the car came to a stop. Were they there already? Surely he hadn't slept for twenty hours.

"Do you want something to eat, Alexander?" his father asked.

"Wh—" Alexander cleared his throat and tried again. "Where are we?"

"Still on the east coast. We've only been on the road about four hours. I was hungry, and your brother was close to pissing himself, so we stopped for a bit. It's a little outlet place so you have a few different things to choose from. Be back in thirty."

Alexander let out a long yawn as he stretched his body like a cat. He put his bag on his back and made his way to the first little place he saw. He went inside, used the bathroom, then ordered some food and a drink. His father was already in the car by the time he got back, and his brother wasn't too far behind. They all got in the car and back on the road, stopping a few more times to gas up and switch drivers. Before long, Alexander was being shaken awake by Misha, and he vaguely remembered falling face first into his hotel room. He guessed he was more tired than he'd thought.

"Alexander! Wake up, shower, and get dressed. We're going scouting in an hour," Misha said.

Alexander rubbed the sleep from his eyes and acknowledged his brother with a grunt. He was starving.

"Food."

"After you're dressed, if you hurry we'll stop and get something on the way."

That woke Alexander right up, and he made quick work of getting himself presentable and ready for his first official hunt. This was one of the final steps in being able to go out on his own with his partner. He couldn't wait until Sam and he could do this without their family watching their every move. Fifteen minutes later and they were on their way. They stopped for food as promised, then made their way to the park where the disappearances were occurring.

"So what's the plan?" Alexander asked.

"Observation only," Misha said. "We *DO NOT* act. This is just a recon mission. We are not to engage for any reason. We are strictly monitoring the creature's habits and routines. We need to know what we're up against first."

"What if it attacks someone? We just stand by?"

"Yes. In this job you make some hard decisions. The point is to stay alive. We have to be smart about this and there will be casualties. It's unavoidable."

"I don't like it."

"You don't have to like it. You just have to follow orders."

Alexander was quiet the rest of the drive. Misha found an inconspicuous parking space, and their stakeout began. They'd brought snacks and drinks because they could be there for several hours before spotting the beast. Two hours later, the creature finally appeared. From where Alexander was sitting it looked just as human as himself.

"Watch carefully and document everything you see with your camera," Misha said. "It's a good thing it's still light out, we wouldn't want it to see the flash."

Alexander had to agree. If it weren't for the claws on the animal's hand, he would have sworn they had the wrong guy. It was the only thing "un-human" about it. Its impressive good looks helped it to blend in with those around it. Alexander watched as the creature leaned its head back and took a good whiff of the air. He was hunting, and Alexander wasn't sure he wanted to know what its prey was. All the training in the world wasn't enough to compare to the terror he was feeling right now. That thing would rip him apart if it caught his scent, and there would be no going back. Alexander didn't let his brother know he was afraid, though. Misha and Alexander did what they were supposed to do, and when the abomination lured an innocent woman to her death, Misha simply started the car and returned to the hotel to inform their father. It didn't sit well with Alexander to just let someone die such a gruesome death, but this was the world they lived in and such irrational thought could get you killed.

After telling their father about what they saw and ensuring him they'd gotten everything on camera, they planned to return to the park as soon as the sun was to set. Alexander was nervous as all hell, and if he was completely honest he may have vomited before they grabbed their supplies and left for the park. He didn't say a word the entire twenty minutes to the park, and neither did his father or brother. Alexander needed to get his head in the game. He couldn't let his family down. He was a Carvanis, dammit!

Misha parked in the same spot as before, only this time the three men got out of the car. Misha and Alexander went one way and their father another. They planned on taking the creature from both sides. Alexander tapped his brother and pointed to where the killer was talking to a young woman. His brother nodded and they were off. Their father reached the spot first and interrupted the conversation. Whatever Alexander Sr. said to the girl caused her to abruptly change course and leave the park. This, however, quite upset the monster. Alexander and Misha arrived just as it was speaking.

"Do you have any idea what you've just done?" it said.

"Yes, I've saved that girl's life from your fangs," their father said.

"You have no idea what you're dealing with, boy," it spat.

"Don't I though, abomination."

"Mooyer!"

"Surprise."

The creature turned to run, but Misha was right there waiting for it. He caught him with a quick two-jab succession. The creature's head jerked to the side, and Alexander followed up his brother's jabs with a few of his own, then he swept its legs out from under it and pinned his knee in its chest. Alexander could feel the sweat pouring down his back and the blood pumping in his veins. The adrenaline rush was almost too much for him to handle, but he was holding it together, barely. Alexander's knife was placed firmly under the creature's neck, and the thing had gone still beneath him.

"What are you waiting for? Do it already," it hissed.

Alexander said nothing. That was his father's job.

"What are you, Mystic, Hyjia, or Dylia?" his father asked.

"None of your fucking business you human piece of shit!"

"Wrong answer. Kill it, Alexander, so we can be done with it."

The creature's eyes widened for a split second as the shock of Alexander's father's words registered in its brain. Then it was choking on its own blood, throat cut from ear to ear.

"Misha," Alexander Sr. said, "call for a cleaner, then we can get back to the hotel, wash up, eat, and then be on the road back home in the morning. Alexander, you did well for your first hunt."

Alexander felt the ghost of a smile on his lips and waited for the cleanup crew. He couldn't wait to get home and tell Sam all about it. He wondered if his friend's first hunt was just as successful as his.

2000

"It's time to meet your fiancée, Nicole Casey," Cassandra said.

"I don't even know this girl, and she's fourteen," Alexander said.

"Nevertheless, you will be married in a few years, and it's time that you start building a relationship."

"Relationship? Are you insane? I have a job to do. I don't have time for this nonsense—and a girlfriend is defined as nonsense."

"You want to be the head of the family one day, don't you?"

"Of course!"

"Then you will need to be married and have heirs."

"This is bullshit."

"I suggest you take that up with your father. This has been arranged since before you were even born. The child they had a few months before you was a boy, but the next one was a girl and thus promised to you. You are a Legacy, and the rules are set out for what you will do and when you will do it."

Alexander counted to ten in his head and when that didn't quiet the rage tearing through him, he did it again. By the fourth time, he was a bit more in control of his tongue. Cursing out his mother would do him no favors. He was resigned to his fate as a breeding bull. That was all these arranged marriages were about. Alexander was surprised none of them had developed any genetic mutations yet from all the inbreeding within the Legacy families. Whose stupid idea was it for only Legacies to marry other Legacies anyway? Eventually they would all be fucking related. Then they would be no better than the creatures they hunted.

"Fine, let's get this over with. Where am I meeting her?"

"We must go to the Caseys house since you're the male. Come on, grab your coat and let's go. It's not a long drive."

Alexander rushed upstairs to get his coat, then was out the door and in the car where his mother was already waiting. Apparently his father would meet them there. At least the girl they were pawning him off to was Sam's sister. That would make Sam Alexander's brother-in-law, meaning they'd get to hang out more often. Just as his mother promised, the trip was less than ten minutes, and before he knew it they were seated in the Caseys sitting room with cups of hot tea in front of them. Alexander didn't drink tea, so he had lemonade instead.

"Nicole will be down in just a moment. She wanted to make sure she was presentable," Melissa Casey said.

"No rush," Alexander replied, bored.

Ten minutes later, the three heard footsteps descend the stairs. Alexander rose from his seat, which was the polite thing to do, and pulled out the chair next to him for Nicole. He would be lying if he'd said she was unattractive. She was very pretty, but he felt nothing upon seeing her. Hopefully, once they started talking he'd feel a spark or something for her. For now, he wasn't happy that he would be stuck with this girl for the rest of his life.

"Hello, Nicole. It's lovely to meet you," Alexander said politely.

"Nice to meet you as well, Alexander," Nicole smiled shyly.

This wasn't going to work. She had no fire in her. What the hell was he supposed to do with this meek thing? His father had gone mad! Two hours later and Alexander wanted to shoot himself in the face. There was no way in hell he was going to marry her. First thing tomorrow morning Alexander was going to tell his father just what he thought about Nicole Casey. He could not be tied to that nitwit for all eternity, and he certainly didn't want to procreate with her. This was a disaster and one he planned to rectify at the earliest convenience. She would just have to be promised to someone else. Yep, he'd made up his mind. He'd never once voiced his opinion about anything, but he was putting his damn foot down for once.

They'd crossed a line tying him to a damn child.

The next morning, Alexander marched into his father's office, told him what was what, and woke up three weeks later in the recovery room bed hooked up to so many machines he was surprised he was still alive. He saw his father out the corner of his eye and tried to piece together what had happened.

"Have you come back to your senses after your little nap?" his father asked calmly.

Alexander did the only thing he could physically do, and that was nod his head and sit back helplessly while his child fiancée held his hand and squawked about him needing to be more careful while he was training. It was official: he was in hell and there was no turning back.

CHAPTER 10

2002

This was it. The last phase of their training before becoming fully qualified as a Mooyer member. Alexander could hardly stand it, and Samuel was bored as always. They were partners on this little incursion, and everything depended on how they handled the situation. Both their families were counting on them to succeed in hunting without a chaperone. It was up to them to drive to the location, stake out the sighted area, record evidence, then either eliminate or apprehend the suspect. There could be no room for error in the task that was laid out before them.

"When do we get our assignment?" Samuel asked.

Alexander could tell Sam was angry by the lack of southern twang in his accent. Samuel was all business when he didn't want to do something, and he lost the backwoods persona he liked to use around all the other members so they would underestimate him. Alexander was one of the few who knew he did that, and he understood why. Being the bastard child of a Legacy wasn't a picnic, and most of the full legacies liked to look down their noses at Samuel. The truth was, Samuel was a better hunter than more than half of the current Legacy members combined.

"We're supposed to meet the family heads in the meeting room in another two hours. What's wrong with you today?" Alexander asked.

"After careful consideration, between my father and grandfather, they've decided that I will be having an arranged marriage after all to some Mason girl. I'm not in the mood for whatever bullshit games they done decided to start playing. I was hoping that since my mama isn't in The Society, maybe they would leave me the hell alone about reproducing the next generation of assholes."

"Now you know how I feel."

"Hey! That's my little sister you're talking about."

Alexander gave him the most annoyed look. Samuel couldn't care less about Nicole and what she did or didn't do. He was just giving him a hard time.

"Fine, you marry the nitwit then."

"Incest ain't my thing. You go on ahead and have at her. I guess I'll take my chances with this Natalie girl. She at least better be attractive."

"I'm sure she's just as geeky as the rest of her bloodline," Alexander said with a sly grin.

"I hate you."

"Liar."

Alexander and Samuel went back and forth calling each other names for the next hour. They even started making fun of what each other's wedding and future children would be like. They were in no hurry to deal with either, but this part of their training ensured they were one step closer to being forced into things that neither wanted. But they were good little soldiers and if either of them had an idea of rebelling and speaking out of turn, all they had to do was remember the three-week coma Alexander had been put in. That always stopped any stray ideas right in their tracks.

The two started the twenty minute walk to the other side of the Society's property, to the meetinghouse. They mentally prepared themselves for the battle ahead. It wouldn't do for the other members to think they were playing around or having fun. It was forbidden. They were to eat, sleep, and breathe The Society and nothing else. For Alexander, none of this had ever been a problem until he met Samuel. The hillbilly was slowly causing Alexander to let his guard down, but Alexander had to be careful not to let it down too much or his family would notice. Once they made it to the meetinghouse, they checked in with the secretary and waited to be called into the conference room to receive their assignment.

The other groups in phase five were also starting to trickle in to receive their final task as well. His idiot cousins were there giving him the evil eye, and Alexander did his best to ignore them. Getting into a fight wouldn't be a good idea right now. It didn't take long for

Alexander and Samuel to be called into the room. Alexander slightly nodded to his father and Samuel's grandfather in greeting and took one of the seats in front of the five council members.

"Good afternoon, gentlemen. Today marks the beginning of the rest of your lives. Your performance on this assignment will follow you around until the day you die. It will determine your rank in The Society, so I suggest you take it seriously and give your all into competently and efficiently completing your task," Alexander Sr. said.

"Here is your folder," Derrick added, "with all the information you need to begin your task. It even has information on what to do should your task prove too difficult for you both to handle. Contact and emergency information is also inside your package. Identification cards, money, a list of supplies, and accommodation reservations. Also, the keys to the car you will be using for your mission. All you have to do is go to the carport to pick it up. Just show the attendant on duty your ticket stub, and you will be pointed to where you need to go. If for some reason you don't understand the instructions or you believe information to be missing, the person you can contact can be reached from the contact information provided. Now I suggest you take the rest of the night to familiarize yourselves with the contents in that folder and devise a plan of attack. You are due to leave first thing in the morning."

"Derrick and I will see you off. You will have thirty minutes before you depart to ask us any questions you may have. After that time, whether all your questions are answered or not, you will be on your way. You are not allowed help from anyone but the person assigned to your case file. Is everything understood for now?" Alexander Sr. asked.

"Yes, Father," Alexander Jr. said.

"Yes, Mr. Carvanis," Samuel replied.

"Good, you are dismissed," Derrick said.

After stopping by Sam's home to grab his supplies for the mission, they headed to Alex's place so they wouldn't be distracted. They settled in his bedroom with the mission folder spread out on the floor between them.

After going over it several times and talking out scenarios with each other, the two had a list of questions they needed answers to before they decided on a solid plan of action. They would go over in explicit detail the approach they would take after they talked to

Alexander's father and Samuel's grandfather with their concerns from the case file. Once they were sure they had the file memorized backward and forward, they went over their questions one more time, then called it a night. They had an early day ahead of them, and they wanted to utilize all of their allotted thirty minutes of help. Samuel was staying the night so Alexander got him settled in one of the empty rooms, then went back to his room to get some sleep. This was the final test before they were left to decide their own paths, and Alexander couldn't wait.

The next day, Alexander and Samuel woke up early enough so they would get the full thirty minutes to voice their questions and have enough time to go over their supplies, grab a shower, and eat breakfast before leaving. Just as they'd said the day before, Alexander Sr. and Derrick were waiting for them in the car.

"So you've had all night to look over the case file. What are your concerns or questions?" Alexander Sr. asked.

"We only have a few questions," Alexander said. "What happens if we come to the conclusion that this girl is not a supernatural creature? What if she's not at her last known location? Are we to just hand over our research as is, or do we write it up into a proper memo?"

"Are those your only questions?" Derrick asked.

"Yes," said Samuel.

The older men gave both Alexander and Samuel an odd look, but it only lasted mere moments. Strange, but they didn't question it.

"If after careful research you conclude that the subject is indeed not supernatural, you are to abort the mission, pack up, and bring the information straight to us. We will then reevaluate the situation with senior Society members to double-check your findings. If the findings prove true, your mission is over and you pass. However, after checking the facts again and we find that she is indeed a Mystic, your mission is considered failed and you won't get a second chance," Derrick said.

"Understood," Alexander and Samuel said in unison.

"If the subject is no longer at its last known location," Alexander

Sr. added, "you are authorized to ask around to determine where it could have gone. If you are unsuccessful in locating it again, you are to return home and a new mission will be given to you. If you do relocate it, you are authorized to follow up. We only ask that you call your case manager and update them on your location. That way you are accounted for."

"And lastly," Derrick explained, "you are not required to write up your notes properly. Your case manager can do it after going over your accounts once your mission is complete. However, if you want to formally write them up, you may. It would be practice for what's to come once you're a full member."

"Thank you," Samuel said. "We think we've got everything covered."

"Good," Alexander Sr. said. "And be careful. Be smart. Be sure. If you get stuck, utilize your case manager as much as you can within the guidelines outlined in your case file. Remember, if the case proves more challenging and the demon has allies, contact the safe house immediately so you can be extracted, and they will take care of the mission. If that happens you will be given a new mission to complete. Drive safe."

Alexander and Samuel loaded the car and performed one more equipment check before they were on their way to Mississippi to complete the last piece of the puzzle into being full-fledged members of The Society.

"How long before we send someone to follow them?" Derrick asked.

Alexander Sr. laughed.

"I've already called the Mississippi safe house and informed them to have someone watch the hotel for their arrival and follow them from there. It's not that I don't think they will be successful in their mission; I'm just not inclined to take any chances with my youngest son's life. He's one of the top runners to take over for me."

"As is Samuel. None of my children look good for the position, so I've moved on to my grandchildren. Sure, the fact that Samuel isn't full blood Legacy will probably be questioned, but there are ways around everything."

"Well, he has my vote. With Alexander and Samuel heading up two of the families on the council, we shouldn't be worried about any stupid mistakes. I've given them a mission that wasn't too easy but not unnecessarily difficult like some of the other teams."

"Good, I'm sure they'll be finished and back before we get a chance to miss them."

Alexander and Derrick knew the boys would be livid if they ever found out they had someone watching them, but they were the future of The Society and all precautions had to be taken regardless of feelings. Investments had to be protected no matter the costs. And make no mistake, those boys were wealthy investments years in the making.

Alexander and Samuel stopped a few times for food, to stretch, to use the bathroom, and once to switch drivers. It was a long drive, but it passed by fairly quickly. They made their way to the hotel address given inside their folder and checked themselves in. They decided to start fresh in the morning and use the rest of the day to go over the file one last time to refresh their memory on the mission. They took turns showering and then grabbed a nice meal from room service. The Society was extremely wealthy, and the hotel was one of the best resorts money could buy. After settling down for the night, Alexander and Samuel discussed what they would do first and agreed that checking out the area where the latest victims were found would be their first stop. Then they would visit the foster home that was the last known address of the subject.

Morning came early, and before long the two boys were back in the car and headed to an abandoned home in the country. Alexander made sure to grab the camera, and Samuel could record their thoughts on their handheld tape recorder. As they walked around the perimeter of the house the only sounds that could be heard were the clicks and snaps of the camera, Samuel's voice as he talked into the recorder microphone, and the echoes of their footsteps as they explored the crime scene. Bright yellow police tape still hung on the edges of doorways and along the front gate. And there was blood still soaked into the ground and splattered in puddles around the house's thick carpeting.

Alexander could only imagine what had happened here, and he knew whatever it was, it didn't happen quickly or easily. The children had fought as hard as they could to escape whatever monster had done this to them.

"What do you think, Alex?" Samuel asked.

Alexander thought for a moment before he answered. What did he think, truly?

"I think whoever did this knew what they were doing, and I would bet money they've done it before. Either this child suspect is a psychopath or she's working with one. There is no way a mere child could cause this much damage. I mean, look at all this blood! That's at least three or four bodies' worth. One little girl couldn't do all this damage by herself, even if she were a Mystic. Surely she wouldn't have the type of power yet to keep that many humans in her thrall."

Samuel searched the house and took everything in once again. He agreed with Alexander's assessment of what they were dealing with. They needed more information before they could proceed.

"I think we need to visit her foster home and talk with a few people who know her," Sam said. "At this point, I would not want to confront this suspect until we know more about her."

"Agreed. If indeed one little girl can do all this damage by herself, then we need serious backup. I've not seen anything like this done by one supernatural in any of the lessons and old missions. This is entirely new territory."

Alexander snapped a few more photos of the house, the property around it, and the bloodstains for their report, while Samuel made a few more observations into the tape recorder. They stayed another thirty minutes or so before heading to the address provided for the foster home. It took them a little under an hour to get from the abandoned home to the last known address for Nancy Donovan. Their cover was they were doing a story on the dangers of child murders and abductions, and they just wanted to see if there was anything Nancy or the other kids could remember. Like if they'd seen any unusual activity from strangers they'd never seen before. They even had a fake business card that had their case manager's phone number for verification purposes in case questions arose.

Alexander parked their car across the street from the residence. Once he shut off the car, the two made their way on foot across the street and up the stairs of the modest home. Samuel rang the doorbell, and they waited for a response. A middle-aged woman opened the door.

"May I help you?" she asked.

"Yes, ma'am. My name is Jason Cross and this is my friend Jacob Simmons," Samuel said smoothly. "We're doing an article for a local paper in Clarksdale, Mississippi, on the dangers children face today, and we wanted to know if it would be all right to speak to Nancy Donovan or another child who may be able to shine a light on the unfortunate murders of those children."

The lady looked at them warily before glancing down at their business card. Reluctantly, she agreed to let them in.

"Come on in. My name is Jessie Ann Clark. You may call me Ms. Clark or Ms. Jessie Ann."

"Yes, ma'am. Thank you," Alexander said.

"May I get you boys something to drank?" she asked with a southern drawl. "Sweet tea? Coffee?"

"Sweet tea will do us both nice," Samuel said.

Alexander was content to let Samuel do all the talking since his accent was better suited to their cover story.

"I'll be right back."

Five minutes later, Jessie Ann was back with three glasses of sweet tea and some cookies. The boys thanked her and waited for her to talk.

"Nancy isn't here at the moment; she's out somewhere with friends. And the other children are running around outside as well. None of them will be back anytime soon. All I know about the disappearance of them other children is what Nancy done told me. She says that she'd left them at the park because she wanted some alone time. That Nancy gets bored of crowds real easy, and she's prone to wandering off from the rest of the group. I say lucky for her, if she hadn't wandered off that day, they'd have found her body out there at that old house, too. Only reason them kids was found at all is 'cause the high school kids still like to go out there and throw parties and such. Nancy was just beside herself when she heard the news," Jessie Ann said.

"That is truly tragic and I bet traumatic for Nancy. But we've heard that it wasn't the first time that Nancy had a run in with a murderer," Samuel said.

"That ain't nothing but gossip! That child's just had a string of bad luck is all. The police even suspect that maybe poor Nancy was the intended target all along. That someone is stalking the poor child everywhere she goes."

Alexander could tell from the way Jessie Ann's face was turning red and the wild look in her eyes that she believed every word she was saying. It was unfortunate because Alexander was convinced that Nancy wasn't what she seemed to be or what people thought she was.

"If the police think that Nancy's being stalked, then why isn't she under twenty-four hour protection, and why isn't she home?" Samuel asked.

"I think it's time for y'all to leave. I ain't got nothing more to say about this. Y'all have a good day now."

Jessie Ann walked them to the door and closed it tight behind them. Samuel and Alexander got into the car and went back to the hotel to come up with another way to find Nancy and speak with her. They would go back later that night to see if Nancy returned, and then figure out a way to get her alone.

"You keeping an eye on our boys?" Alexander Sr. asked into the phone. "Good, don't let them out of your sight. You should be able to hear if anything goes wrong from the room beside them. You smell trouble you get them out. Am I clear? Good."

Alexander hung up the phone without another word and forced himself to get some work done. The boys would be home soon, and he could stop worrying about them getting killed on their first solo mission. It was just nerves. The boys were going to be fine.

Alexander and Samuel were going over the notes from that morning when their hotel door was suddenly ripped off its hinges. The two boys barely had time to look up before they were both lifted up and tossed into the wall by an invisible force.

"I heard y'all was looking for me," shrieked a shrill voice. "Well, surprise, bitches! Mm, what is that I smell? Could it be Mooyers? And it looks like they sent the C team. That's a shame. I thought I was going to be in for more of a challenge," Nancy said.

"Let us down, you demon child!" Alexander shouted.

"Ah, see that's were y'all messed up. I'm far from a child. Try one thousand years old. Oops, sucks for the two of you. No matter, I'll be sure to send your little Society a postcard."

The last sounds Alexander heard were footsteps, shouting, and a loud, sickening thud.

For the second time in his life, Alexander woke up hooked to more machines than he'd ever thought existed and fucking Nicole sobbing over him like he'd died. This shit was getting old. Alexander tried to think of the last thing he could remember, but he was drawing a blank. How did he get here, and what the hell happened?

"Thank God! Alexander, he's awake!" Cassandra shouted. "Nicole, stop that incessant wailing and move out of the way."

"What happened?" Alexander asked his mother.

"Shush, sweetheart. Don't try to talk. Your father will be here soon, and he'll tell you everything. Don't worry. You just rest until he gets up the stairs."

Alexander could hear the heavy footfalls of his father's boots, followed by another pair behind him.

"Where's Samuel?" Alexander asked.

At the sound of Sam's name, Nicole cried louder.

"Will someone please shut her up?" Alexander said.

"Nicole, go home. I will call you when Alexander is feeling better," Cassandra said.

Nicole made her way out of the room, loudly. Damn, but that girl had a pair of lungs on her, and Alexander wasn't in the mood for her shit.

"You didn't answer my question, Mother."

"Alexander, finally. You're awake," Alexander Sr. said. "We thought we'd lost you."

Alexander's entire family had shoved their way into the recovery room. What the hell was going on?

"Someone had better start talking. Quickly."

Alexander's father cleared his throat.

"Well, it seems our intelligence was faulty, and the ones who provided it have been sufficiently dealt with. What we thought was a child was really a thousand-year-old creature with the body of a child. She liked to pass herself off as a child, as it made it easier for her to lure her victims. After Samuel and you questioned the foster mother, Nancy paid you both a visit. She killed Samuel. His neck snapped instantly when she threw him into the wall the second time. The only reason you're not dead right alongside him is because the surveillance team heard the commotion and got to your room just in time. The distraction caused her to shift a little before tossing you into the wall again. You got hurt pretty badly. You have some broken bones and a fractured skull, and were pretty touch and go for a while. Alexander, are you listening to me?"

No, he wasn't. He'd stopped listening after hearing that Samuel was dead. It was supposed to be a simple mission, and now his only friend was dead. Alexander hadn't realized he was crying until his father ushered all his brothers and sisters out of the room. The only person left with him was his mother, to witness something Alexander had never done before. She just let him cry until he couldn't cry anymore. And to think it only took eighteen years for his first set of tears to make their presence known. Guess he wasn't immune to emotion after all.

CHAPTER 11

2011

"So why are we going to this dinner at Derrick's again?" Alexander asked his father.

"Because he has a new recruit he wants you to train."

"Why me?"

"Because you are the best."

"And why exactly does Nicole need to be there?"

Alexander watched as his father sighed. He knew he had to marry her eventually, but did she have to be near him all the time?

"You have got to get over whatever problems you have with Nicole. She will be your wife and the mother of your children. Do you think I wanted to be married to your mother? I did it because that is what my father set up. It is the way things are done."

"Maybe the way things are done should be changed. Other rules have changed. Why can't this one be changed as well? We should be able to pick which other Legacy we are to marry."

"Well. if you happen to take over after me, change it."

Alexander's mouth hung low in a grimace. He'd told his father after what had happened with Samuel, he never wanted to sit on the council. And he meant it. His father still seemed to think he would get over it, but he wouldn't. Not ever.

"Let's just get this over with."

They were silent the rest of the car ride to Derrick's. It looked like they'd arrived before this newest non-Legacy recruit. Good, that way he could watch from the sidelines whenever this person arrived. Seated in Derrick's living room, Alexander tried his hardest to ignore Nicole, but either she was extremely clueless or she was doing it because she knew it annoyed him. Either way he just sat there and nodded his head every so often. Alexander watched as Derrick opened the front door to usher in the prettiest girl Alexander had ever seen. At first glance she looked just like Nicole but prettier. Alexander could hear his heart trying to beat out of his chest. Who was this woman? He involuntarily started moving toward her, but once he realized what was happening he grew angry.

What the hell was he thinking? She wasn't a Legacy, and worse, she was some idiot who'd happened to be in the wrong place at the wrong time. This was who they wanted him to train? This peasant! Alexander was further brought out of his childish daydreams by the sound of Derrick's voice.

"Isobelle, you've meet my wife many times and Alexander, but this is his youngest son, Alexander Jr., and his fiancée—my granddaughter, Nicole Casey."

Isobelle... Alexander played the name around in his head and nearly said it out loud when the strangest thing happened. The girl looked as if she'd seen a ghost. Sweat beaded on her forehead, and she looked as if she would pass out at the smallest hint of movement. Again, Alexander asked himself if this was the person they wanted him to train. If it was, she was in for a rude awakening. He would not train lightly with her regardless of whatever issues she had. After she passed out, Alexander couldn't keep quiet any longer.

"I'm sorry, this is who you would have me train? She's hardly worth all the trouble."

"Shut up, boy!" Derrick growled.

"Fine, but don't blame me if she's washed out of the program and forced to either commit herself to an institution or we have to kill her."

"No one is killing anyone, and she's definitely not being placed in a mental ward."

"So we're making exceptions now? Since when?"

"Alexander, take your son home. We will do this at another time," Derrick said.

"I'm not training this waste of time."

"You will do what you're told!"

Alexander was about to open his mouth but his father shook his head.

"We will try again tomorrow, Derrick. Same time?" Alexander Sr. asked.

"Yes, same time."

Alexander Sr. rushed Alexander out of the house before the boy had a chance to wonder what the hell had just happened. But Alexander was more determined than ever to get to the bottom of what made this girl so special, no matter the consequences.

PART THREE

ALEXANDER & ISOBELLE

CHAPTER 12

"Who the hell is she, and what do you think I'm supposed to be able to do with her?" Alexander asked his father. "Did you see her in there? Passing out only seconds after coming through the door. What kind of investigator is she supposed to make?"

"She is the head of her class and even outshines most Legacies. Tonight was a fluke," Alexander Sr. said.

"A fluke! Father, really, the girl passed out for goodness sake. Why must I waste my time training her? I should be in the field."

"You haven't been the same since the night Samuel died."

Alexander sucked in a breath through his teeth. If they weren't in a car he would have left the conversation, and his father knew it. He didn't like to talk about Samuel, and he didn't know why his father insisted on bringing it up so often. It hurt too much and in his line of work, emotion could get you killed. Sometimes he wished he had died that night, too, so he wouldn't have to live with such pain. Sometimes he caught himself wondering if Samuel would be feeling the same had it been him who lived instead.

Alexander knew he was being foolish. The past was in the past and this was now. But now he was being forced to train some weakling who definitely didn't deserve his training. Sometimes he found himself wondering if it was worth it. His life wasn't for the weak, that was sure. Alexander often dreamed of a normal life, but he didn't know the first thing about normal.

"Are you going to say something or just stare out that window and sulk?" Alexander Sr. asked.

"I don't want to talk about him."

Alexander couldn't even say his name out loud anymore. He felt pathetic, weak. Some nights, he'd wake up screaming, reliving the violence of the attack. A few months after he'd woken up from his injuries, he started remembering things here and there. It wasn't much, but it was enough to make him wish he would just forget. Nancy hadn't gone out quietly, and she took more than just Samuel that night. No matter how hard he tried to replay that day in his head, Alexander didn't understand how she'd found them so quickly. He would probably never get the answers he was looking for. The case file was nowhere to be found and no one would talk about it. Alexander had a feeling his father and Derrick made it that way so he would never really know what happened that day. Maybe he didn't need to know. Most importantly, did he even want to know? Not likely—it wouldn't bring his friend back either way. So there was no point in seeing the gory details in photographed stiles of color. He was better off just letting it go. Unfortunately, some things were easier said than done.

Isobelle woke up with a pounding headache. Where the hell was she? Had she missed the dinner at Derrick's? She scanned the room, trying to get her bearings, but nothing was familiar. When she spotted Derrick and Kalliope standing over her, she smiled. Now she just needed to know what had happened.

"Oh good, you're awake," Kalliope said. "How are you feeling, dear?"

Isobelle studied the petite woman who had been like a surrogate grandmother to her the past few years. Kalliope looked ravishing as usual with her strawberry curls meticulously held in place with various clips, combined with the bluest eyes and slightly tanned skin. Isobelle could see why Derrick was madly in love with the woman. If Isobelle was completely honest, she was pretty infatuated herself.

"I'm trying to piece together what happened before I blacked out."

"We believe you had one of your episodes," Derrick said. "It was all we could do to usher Alexander Jr. out of the house. I'm sorry to say his opinion of you isn't very high. He says you would be a waste of time."

"He doesn't even know me! Also, what time would I be wasting exactly?"

"His. The reason we were having this dinner tonight was to introduce you to your new personal trainer. You're far too capable a fighter to fall in with the other recruits. I believed you would do better with one-on-one training with a senior member of The Society. Now I'm afraid you'll have to work twice as hard to earn Alexander's respect and admiration."

"Great, just what I need in my life—some uppity spoiled asshole. So when are these lessons supposed to take place?"

"We have rescheduled dinner for the same time tomorrow night. Do you think you will be up for it?"

"Of course. I'll be here."

"Good. Do you want to talk about your vision?"

Isobelle thought about it for a moment and decided that, no, she did not want to talk about what she'd seen.

"Not at the moment."

"Very well. Are you okay to drive yourself home?"

"Yes, I just have a bit of a headache. I'll take care of it when I get home. I'll see you both tomorrow, hopefully without incident."

Isobelle let Derrick walk her to her car. She assured him she was fine, and after several minutes of back and forth, she was on her way home. She was still reeling from that vision and didn't want to dwell on it any longer than she had to. The drive back to her apartment was uneventful, and before long she'd had a nice, hot bath, a glass or two or wine, and was off to bed. She wanted to make sure to mentally prepare herself for coming face-to-face with the sexiest man she'd ever seen. Once she was under the covers, it didn't take long before she was fast asleep and dreaming of things better left alone.

As soon as she looked into those blue-grey eyes, nothing else mattered. The vision took her with a strength she had not felt since she was a child. There, as clear as day, was her future and those blue-grey eyes were in it, along with another pair of

blue eyes she didn't recognize. Looking into them gave her pause. She then saw someone else in the shadows but couldn't make out who it was. They were too far away to tell. A shiver worked its way up her spine and suddenly Isobelle was freezing. Who was this second man, who was the person in the shadows, and what did this vision mean? She couldn't help but be drawn to all of them, but there was a hatred surrounding one that threatened to consume them all.

Suddenly everything went dark, and Isobelle found herself calling out two names. One she vaguely recognized and the other she'd never heard before. James and Alexander. She didn't know the third, and the name wasn't coming to her. She called to them as if she was afraid to lose them, but it couldn't be. These men meant nothing to her. They were strangers. Two she'd never met, and the other she'd only just briefly glimpsed. Then, all she felt was unimaginable pain. Every part of her body sang a song of blood and pain. Everything around her was in ruins. People lay dying in the streets, and the world threatened to consume itself. Destruction and chaos surrounded her, and no matter where she looked, she was alone. James and Alexander were being pulled away from her, the other was nowhere to be found, and for some reason it made her feel desolate. She still didn't know why she should care, but with every breath she took they were being forced farther and farther away from her. Isobelle screamed, and she kept right on screaming until she couldn't scream anymore.

Isobelle woke up covered in sweat. The blanket and sheets were tossed haphazardly around her bed, and her nightgown molded to every crevice of her body. Her heartbeat was still beating frantically from the vision she'd had hours before, which were now plaguing her dreams and turning them into nightmares. She glanced at the clock beside her bed and winced once she took in the time. Three in the morning and she had the feeling that sleep would not return quickly. Isobelle resigned herself to her fate and headed to the bathroom to take a quick shower to wash the lingering effects of the vision/nightmare she'd had. Hopefully the hot water would succeed in washing away her troubles the second time around. After spending a considerable amount of time in the shower, Isobelle finally redressed into a dry nightgown. She stripped the bed of the wet sheets and blankets and tossed them into a basket. She then lit a chamomile candle to help her relax and lay back in bed. It took far longer than she'd have liked, but thankfully this time her sleep wasn't interrupted in a fit of anger and terror.

Due to the excitement of her night terrors, Isobelle woke up later than usual. This unfortunate event succeeded in throwing her entire day out of proportion. Luckily, she had managed to catch up quickly enough to arrive fifteen minutes early to Derrick's. This time she was determined not to make a spectacle of herself. It wouldn't do for her to act the fool a second time in front of her new personal trainer. As it stood now, she would have to apologize for her black out. Hopefully he wouldn't give her too hard of a time about it.

Isobelle did her best to control her breathing and prepare herself for the sight of Alexander. She rang the doorbell and didn't have to wait long for Kalliope to answer the door.

"Isobelle dear, come in, come in," Kalliope gushed. "You're looking much better than yesterday. Let's go to the sitting room where everyone is waiting."

"Everyone?" Isobelle gasped.

"Yes, the same people who were here yesterday."

Isobelle tried to hold in her embarrassment as best she could. How to explain to everyone what had transpired? She couldn't think straight.

"Isobelle, come meet Alexander and Nicole," Derrick said.

"Hello, it's nice to properly meet you this time," Isobelle joked.

Maybe if she brought it up first, it wouldn't be such a big deal.

"Oh it's quite all right!" Nicole smiled. "I can just imagine how much energy it takes to train so much later in life. It's different when you're born into things."

"I thought I was in amazing shape until I started the training program for The Society. Their workouts made mine look like a complete waste of time," Isobelle said.

"It seems you're still wasting time," Alexander sneered.

What the fuck was his problem? Isobelle's mismatched eyes flashed with anger so quickly that anyone not paying attention would have missed it. But she was sure Alexander had seen her displeasure. He hadn't taken his eyes off her since she'd arrived.

"I'm sorry. Exactly what time am I wasting, or, better yet, whose?" Isobelle asked.

"Mine."

"How am I wasting your time?"

"Because these fine gentlemen would have me train you, but after that spectacle I witnessed yesterday I can't be bothered with such weakness," Alexander said.

"Weak? Weak! I'll show you weak," Isobelle huffed.

"Really? What are you going to do? Pass out on top of me?" Alexander mocked.

"You're an asshole."

"I don't like you. I don't think you belong here, and I don't think you should be shown special favor, regardless of who you know. I won't take things easy on you, and we won't work up to anything. You either keep up or get left behind. Either way, I don't care. In fact, I take that back. I'm kind of hoping you fail just so I can laugh in your face at your execution."

Isobelle couldn't help herself. She laughed. Loudly. This arrogant son of a bitch thought he could intimidate her with his words and I-don't-care attitude, but he was sorely mistaken. Isobelle hadn't met a challenge she couldn't overcome and now would be no different.

"I'm sorry, was that little speech supposed to frighten me? Get over yourself. Now if you'll excuse me, I need a drink before dinner."

Isobelle exited without a backward glance, but she would have bet money that Alexander Carvanis Jr. never once took his eyes off her. Even though it shouldn't have, the thought of it was almost enough to bring her to her knees. She was halfway to falling in love with a man who would dance on her grave the first chance he got. And she couldn't even bring herself to care one way or the other. It was going to be torture training with this man. Complete and utter torture.

CHAPTER 13

"Again!" Alexander yelled.

Isobelle was about to lose her cool. It was the only word that smug bastard had said since they started training together this morning. After the dinner at Derrick's a few nights ago, Alexander's father finally managed to wear him down enough to agree to work with Isobelle. And he was being a total dick about it. All he did was bark out orders, and Isobelle was ready to punch him in the face instead of the bag she was training with.

"Is. All. That. Yelling. Necessary!" Isobelle grunted.

Say what you wanted, but the training routines Alexander was putting her through were rough. Every night she went home exhausted, and during the day she could barely stay awake to watch the videos or read the history of The Society. Alexander was not making things easy for her in the slightest. He was a hard ass, and she swore he got off on tormenting her.

"Do you want to be the best?"

Isobelle grunted in response.

"Then yes, the yelling is necessary. Now take some laps for the next twenty minutes, and we'll be done for the day. Tomorrow we spar, so be prepared. I *will not* take it easy on you."

"Aye, aye, Captain!"

Isobelle smirked to herself when she heard Alexander mumbling about ringing her neck. If he insisted on being a jerk, Isobelle would follow suit. All he had to do was tone down the hatred a smidge and they would get along great. If he wasn't so damn pigheaded he'd get over himself, but that was apparently asking for too much, so Isobelle was stuck getting lessons from a pretentious prick. She was way classier than he'd ever be, and yet no one saw her walking around with a stick up her ass.

Twenty minutes later, Isobelle was getting the evil eye from Alexander. She just rolled her eyes and continued on to the shower room. She took her sweet ass time cleaning up and finally dragged herself out so that she could make her way home. To her surprise, Alexander was still there.

"What? Forget an insult and decided to stick around and tell me," Isobelle said.

"No, we've been summoned by the Council. Let's go," Alexander said.

Isobelle watched his back for several seconds before his words registered. What the hell could the Council be summoning them for? Isobelle hadn't even completed her training requirements yet. She jogged to catch up with Alexander after stopping to put her bag in her car. She then opened the passenger side of his red sports car and got in.

"Nice car. I'm surprised. You seem far too ridged for a car like this," Isobelle said.

"Don't let my looks fool you. There is more to me than you know," Alexander said.

"Well, of course there is. You don't like to talk to me."

"And yet you insist on trying to talk to me."

"You are the rudest person I've ever met."

"Sorry, everyone can't grovel at your feet, princess."

"You don't even know me."

"I know all I need to know."

"Really? And what do you know?"

"That the only reason you're in The Society is because of Derrick Casey, and I intend to find out exactly why he's so fond of you."

"He mentored me a lot while I was in college. He wanted to help me reach my potential is all, and when I got in trouble I dropped his name.

"I don't buy it. Something else is going on. His protection of you borders on the obsessive. He knows something, and I want to know what it is."

"You're wrong."

"If you say so."

The rest of the trip passed in silence. Isobelle had nothing else to say. Alexander was on some sort of witch-hunt, and she was his suspect. Well, she had news for him: there was nothing special about her. At least he would never know there was. Derrick had promised her that much, and she trusted him to keep his word. He'd kept her safe this far, and she had no doubts that he would continue to do so.

Isobelle was brought back to the present by the screech of tires and being jerked in her seat from the sudden stop. She looked up and saw they were at The Society meetinghouse.

"Nice driving skills. Next time try not to kill me," Isobelle said.

"If I had it my way, there would never be a next time."

Good looks would only get him so far, Isobelle said to herself.

She followed Alexander inside and took a seat in the waiting area while he informed the secretary of their meeting. Once he told her what she needed to know, he took a seat next to her while they waited. Thankfully, they didn't have to wait long or Isobelle might have done something stupid. Like touch him. She would not have been able to explain that impulse had she followed through with it. The only thing she did follow was Alexander into the conference room.

"You wanted to see us," Alexander said flatly.

Isobelle gaped at Alexander, her mouth hanging open. They hadn't even sat down yet. He was so disrespectful! His fuck-everybody attitude was starting to grate on her nerves. Isobelle looked at the Council and said something she probably shouldn't have.

"I'd like to apologize for Alexander's rudeness. It was uncalled for and very unprofessional," Isobelle said.

Isobelle noted the way the Council members' eyes went wide in shock, but they recovered fairly quickly. Alexander, however, was another matter entirely.

"Have you lost your fucking mind?" Alexander exploded. "Don't you ever assume to speak for me, little girl. Perhaps I've not made myself clear enough. I don't fucking like you, and if you *ever* pull something like that again I will end you. I don't give a fuck whose dick you're sucking or who you think you know. You do not speak for me. Now why the hell did you call us here?"

Isobelle was speechless for a second before her rare temper

exploded.

"Just who the fuck—"

"SILENCE!" Alexander bellowed. "I've had just about enough of your shit today. Do not speak unless you're spoken to. Speak again and I will not be responsible for my actions. Derrick, muzzle your pet before I do it for you."

"Well," Alexander Sr. piped in, "as intriguing as this all is, we called you both here to let you know you will be partners once Isobelle's training is over and her completion ceremony is complete. And before you say anything, Alexander, it isn't negotiable. Either you are partners or you are both riding desks for the rest of your involvement in The Society. You'll be lucky to be assigned as case managers. You're dismissed."

Isobelle didn't want to be partnered with that ass hat, but she didn't want to be strapped to a desk either so she kept her mouth shut. But she was not getting in the car with him after his little display. She didn't care if she had to walk to her car. She stormed out of the conference room in a daze. This day just kept getting better and better.

"Isobelle, hurry up and get in the car before I leave you," Alexander shouted.

"Go fuck yourself! I'll find my own way home," Isobelle said.

"Excuse me?"

"Fuck off and leave me alone."

Isobelle was pulled into a secluded room and pushed up against a wall. She was held firmly in place by one of Alexander's knees and forearm. He gave her the strangest look before his mouth came crashing down onto hers. She stood there, stunned for several seconds before she grabbed him by the back of his neck and pressed her body closer to his. His hands came down to rest on her behind and he squeezed. He picked her up so quickly that she skipped a few breaths and then could feel something solid and cool pressed up against her back. He'd moved her on top of the table that was in the room. She could feel him through his pants, and the rubbing motions he was making were driving her insane. Isobelle had never been intimate with a man before, and she was all but purring like a cat.

Alexander's hands slid up under her shirt, blazing a path to her breasts. Just as quickly as they were there, they were gone and her shirt was being ripped down the middle to expose her in a way she'd never been exposed before. The look in Alexander's eyes was one of possession. In that moment, he owned every part of Isobelle and nothing else mattered. He started to attack her nipples with a vengeance, and Isobelle arched her back up to meet him. She was greedy for his touches, his kisses, and most of all his eyes. She wanted his eyes on her, always.

Isobelle felt herself fumbling with the buttons on Alexander's slacks when just as quickly as he'd attacked her, he pulled away. The loss of his skin on hers was so drastic that she shivered in its absence. The look on his face was a mix of horror and longing. Isobelle didn't understand.

"Alex, what's wrong?" Isobelle asked.

She was panting but she'd managed the words. He was silent for a long time, too long.

"Don't call me that. This," Alexander said, pointing between the two of them, "was a mistake that will never happen again. Either get in the car or walk home. I don't care. Either way I'm leaving in the next two minutes."

Isobelle watched as Alexander walked out the door without a backward glance. She looked down at her ripped shirt and the thought of walking out behind him in the state she was in reduced her to tears. For the first time in her life she was ashamed, and for that Isobelle might never be able to fully forgive him. With as much dignity as she could summon, Isobelle held her shirt closed with her hands, walked out the room Alexander had pushed her in, past The Society's secretary, and left the building to start her extremely long walk-of-shame to her car. Because, true to his word, Alexander had left when she hadn't come out in time. She was falling in love with a complete and utter asshole, and she had no idea what she was going to do about it.

Alexander sat outside his condo unable to move. All he could think about was the way Isobelle had felt pressed up tightly against him, the way she smelled, and the taste of her skin. He wanted her. More than he'd ever wanted anything in his life. But it was never meant to be. His heart could never be hers. They could never be together. His father wouldn't allow it for one, and for two, she wasn't even a Legacy. He'd screwed up back there in that empty room. He'd acted irrationally for the first time in his life, and it had almost cost him everything. From now on he had to play it cool. He could not get involved with Isobelle Mina. She would end up being the death of him, and he wasn't about to throw everything away for some chick, even if he felt like his heart was being ripped from his chest. Was this what love felt like? If it was he didn't need the hassle. No, he didn't have time for any more feelings. The last time he'd felt something, it hadn't ended very well.

CHAPTER 14

2012

This was it. The day she'd been waiting for—her completion ceremony for the training program of The Society. She swept over the crowd, searching for Alexander, and cursed herself when butterflies fluttered in her stomach upon seeing him. She couldn't keep doing this to herself. Ever since that day in the empty room, he'd been careful to give her a wide berth. In truth, she wasn't sure why she still got so excited whenever he was near. The embarrassment of that day should have been enough to hate him forever, but she just couldn't get him out of her head. Maybe it had something to do with that vision all those months ago. It didn't matter; he seemed to be paying much more attention to his fiancée these days. If Isobelle didn't know better, she'd say he was over selling it.

She wanted him badly. Never in her life had she ever felt the way she felt about Alexander. He was the one for her. She knew it in her heart, but sadly he had other ideas and they didn't include her. So she suffered in silence and resigned herself to a life spent alone. Isobelle shook herself to dispel her thoughts. The ceremony was about to start and she couldn't afford distractions. She watched as Alexander Sr. took the podium.

"Good morning, fellow Society members. Today we gather to welcome into our ranks our newest members. These ladies and gentlemen have endured rigorous training and have been tested beyond what they believed capable. I have the utmost faith that most of them will go on to achieve great things for us all. Now for the reason we've come here today, and that is to publicly congratulate the latest batch of survivors. When I call your name please come forward."

Isobelle watched as each graduate who was called got up, received their medallion, shook the hands of each family head, and sat back in their chairs. She waited patiently for her name to be called, but then something strange happened. Alexander Sr. stepped back and Derrick Jr. took his place. It was strange because he wasn't even on the Council and yet he was about to speak.

"I'm sure you all are wondering why I'm up here today, but this next member holds a dear place in my heart. She may not know the reasons why, but her accomplishments have made me very proud. It's my great pleasure to present to you Isobelle Catherina Mina."

Isobelle sat in her seat in shock. She'd barely spoken to the man all the years she'd known his father. She could count the number of conversations they'd had on one hand, and yet he was speaking for her and saying he was proud of her. But why? Isobelle needed answers.

"Isobelle, it's your turn to get your medallion," one of the other recruits said.

"Oh, yes, thank you," Isobelle stammered.

She forced her legs to climb the stage. She shook all the hands of the Council, exchanged a brief hug with Derrick Sr., and stopped awkwardly at Derrick Jr.

"Isobelle, congratulations on your achievement. We must get together more often to talk," Derrick said.

"But I don't understand," Isobelle replied.

"You will when the time is right. Just trust me and if that's too far of a stretch, trust my father. Everything will be explained in due time. Keep your medallion close to your heart. It is the perfect symbol for our Society."

Isobelle was startled further when he leaned in and kissed her cheek. She didn't know how long she would be able to wait for explanations, but for now she walked out on a little faith that Derrick Sr. would protect her from any foolishness. Isobelle couldn't help but seek out the face of Alexander, and the look he gave her caused her heartbeat to still. He looked devastated, but she didn't understand why. She wanted to run to him and offer her comfort, but she knew it wasn't possible. So she did the only thing she could do: sit back and wait for the conclusion of the ceremony.

A half an hour later, Isobelle found herself alone in a corner at the ceremony reception. She really just wanted to go home, but she had to at least show her face for a little while. She would give it twenty more minutes before she would head home. Isobelle swallowed a shriek when she was grabbed by the arm and dragged to the balcony. She looked up to find blue-grey eyes boring into hers.

"Are you insane? You nearly scared the life out of me," Isobelle scolded.

"Tsk, tsk. Had I been the enemy, you would have been dead. Pay attention to your surroundings or you're going to end up on a missing poster," Alexander Jr. said.

Isobelle huffed. She wasn't in the mood for his games.

"What do you want, Alex?"

"I told you not to call me that for one. For two, to offer my congratulations."

"I doubt it. Why are you really here?"

For a moment, Isobelle thought he wouldn't answer, but when he did, it was enough to shock her.

"Are you sleeping with him?"

"With who?"

"Don't play stupid with me, Isobelle. You know exactly who I'm talking about. Or did that little display the two of you put on at the ceremony mean something else?"

"I have no idea what you're talking about, and who I sleep with isn't any of your concern. For the record, I'm just as confused as you are about that display."

"Don't lie to me," Alexander growled.

"Oh, get over yourself. You had your chance, and you blew it. Now if you'll excuse me I'm going home. I have a hunt to prepare for. I suggest you do the same. I'll see you next week. Go find your fiancée and bother her for a while. You do remember your fiancée, don't you? You know the one who sort of looks like *me*."

Isobelle couldn't believe the nerve of that man. How dare he try to dictate to her and accuse her of things? He was the most infuriating man she'd ever met. She'd hit him below the belt on those last words, but she didn't care anymore. She did not know how she was going to survive missions alone with him for the next who-the-hell-knew how long. This partnership was already complicated. This was not what she'd signed up for. She would bide her time and in a few years ask for a reassignment. All she had to do was build a solid reputation for herself and the sky would be the limit. Yes, she would obsess over her job, and before long her feelings for Alexander would be but a distant memory.

Alexander wanted to punch something, or someone, preferably Derrick, Jr. As if he didn't have enough harlots falling all over themselves to get to him. Now he was honing in on what was his! No, that's not right. She wasn't his, but by god he wanted her to be. He needed to focus on something else besides his growing attraction. He needed a distraction. Alexander closed his eyes and forced himself to think. He needed something to temper these feelings that were taking root in his very soul. He could not have Isobelle imbedded in his bones. Then he remembered the first night he'd laid eyes on her. Something had happened. She'd had some sort of episode. He focused his thoughts on that and grabbed on tightly. She was hiding something, and his new mission would be to find out what. That should help to remove the feelings that were constantly growing inside of him. He'd focus on ruining her reputation instead of how soft she felt or how good her skin had tasted. NO! He would not be controlled by his emotions a second time. He had work to do. Starting with their first official hunt together.

"I will find out your secrets, Isobelle. If it's the last thing I ever do."

CHAPTER 15

What was that noise? It was loud and sounded like banging or kicking. Isobelle was in the place between dreaming and being awake. Was she dreaming the noises or were they real? Then the ringing started. She couldn't think clearly, and she was so warm and comfortable. The noise would stop eventually. She was sure of it. Minutes later, Isobelle was jerked awake by a loud crashing and heavy footsteps. The sight of Alexander with a gun in his hand caused her mouth to part open and her hand to fly to her chest to try to calm her raging heart.

"Ahhhhhhh!" Isobelle screamed.

"I could have killed you, Isobelle! I've been knocking on the door for ten minutes and your phone just rang and rang," Alexander screamed.

Ah, so those were the noises. Once she was calm enough to speak without shaking all over she addressed his concerns.

"I was sleeping and thought I was dreaming those noises. You didn't have to kick my damn door down."

"We were supposed to be on the road an hour ago!" Alexander shouted.

"No need for theatrics. I must have overslept."

"Overslept? Overslept! That's all you're going to say?"

"No. Get out of my room so I can get dressed. My gear is next to the door. Be a lad and load it up in the car, will you?"

Isobelle gave Alexander a little smile. He snorted in disgust but left her in peace to get dressed. She heard him on the phone requesting someone to come fix her door and to leave the new keys with Derrick. There was a pause and then she heard him say it was none of their business how the door was broken in the first place. She stifled a laugh and made her way to the bathroom to get presentable, and then grab her toiletry bag so they could get on the road to Vancouver. Isobelle had never been out of the States before, and she couldn't help the bubble of excitement. The fact that she was going to be holed up with Mr. Grumpy couldn't even quash her delight of going to Canada for the first time.

The Society had made sure she had all the proper documents months ago, because sometimes their missions brought them out of the country. There were members all over the world and compounds in most foreign companies under the guise of legitimate businesses. It was one of the reasons The Society was so wealthy; plus, it provided for an amazing cover to stake out potential paranormal activity and to send investigators out to handle the problems that arose. It was a new way of doing things, and so far, worked like a charm, with some of the business being a hundred years or older. Isobelle hoped to one day tour the bases in Italy, Spain, or Ireland for a year or two. But those assignments were only given to members who had been in The Society for several years if you weren't a Legacy.

Half an hour later, Isobelle was in the car, and Alexander was barreling through the streets to get to the private airstrip owned by The Society. They would be taking one of the private planes under the guise of a belated honeymoon trip. That way no one would question their presence in the country. It would also give them the freedom to survey at will instead of pretending to be in the country for work. For the last week, Isobelle had thoroughly studied the case file and committed it to memory. A small pack of Dylias had been spotted in the area, and the body count was slowly increasing. Isobelle and Alexander's mission was to catch them in the act, record the data and make notes, follow them to their dwellings, and convene with the members living in the area to take the pack out. They were to question the monsters first if they were able, but the kill order had been granted without hesitation.

Isobelle hoped to be able to question them first, but she wouldn't hesitate to kill them at a moment's chance. She would not be caught on the wrong side of this situation, and she wouldn't be surprised. She'd studied the tapes and knew their tricks. She was ready, and if perhaps she really wasn't, she would be when the time came. The trip to the airstrip didn't take long with Alexander's reckless driving. Isobelle really needed to insist on driving or she'd be dead before her time.

"The baggage attendant will get our bags and store them under the plane. Take only the ones you want on the plane with you," Alexander said.

Isobelle nodded her thanks and grabbed her backpack that had her laptop, notepad, music player, and travel amenities in it. They would be in the air a few hours, and Isobelle would get as much research done as she could. She also wanted to look into law school classes online since she hadn't had time to attend anything during her training. Now she wanted to get back into things since she would have more free time since she was a full member.

"What are you doing?" Alexander asked.

"If you must know, I'm looking at applying to law school again but for online classes, or maybe something hybrid," Isobelle said.

"Yes, because we don't have enough lawyers in The Society," Alexander deadpanned.

"What's your background then, genius?"

"I have several. Computer Programming, Graphic Design, and Psychology."

"What the hell do they teach you growing up in The Society?"

"Everything. Go to law school if you want but I also suggest you look into other programs as well. One can never have too many degrees."

Isobelle thought about that for a moment and decided to look into Mythology degrees as well. The rest of the trip passed by with nothing but the clicking of keyboards and barely audible music from headphones. Before long, the pilot was announcing their descent into Vancouver and turning on the fasten seatbelt sign. Isobelle started collecting her things and putting them away, then sat back and waited for the plane to land.

"When will we get to tell her, Father?" Derrick Jr. asked.

"Soon. Give it a few years, son, and we will tell her everything," the elder Derrick replied.

"I can't believe Bethany used me like that and kept my child from me. Isobelle should have been raised here just like Samuel and the others had."

"Yes, she should have. But she's with us now. I hope to mold her to sit on the Council alongside Alexander. Had I known about her sooner, she would have been promised to him instead of Nicole. I see the way he looks at her, and we all saw the tape from the room. They have a chemistry that he will never have with Nicole, sad to say. He doesn't even love her and will never even at least respect her. Isobelle is a better fit, but what's done is done."

"It could be undone just as easily. Nicole will do what she's told."

"You underestimate Nicole. She knows the track that Alexander is slated on and will not give up as easily as you believe. She may like to appear dumb and naïve to everyone who's watching, but underneath it all she's a snake, and she will strike if she feels threatened. It won't matter to her that Isobelle is her little sister. In fact, that may make matters worse. Being passed over by a younger, prettier sibling. And a half one at that whose mother isn't a Legacy like hers."

"Something must be done, Father."

"Give it time...things will work out as they should."

"I follow where you lead."

"Good, now ensure that as soon as Isobelle and Alexander land they are protected. I will not have a repeat of the Mississippi debacle. I will not lose another grandchild to those monsters."

"Yes, Father. It will be as you say."

As soon as the plane landed, two senior members of The Society met Alexander and Isobelle and escorted them to the safe house they would be staying in. After what happened in Mississippi, a lot of protocols were changed. Alexander wished they'd thought of those changes before his best friend was murdered. Years later and he was still bitter about it. Some days, if he tried really hard he could still hear Sam's voice and that damn accent he'd hated so much. Now he would give anything just to hear it one more time. There was still a hole in his heart were Samuel's presence had once been. He didn't think it would ever be filled again, but then he'd met Isobelle, and slowly that hole was shrinking.

If he'd not fought it, that hole would have already been gone and Isobelle firmly placed inside it. But it could never be, and dwelling on things that couldn't be weren't doing him any favors. He needed to focus on the mission. That's how Alexander lived his days now, from mission to mission. He couldn't afford to live it any differently, but a part of him wished he could. A part of him desperately longed for things that would never be. He just wanted to spend his days in peace and not hunting down supernatural killers. He had to bury that part and never let it show its face to the world. He'd almost risked it all because of that day in the empty room. It was a blessing and a curse that his rational part had prevailed. Had it not, he wasn't sure what would have happened, but it wouldn't have been good.

Alexander suggested they get some rest before starting their mission first thing in the morning, and Isobelle agreed. They ordered takeout and sent one of the junior members to pick it up. They then went over the plan.

"I say we start at the site of the last murder, which reminds me—do you have a map, Charles?" Isobelle asked.

Charles Mason was one of the senior members that had picked them up from the airport.

"Yes, what will you do with a map, dear?" Charles asked.

"I'm going to place pins on the areas where the bodies were found and see if we can't find a radius that may tell us where the pack could be hiding. Depending on how far each body was found from certain places that could be used as cover, we may be able to pinpoint their location a bit faster or at least have a good starting point."

"That could work," Alexander said.

Alexander watched as Isobelle pinned the map on a wall and started to place pins at each location where the local police had found the victims' bodies. It didn't take her long before she had them all plotted. He watched as she took her time to study the map. When the door to the safe house opened, he nearly jumped out of his skin. But it was only the food. Good, he was starving. They hadn't eaten all day.

"Isobelle, come and eat. Then we will look at the map together," Alexander said.

"Dammit," Isobelle murmured. "I think I may have a connection."

"If that's true you'll still be able to make it after you eat. We haven't eaten all day. Once your stomach is full, you may be able to think a little straighter."

"Fine. But only because my stomach has chosen this exact moment to protest loudly."

After an hour of small talk, Alexander watched as Isobelle returned to the map. She would let him know when she saw anything and if she didn't, then he'd take a look at the map himself. He didn't have to wait long before she was shouting in triumph.

"I take it that means you think you've cracked the case?" Alexander asked.

"As a matter of fact, yes it does. All the bodies have been dumped within a ten-mile radius of each other, and there is only one building in the middle of said circle. I'd bet money that this"—Isobelle pointed with her finger on the map—"is the place we'll find the pack."

Alexander studied the location. For now he agreed with Isobelle's assessment. If it proved wrong, it would have been a good start anyway.

"Good, while we check out the last dump site, two of the junior members will stake out the building from a distance. We don't want to get too close until we've gathered enough members to block the site in. The Dylia have a very strong sense of smell that rarely fails, so we need to be very careful. I have no intention of becoming werewolf food. I'm going to bed. I'll see you bright and early in the morning."

CHAPTER 16

"Do you have everything?" Alexander asked.

"Yes, for the fifth time, I have everything. Can we go now?" Isobelle asked.

"Hey, I'm just trying to make sure you don't embarrass yourself on your first official hunt. It's not like you got the practice I did with my father and older brother."

"Whatever. Let's go. We're burning daylight."

"Suit yourself. Don't whine if you realize you left something important behind."

Alexander pulled out of the safe house driveway in the piece of shit car The Society had bought for them. He hated any car that wasn't his baby, and this hybrid Toyota was definitely not going to reach the speeds he was accustomed to. He would have to talk to his father about getting him appropriate cars in the future when he was in the field. Eventually, they arrived at the site, and he pulled into a discreet parking stop. The police tape could still be spotted blocking the scene where the body was found. Luckily, one of The Society members had transferred to the Canadian police, so they were able to sign off on investigating the scene without issues.

"I'll photograph the area while you walk the scene and record your notes," Alexander said. "Once we are both satisfied, we'll go back to the safe house to see what the junior members staking out the abandoned warehouse have to say."

"Sounds good to me."

Alexander and Isobelle worked for the most part in silence for the next two and a half hours. Once they were both sure they'd learned all they could from the dumpsite, they packed everything up and returned to the safe house. They were both lost in thought so conversation on the way back was scarce. The return trip didn't take nearly as long as the first. Alexander thanked his lucky stars for small favors. He was ready to get out of that thing people called a car. He was a proud car snob and never hesitated to make his displeasure of a car known.

Upon walking into the safe house, Alexander searched for the junior members. They hadn't arrived yet.

"I'm going to go rest for a bit. Let me know when they get back with any information," Alexander said.

"Sure, I'm going to order some food and pick it up. Do you want anything?" Isobelle asked.

"Something quick is fine. Thank you."

"You're welcome."

Alexander made his way to the room he was using and wasted no time in undressing and getting under the covers. A nap was calling his name, and he had every intention of answering. He was asleep as soon as his head hit the pillow.

"Alexander, wake up, they're back from the scouting mission," Isobelle said.

"What time is it?" Alexander asked.

His mouth felt like a sandstorm had blasted through it. It was itchy, and his throat was dry.

"You've been asleep for the last four hours."

"Water, please."

A few minutes later, the cool liquid was traveling blissfully down his parched throat.

"Thanks. Four hours, seriously? What were they doing out there, and why didn't you wake me earlier?"

"Not sure what they were doing. I haven't asked them yet because I wanted to wake you first. And I thought you could use the rest. Not much we could have done anyway until we got the scouting report back. Now get up and let's go. I'll get your food out of the refrigerator."

"Yeah, okay. Give me a minute. I'll be right there."

"Hurry up."

Alexander didn't miss the covert looks Isobelle had been giving his virtually naked body. All he had to do was look under the blanket at his fully erect cock. He was going to need more than a minute to make sure that thing went back to sleep. By the time he was presentable it was ten minutes later. All heads turned to him when he walked into the living room. Fuck them, they didn't know his struggles.

"Stop staring at me and give the goddamn report!"

"Yes, sir," Jace Singer said.

Jace was one of Alexander's cousins. Didn't mean Alexander was going to give him special treatment. If anything, he was harder on family. He expected more from them.

"Stop wasting time and speak."

"Ah-ah, right. We took photos, so I'll just pop the memory card into the computer and put it on the screen so we can go through them. We'll offer commentary as we go."

Alexander started to eat the sandwich and chips that Isobelle had brought back for him. It was his favorite: ultimate club on sourdough with a pickle on the side. He didn't dwell too long on how she'd known his favorite sandwich. He didn't really want to know, so he just sat back and enjoyed. He was done devouring his food before Jace even started his little briefing.

"What the hell is taking you so long?"

"Sorry. It's ready now."

"Then get to it. We don't have all day. I would like to go home as soon as possible."

"Right. If you'll all turn your attention to the photos, you'll see that indeed this is the place the pack has made its home. You'll find some in their human form as well as a few running around in shifted form. We had to make sure to maintain a good distance or they would have smelled us for sure. Their sense of smell is more acute and accurate in wolf form. From what we could gather, with limited observation, there are at least fifteen of them, both male and female. We will need to call in more reinforcements if we're to take them all down."

Alexander studied the pictures some more before he spoke. It would be Isobelle and his call.

"What do you think, Isobelle?" Alexander asked.

"I think waiting one more day for backup wouldn't be a waste of time. I say we send another team to keep an eye overnight to ensure they don't move, have someone relieve them the next day, and wait for us to get there that night to take them all out."

"Sounds like a plan. Jace, make the call, and Charles, get two more teams ready. Let them know which shifts they'll be taking, and tell them to call with any changes or Intel. We don't want any mistakes on our side."

"Got it," Jace said.

"As you say, Alexander," Charles said.

Now all they had to do was wait for their backup, and they would be taking out an entire pack the following evening.

"Okay, people, the surveillance team says the pack hasn't made a move, so we're good to go. Make sure your earpieces are working, and once you're in position sound off to Central. Once Central hears from everyone, the go-ahead will be given and we'll move out. Be fast, be accurate, and most importantly, be safe. I don't want any casualties from us tonight if we can help it. Watch each other's backs. Isobelle, you and me, like glue. Do you hear me?" Alexander asked.

"I got it," Isobelle huffed.

"Don't roll your damn eyes at me. I'll stick you in the damn van and make you stay there."

"I said I got it. I'm ready."

"You better be. Let's move, people."

They loaded up into five SUVs loaded to the max. Hopefully that was enough armed members to take out a pack of Dylia, and if not, Alexander just hoped he died quickly. He did not want to suffer and be played with. The ride was over before long, and they were quietly making their way to their positions around the compound. Isobelle was barely a foot behind him, which was good. That was about as far as she was allowed to be. They got into position and called it in. Alexander could hear several other calls coming in and waited for them all to be in position. Ten minutes later, Central told everyone to stand by while they made sure everyone had checked in.

"Okay, everyone's in position. Get ready to move in five, four, three, two, go! Go! Go! Go! Go!"

Alexander sprinted from his position with Isobelle hot on his heels. Dylia could be seen coming out of windows, only to fall back once the bullets started flying. Alexander had his gun out and at the ready, and got off several shots once the front door was swung open. He heard Isobelle open fire from behind as well. They didn't stop firing until the Dylia stopped pouring out of every available exit. Alexander and Isobelle covered each other as one reloaded. Several minutes later, all was quiet. Alexander tiptoed toward the doorway, his gun still at the ready. He saw several other members slowly approaching open windows as well, stepping over the piles of bloody Dylia bodies—some in human form and others caught trying to transform. But what Alexander saw inside the building was truly awful. He swung his head back toward Isobelle, who was approaching the door behind him.

"Alex, what are you doing? Let me in," Isobelle said.

"No, you don't need to see this," Alexander said.

"What are you talking about? I'm already seeing dead bodies."

"No, not like this. Get back, Isobelle."

"No."

Isobelle shoved past Alexander and entered. Seconds later he heard her footsteps retreating and retching sounds coming from outside. Alexander closed his eyes and took in a deep breath. He told her not to fucking come inside. Didn't matter what anyone said about war, no one wanted to see dead babies and children. Nobody. Especially if they were dead because of bullets from guns carried by your team member. And that included him, but this wasn't his first rodeo so he was a little better prepared. But Isobelle, this would haunt her for a while. Alexander walked out of the warehouse, shaking his head in pity.

"Somebody call a cleanup crew and get this shit out of here! Charles, call the fucking pilot, Isobelle and I are going home. Tonight."

Their mission was done, and there was no more need to stay here. He was over Canada already.

CHAPTER 17

NEW YEAR'S EVE, 2012

"We have a new case, a few brutal murders. Blood everywhere. Mostly males and a few females with the same basic M.O.," Alexander said.

"What do they think it is?" Isobelle asked.

"Could be any one of them honestly, but the Council thinks that a Mystic wouldn't let all that blood go to waste."

"Makes sense in theory, but I don't want to go assuming stuff. That can get you killed quicker than anything else."

"Good, I see you're learning."

"Where are we going this time?"

"Nowhere. The kills are in our own backyard."

"This should be interesting."

It didn't take long to get to the latest victim's home. It was a fresh crime scene so they would get to see everything in its original state for once. Only downside to that was they couldn't take pictures and do their normal walk around to play out the crime and record the notes. They would have to just remember as many details as they could and have their contact on the inside send copies of the case file.

Isobelle took a deep breath and let it out slowly. She was still struggling with the aftermath of Canada and had to mentally prepare herself to see things she might not want to see. Once she was sure she had her shit together, she went inside the house.

"Do you need to sit this one out?" Alexander asked.

"And mess up my close rate? I don't think so," Isobelle said.

"Mm, wouldn't want that now, would we?"

"Nope."

"I'm watching you."

"Please don't."

"There is something unnatural about you."

Isobelle laughed in his face. It was either that, or react to his words and agree with his assessment. She'd been getting glimpses of information here and there for the last few cases and was able to impress more than a few people, while also pissing just as many off with her accomplishments. Alexander was one of the people she was pissing off. No surprise there. He was always pissed off at her for one reason or another. Sometimes it was like he almost cared and then just as quickly he was back to being the asshole. She was starting to get whiplash from his constant emotional shifts.

"Only thing unnatural," Isobelle said and looked around to see if anyone was around, "are the things we hunt. I am not one of those things."

"If you say so."

"I do. Now can we get to work?"

Isobelle climbed the stairs and entered what she hoped was the bedroom. A few cops were hanging about and when they saw her she just smiled casually, as though she belonged there. She looked into the room and... holy shit storm! There was blood everywhere. Someone had a field day with the victim's blood and used every spare drop of it to redecorate the entire bedroom. Blood was on the walls, in the carpet, soaked into the bed, and just everywhere. There were barely any spots that hadn't been dipped thickly in the victim's blood.

"You poor soul. Who did this to you?" Isobelle said to the indiscernible corpse.

Isobelle knew she couldn't get away with touching anything, but she was itching to place her hands on a surface and hope for a tiny vision. Yes, she hated her visions. But for once she could use them for a bit of good and have no one question her or look at her like a freak. The other members just merely believed she was following her instincts. It helped that most of the time she was right, and it wrapped up the case that much faster.

"What do you think?" Alexander asked from the hallway.

"I think we have a psychopath on our hands."

Isobelle looked at the file as it slid across her desk. Whoever was killing these people needed to be caught and fast. She was tired of being three steps behind this asshole. Months had passed, but she and Alexander were no closer to a suspect. The investigation was wearing on her, making her question her own abilities as a detective. Alexander's nagging in her ear didn't help the cause either.

"Good, I see you've gotten your file. Have you looked at it yet?" Alexander asked.

"I just got it. Can I have a minute to myself?" Isobelle asked.

Isobelle hated that damn look he gave her. The one that said I'm better than you because my family's a Legacy and yours isn't.

"Fine," Isobelle snapped.

She looked through the file and nearly vomited. Similar M.O. as before—a room painted crimson with several victims' blood. Isobelle got up, grabbed her coat, and rushed out the door. She knew without looking that Alexander wasn't far behind.

They pulled up to the crime scene thirty minutes later and the place was already swarming with cops. Just what they didn't need—a bunch of officers who didn't realize that they were looking for a non-human killer. Isobelle and Alexander would have to censor their words and actions. They couldn't let on that anything supernatural was really happening.

Isobelle found the room the victims were murdered in and had déjà vu. There was so much damn blood, just as before. Who was this madman, and what was the point of these murders? Isobelle slowly looked around the scene. It was too much. It had to be staged, but why? Isobelle turned to look for Alexander, but a rookie cop spotted her first.

"Excuse me, but you aren't supposed to be up here. Who are you anyway?" the rookie asked.

Shit! Where the hell was Alex? She didn't want to say anything in case he'd told a different story about their identities. She needed to think fast. Before she could come up with anything she heard his voice from the stairs.

"Detective Mina? There you are. I told you to wait for me. Rookie, move the hell out of the way and let us do our job," Alex barked.

"Now wait just a damn minute! Who are you people? You aren't allowed up here. No one said you could be here," the rookie argued.

"If you don't like it, talk to your chief. He knows who we are. You don't need to unless he feels you do. Now get the hell out of my way before I move you myself."

"This isn't over, asshole."

"Spare me the empty threats, rookie."

Isobelle watched in muted shock as the rookie huffed and puffed his annoyance down the stairs. She looked at Alexander and just shook her head.

"Was that really necessary?" she asked.

"What? You broke protocol and would have gotten us busted if I hadn't already talked to the chief. Next time wait for me."

She didn't dare reply when he got like this. Nothing she could say would make a difference. So she just told him her thoughts on the crime scene. He listened with a thoughtful expression on his face. She held her breath waiting for his answer.

Alex surveyed the scene before him, thinking on Isobelle's words as he did. The scene did look forced. Staged. The killer had fun with these two. Looked like he took his time. Magic was also definitely involved. For no one to have heard the screams the couple no doubt made, magic had to be used. Only good thing was that the magic used eliminated some species as the culprit, and he now had an idea of where to look. He turned to Isobelle to give her his thoughts.

"This scene was indeed staged. Question is who exactly was it staged for and why? If we find out the answers, we find the killer," said Alexander.

"Do you have an idea of who did it?" Isobelle asked.

"No, not for sure, but I do know magic had to be involved and only a handful of these monsters use magic that we know of."

"Okay. I will be downstairs. I've seen enough."

Isobelle fled to the car to wait. He would take as long as he needed. While she waited she would look over the other scenes in her files for similarities they could use.

As soon as Isobelle walked in the office Alexander sought her out. She didn't have time for his drama right now. She was late, and she just wanted to sit at her desk and do her job. The murders were still weighing heavily on her, and she needed to solve this case already.

"Where the hell have you been?" Alexander asked.

Isobelle looked at him in a way that said, "You had best change your tone." It only caused his scowl to deepen. Apparently, the look didn't work on him. Isobelle gave out a long, tired sigh, then sat in her chair and turned her back to Alexander. She heard his foot tap and a few minutes later, he spoke.

"Well, I'm waiting. Are you going to tell me or not?"

"Not," Isobelle replied.

"This conversation isn't over, Isobelle. I WILL have answers."

"Well, Alexander, I don't fucking answer to you, so I suggest you find something else to do."

It was only after Isobelle heard Alexander stomp off that she turned back to her desk. She knew he wouldn't let this go, but she just couldn't deal right now. She needed time to think, and Alexander was wasting that time.

Isobelle picked up the phone and called her boss to explain her absence before Alexander gave his version of why he thought she was late. Even though Isobelle had a crush on Alexander, she still knew what an ass he could be. She had the feeling he was waiting for her to screw something up just so he could nail her ass to the wall. Well, she wouldn't give him the satisfaction.

Alexander was pissed. Just who the hell did she think she was talking to him like that? He was a fucking Legacy! He needed to find out everything he could and nail her ass to the wall. Once he got back to his office, he found the old journal he had been reading on Seers and read the other entry from Jacobi Carvanis. His ancestor had kept several journals from his time in The Society, and Alexander had officially read them all. Once he was finished he needed more. Surely there was something else in the way of Seers.

Alexander rushed out of his office at once with his coat and personal items. No point in delaying his search. In fact, he might take a much-needed vacation so he wasn't rushed. With that thought in mind, he made a detour to his superior's office and knocked once on the door. The faint "enter" was all he needed to hear to open up and rush in. He wasted no time with pleasantries.

"I need a few weeks off, Father. I have some business I need to attend to," Alexander grunted.

"Is that the proper way to greet your own father?" Alexander Sr. asked with a frown.

"Of course not," Alexander said with a sigh. "I'm just in a hurry and don't have time to talk just now."

His father looked at him from the corner of his eye like he used to when Alexander was a child. He didn't like it then, and he definitely didn't like it now. Alexander Jr. wished the man would stop the theatrics and get on with it. He had journals to find. When he didn't twitch under his father's heavy stare, only then did the man finally speak.

"Fine, but you only get one week. You can't leave Isobelle alone too long or she might outshine you in your ridiculously ill-timed absence," his father said curtly.

"Ha! That's hilarious, old man. The day that street trash surpasses a Legacy, especially me, is the day you can put me out of my misery," Alexander said with much confidence.

"Careful, Son. Pride cometh before the fall," his father stated before he waved his hand, indicating the conversation was over and the boy was dismissed.

Alexander hated that fucking quote. He hated it even more hearing it from his father. That little saying could kiss his ass. He had other things to worry about besides his pride, like his reputation. If he didn't find out what Isobelle was hiding before anyone else did, as her partner, he would never be able to live with the shame. He would be damned before he was made to feel ashamed by Isobelle Mina—in this life or the next.

After studying the crime scene photos from that double murder for the third time that night, Isobelle pored over every piece of evidence that she came across. If she didn't find a way to solve this thing, she just knew that Alexander would find a way to make it her fault. She couldn't live with disappointing him. In fact, she hadn't seen him since this morning. She'd give it a few more hours then go looking of him. She would solve this case one way or another. What she wouldn't give for her therapy-inducing dreams to give her a lead, any lead. It didn't even have to be a big lead. She just needed to put these damn cases behind her. They were the most brutal she had ever seen.

Isobelle was determined to solve this case by any means necessary. If she had to endure those terrifying, creepy-as-hell nightmares she sometimes got, she was all for it on this one. Where in the hell was Alexander? He was supposed to be helping her on this. Isobelle went to the boss' office. She knocked once and entered.

"Excuse me, sir. Have you seen Alex?" she asked.

"Ah, Alexander is taking a week off. Is there anything I can help you with?" Alex's father asked.

"No, sir. I just wanted to talk to him about our unsolved case. I'll just keep looking until I find something," she said and walked out without a goodbye.

That man gave her the willies. Where Alex made her heart beat in anticipation, his father made it beat in fear. The man was insane, not to mention he was also a major asshole about this Legacy stuff. So what if she wasn't born into this life? She was damn good at her job. She would show them all by solving this case without Alex's help. She needed to go back and look at the last victims' house. Let's see how much they turned their noses at her then. She would show them all that even someone as commonly born as her could outshine a fucking Legacy.

CHAPTER 18

Alexander decided that there had to be more journals at the Carvanis House. The place was off limits to a lot of people because of secrets the family didn't want getting out, secrets that an uncle of his had written centuries ago. It took some doing, but he finally found five journals written by Nathaniel Carvanis. He slipped his way out of the house unseen and made his way home to read the journals uninterrupted. He was determined to find out as much as he could in the next week, regardless of the consequences.

Alexander rushed inside the house and to his bedroom and opened the first journal he was able to put his hands on. He intently read the pages, and each passing word had him ready to kill. This wasn't possible. He couldn't believe the words he was reading. His uncle had protected a pregnant Mystic! The man had turned his back on his family and possessed some sort of unexplained powers. Alexander threw the offensive book across the room.

Alexander's emotions were all over the place. He didn't know whether to be disgusted or use these journals for insight into a world he would never be that close to. He could learn so much from these journals, more than he thought was possible, but at what cost to himself?

Could he read about a coward who carried the Carvanis name and wrote every unspeakable act in a journal forever preserved in history? He was conflicted. Alexander paced his bedroom like a caged animal. In the end, the only thing he could hear were the words his father had spoken to him days ago. "Pride cometh before the fall." He snatched the journal up and prepared to delve deeper into unknown depths. He only had three damn days.

Isobelle walked around to the back of the townhouse so that fewer people would spot her picking the lock on the door. Everything had been locked up tight after the last baggie was zipped up and hauled down to the compound controlled by the Mooyer Society. Pulling out her tension wrench and pick, she bent down and set to work on the lock. It was a pretty simple deadbolt lock and would be fairly easy to open. Applying pressure with the wrench, she inserted her pick and rotated it around while turning the wrench clockwise. After a series of three clicks, she felt the lock give.

She quickly made her way inside and closed the door, placing her lock picking tools back inside her inner coat pocket. She pulled out her low light flashlight and turned it on. Starting from the back door entrance, which was located in the kitchen, she proceeded to go through the house with a fine-tooth comb. She wasn't expecting to find anything, but every little bit would help. She was looking in every crevice and crease and laying her hands on every surface she could find. Nothing downstairs, not a single fucking clue. She slowly made her way up the stairs and let her hands linger a bit on the way up.

She started in the bedroom where the murder took place. It looked as if nothing had happened, but she knew better. She had seen the bodies. They had been beaten and broken beyond physical recognition. She could still see the scene as clearly as the first day. Already decomposing and a few hours old before the cops had even known there was a crime scene. Isobelle took a deep, cleansing breath to clear her mind and help her focus on what she was supposed to be doing. She then ran her hands along every inch of the place. She was about ready to scream when she felt the spine-tingling tell of a vision.

She could see two females. They appeared similar to one another, except one was a die-hard redhead and the other had hair as dark as a raven's. The redhead had the most stunning green eyes she had ever seen, while the darker haired one's eyes were a vivid blue. They could have been twins if not for those striking differences. They were both beautiful and moved with a natural grace. They were frantically removing certain things from the bedroom, and the redhead seemed to be in a panic. Isobelle could see their faces just as clearly as if they were standing next to her. She would be able to recognize them if she ever saw them.

She couldn't determine their species, but she knew they weren't human. It was in the way they carried themselves. Their presence screamed predator. Monster. Killer. The dark haired one had a hard glint in her eyes, like she was barely holding herself in check. Just as suddenly as the vision came, it was gone. Isobelle let out the breath she was holding. At least this trip wasn't a complete waste of time. She couldn't share what she learned, but at least she had a clue. She wasn't sure if these were the animals that had killed the poor couple, but they knew something about the murder.

"Why were you here? What did you two see?" Isobelle asked herself.

She would just have to hope that another clue presented itself, and soon. She wanted to blow this case out of the water. She finished searching the rest of the house in case she got another reading. Nothing else was seen. Ah, well, at least this trip wasn't a total bust.

Isobelle returned to the compound to see what else she could find out tonight. She was so close she could taste it. She would not be deterred. She would solve this case just like the others. No matter what it took.

Alexander was shocked. He'd read things that he had no idea were even possible. No wonder his family had hidden these journals. He needed to talk to someone about what he'd read, but to who? Only one name came to mind: Isobelle. But would she believe him? He knew she at least wouldn't betray anything he said to anyone else. He was starting to question his years of training, the many years of brainwashing and control forced upon him. He was a Legacy, but was that a good thing?

Alexander scooped up the journals and placed them in his bag. He grabbed his car keys and headed out to Isobelle's place. She should be home from the office by now. If not, he would wait for her.

He reached her townhouse in an hour with traffic. He rang the bell several times before hearing that "she was fucking coming and to hold his damn horses." She opened the door with a look of annoyance. When she saw it was him, she wore a look he couldn't quite decipher. He didn't have time. He pushed past her and let himself in.

"Why, yes, Alex. Come on in," Isobelle muttered as she closed the door.

She followed him into her living room and sat on the couch opposite him.

"So, why are you here? You leave for a week without informing your partner, and now you just show up out of the blue," Isobelle said.

"I need to tell you something," Alex said.

"Really? You never tell me anything. I'm not a Legacy," Isobelle said mockingly.

"That's why I can tell you, because you aren't one."

"You don't have to throw it in my face, asshole." Isobelle got up to show him the door.

"Will you just stop and listen? I'm glad you aren't one because what I have to tell you could get us both killed."

That stopped her dead in her tracks. She slowly turned around and walked back to the couch.

"I'm listening."

"Okay, let me start from the beginning."

And he did. Holy shit did he ever. Isobelle sat there speechless for what seemed like forever before her temper got the best of her.

"Of all the low and hateful things in this world to do to a person, you wanted me dead!" she shouted. Before she knew that she was moving, she had slapped him. The look of utter shock on his face was something she would carry proudly with her for as long as she lived. "How could you, Alex?"

"Isobelle. I'm sorry. Please. There isn't anyone else I can talk to about what is going on in my head right now. There are still so many things that don't make sense. Please?" Alexander begged.

"How can I trust you? I knew I wasn't your favorite person, but this? What you've just told me." Isobelle just shook her head. "I need a glass of wine if we are to continue this conversation."

When she returned, Alexander handed her one of the journals.

"Read this," he said.

Isobelle picked up the journal and read it. Then she handed the book back to Alex with shaking hands.

It was now time for her to pay the piper. She may be angry with him, but he had shared something sacred with her today. It was only fair that she did the same. She took a long, deep breath and started to speak.

"I need to tell you something before this continues, and we discuss that 'Prophecy' and its potential meanings," Isobelle said.

She told him everything, things she had never told anyone. She told him about the visions, past and present. She told him about seeing the redhead twice now in only a matter of days. He listened to everything with a look of great intensity. His face never left hers as she recounted things that could get her killed in The Society they both worked for. They both had secrets that could destroy them.

"Well, what do you think?" she asked.

"I think we are both in deep shit."

Yes, she thought so, too.

"We need to make arrangements. We can't stay here for long," Alexander said.

"Where the hell can we go that they won't find us? We need to find those Mystics. Seeing as I'm not wholly human, they might help," Isobelle reasoned.

"Yes, let's find them so they can KILL me on sight!" Alexander said. "How are we going to find them anyway? Do you think your visions will lead us to them?"

"They won't kill you. I won't let them. And it's worth a damn try. We need to find them soon," Isobelle said.

"We need to pack a bag with essentials just in case. We also need to act no differently at work. We can't afford to be found out before we can secure a way out. Oh my god! My family is going to lose it," Alexander realized. "I need to use your restroom."

Isobelle told Alexander where it was, then she heard him throwing up. She went in and placed a cool compress on his neck. She'd never seen him like this. It was starting to scare her a bit. Then the doorbell rang.

"Are you expecting company?" Alexander panted out.

"No. Stay here and be quiet. I'll go see who it is," Isobelle said.

Isobelle walked to the door and looked out the peephole. What appeared to be an inhumanly beautiful man was standing impatiently outside her door. He didn't look like a contract killer, but then again, did they ever?

"Who is it?" she called through the door.

"My name is Kain. Please open the door, and I will explain why I'm here," came the reply.

"I don't know you, and I don't want any cookies or anything else you may be selling," Isobelle stated.

Kain found his patience snapping.

"Open this damn door, woman, or I will open it for you!"

Shit. Isobelle did not want to open the door. After a few moments of silence, she slowly eased the door open.

"Move," Kain said as he pushed his way inside.

"Excuse me! You can't just walk in here like you own the place."

"Shut up and listen. I need you to come with me. You aren't safe here."

"Bullshit! I'm not going anywhere with you. Who's authority are you working on? What Mooyer sent you?"

"Mooyer? Woman, are you insane? I wouldn't be caught with a damn dirty Mooyer. Nathaniel Carvanis sent me. Let's go."

"Filthy fucking liar!" Alexander bellowed from the hallway. "If that were true, he would be over four centuries old."

"Okay..." Kain replied. "What is your point, human? And how do you know that name?"

"My point? Wait. What the hell are you? I know that name because I am Alexander Carvanis."

Kain was officially annoyed, so fuck it. He grabbed them both and teleported home. Nathaniel could deal with the both of them.

Isobelle slowly looked around her new surroundings. Her eyes locked onto the red-haired woman that she'd seen in her visions. She also recognized Nathaniel Carvanis. She'd had visions of them both. Jennifer, that's what she believed the redhead's name was. Isobelle looked over to see Alexander's mouth open in shock. Poor guy had too many shocks in the last few days.

"Alex, are you all right?" Isobelle asked.

"I asked you not to call me that," Alexander grimaced. "This is outrageous! How long do you people plan to keep us here? People will come looking."

"Don't worry, son. They won't find you," Nathaniel assured. "I know what's happened the past few days. You can't possibly go back now. They would know something has changed the minute you step foot at The Society. I have just the place to stash you both, and they will never think to look for you there."

SAFE HOUSE, 2013

"Okay. I'm to take you to the safe house, and we will contact you when we need to," Kain said.

Isobelle and Alexander nodded their agreement. They had been taken to a small, inconspicuous house for their base of operations.

"There should be enough food and water to last a month. We will come and check on you both in a few weeks and take you to restock everything. Here is a disposable with Nathaniel and my numbers in it. Use it only in case of emergencies. Other than that, see you in a few weeks," Kain said and vanished without waiting for a reply.

"What now?" Isobelle asked.

"Now we rest and figure out something in the morning," Alexander replied.

"Of course. I could use some sleep. See you in the morning." Isobelle yawned and climbed the stairs in search of a bedroom.

Alexander did a quick check around the house. He would do a more complete sweep in the morning, but for now it was time for bed. He made his way upstairs and found an empty room. He was asleep as soon as his head hit the pillow.

"Isobelle, what are you cooking? It smells great," Alexander said in in the morning.

"Just some eggs, bacon, and toast. Something simple. We need to eat, but I'm not too hungry. So much is going on, and I don't know what to feel right now. Plus, I slept like shit," Isobelle answered.

"I know what you mean. I feel like my world has been turned upside down. Everything I knew, everything I was taught, isn't black and white anymore. Reading those journals left me feeling like I don't even know myself. I have to figure out who I am as a person," Alexander confessed.

Wow. Isobelle was floored. This was the most she had heard him speak in the years they had been partnered together. She was noticing certain changes within him—he was becoming less of a prick…softer. She decided they both needed a distraction from the stress for a while.

"I'll tell you what—today we won't worry about Mooyers or "The Tarnished" assholes. Today we are just two regular people hanging out. Let's eat some breakfast and watch some of the movies Nathaniel has in the den. We will make a day of it, just laze around without a care in the world, wallowing in denial. Tomorrow we can freak out. What do you say?"

"You know what? Why the hell not? I've never had a day where I wasn't training to become a Mooyer. A day of just relaxing and not worrying about who's trying to kill who sounds like a good idea."

"Then it's settled. We will watch some movies, pop some popcorn, and play in that ridiculously huge backyard. Now eat up. I only have one day to show you how your childhood should have been."

Afterward, Isobelle took in the look of content on Alexander's face and gave herself a mental pat on the back. She was glad she was able to give him something he had never had before. She was even more ecstatic that she got to experience it with him. No matter what happened after this, she would always have this day. She would always remember the joy on his face as she chased him around the backyard. No one would be able to take this day away from her, no matter what was still to come, and there was a hell of a lot still coming, but she wouldn't burden him with those problems tonight. Tomorrow they would go back to the shit storm surrounding their normal, everyday lives.

Just as they were about to settle into the couch to watch a movie,

Isobelle heard a noise coming from behind her.

When she turned to see who had entered, she shrieked. "Oh my god! How did you get in here? Who the hell are you? "

Alexander quickly turned and saw a dark figure standing behind the couch. Well, there went their one fucking day of normal. Alexander grabbed Isobelle's arm, pulled her off the couch, and dragged her to the wall. Where the fuck was his gun? He left it upstairs like a fucking idiot. He should have known better. The world he lived in didn't have normal days.

"She asked you a fucking question!" Alexander snarled.

"That she did, but you see, I ask the fucking questions around here. Tell me your names," James demanded.

Isobelle raised her chin in defiance. "I'd rather die," she spat out.

"You just might," James mumbled. "We can do this the hard way or the easy way. I can find out your names simply by reading your minds. I'm trying to be nice."

Isobelle glanced at Alexander. He just shrugged his shoulders. They both knew that whoever this man was, he wasn't human. Running would prove futile.

"Fine, asshole! I'm Isobelle Mina, and this is Alexander Carvanis," Isobelle snapped.

James jumped back two feet and hissed. "Mooyers!" James shouted.

"Former, so get over yourself. Do you have a name or are you going to leave now?" Isobelle challenged. Alexander just stood there with a stupid smirk on his lips.

James smoothed his hand down his suit jacket. He was a pure blood. They didn't scare him.

"James. James Johnston. Maybe you've heard of me," James said with a flashing smile.

Oh, hell! They were screwed, Isobelle thought to herself. Alexander sharply shook his head in denial. This couldn't be happening. This couldn't be their fate. They would have been better off letting the Mooyers deal with them. At least their deaths would have been quick, instead of filled with torture.

"Whatever it is you are planning, we want no part of it," Isobelle stated.

"Oh, sweetheart. You say that like you have a choice," James chuckled. She was cute.

"I'll kill myself first before I let you torture me," Isobelle said.

"Isobelle, please don't give the monster any ideas," Alexander pleaded.

"Mm, torture. I like the sound of that," James said with an evil laugh. He pushed enough power into both his mates to knock them unconscious but not kill them. He had no idea what he was going to do with them, but walking away now was no longer a choice. They were his, and he was keeping them.

PART FOUR

THE PRESENT

CHAPTER 19

James was never one to believe in fate, or in mates for that matter. He had been screwed over one way or another his entire life. The only time he felt like all had been right in his world were his centuries spent beside Kain. But even that had turned to shit. James let out an extremely long sigh. He needed a place he could take the two humans. It definitely wasn't going to be that fucking warehouse. He wasn't sure if his townhouse was still his after the nine months he had spent in Hell. He had of course paid cash for it outright, but he didn't know what to expect if he went back there now. Besides, he needed something with a basement. He would need cages. Well, actually one big cage, a prison specifically. For now he would have to take his mates to the warehouse and task Krista with finding them another place to stay. James picked up the two humans and teleported back to the warehouse.

"What are they doing here?" Krista asked.

"None of your fucking business. You aren't in charge of this operation, little girl. I am. Now go find us somewhere respectable to stay and preferably with a basement big enough to build a prison. And don't take your time about it either. I need it found two days ago," James growled.

Krista gritted her teeth. Who the hell was he to command her? She felt the calming vibes coming from her mates. She knew they were right. They had to bide their time, but she was pissed. Every minute she spent with her father she wished she had left him in Hell.

Honestly, what could he have done to her from there? Krista should have taken the risk. Now she was a pawn in whatever her father had planned. She tried a different tactic.

"Surely you wouldn't want The Mooyer Society to come down on our heads for kidnapping a Legacy member?"

"Fuck those assholes. They weren't worth my time when they first formed, and they aren't worth my time now. If anything, it is they who should be afraid of us. Your grandmother cursed the entire Carvanis line, so I'm not worried about what the head of that family will do."

Krista couldn't contain her shock. Her grandmother had done what? Just how fucking old was James anyway? She was battling between waiting to know everything he knew and slitting his fucking throat. She settled on finding a new place to stay for now. James was right that the warehouse was disgusting and vile. They needed to move from it, but she wasn't happy that James insisted to tag along. Plus, what the hell were they going to do with two fucking humans? One of whose blood called to Krista like a siren's song. She needed another taste, just a small one. James wouldn't know.

Krista's arm was broken. She tried to stand up from where she was on the floor, but she was dizzy. She looked over to where her mates were. They were both shifted. That was odd. She couldn't remember what happened.

"Wh—" Krista cleared her throat a few times. "What happened? Why are you both in shifted form? Where is my father?"

Nathan was the first to shift back. He was livid! He wanted to kill James for what he'd done. It was unprovoked and unnecessary.

"Your father is what happened. He's insane and needs to be dealt with. He flew off the handle in a rage out of nowhere," Nathan growled.

It didn't make any sense. Krista didn't understand what had happened. Had he heard her thinking about draining the woman dry? Probably knowing her luck. Great, now she would have to be careful with her thoughts when in his presence.

"I think he heard my thoughts. I wanted another taste of the virgin's blood. We will have to be careful of our thoughts around him. Did he say where he was going or when he would be returning?"

"No, the psycho just said to find the place he asked for and he would find us. Your father needs help. Surely Kain knows how to control him," Taser said.

Krista laughed, or tried to. It hurt to breathe, let alone laugh. No one controlled her father, especially if he didn't want to be controlled.

James didn't know why he was here, but he had no choice. He needed a place to lay low until Krista could find a better place for them to stay. He didn't want to have to keep beating her ass for looking at what was his like she wanted them for herself. They were his to deal with as he pleased, but he needed to keep them somewhere. He knocked on the door in front of him, then looked behind him to make sure his mates were still knocked out cold. It didn't take very long for Kain to answer the door. James gave him a bright smile.

"What are you doing here? I told you where they were," Kain said.

"Yes, you did. I found them. I just need a tiny favor for a few days maybe."

James frowned at Kain's laughter. He was serious.

"What? You're serious?"

"Of course I'm serious! Krista wants to drain one of my mates dry. I need a place to lay low until she finds a suitable place where I can build a cage."

"Okay, what does that have to do with me?"

James huffed. Why was he being so difficult?

"I was hoping you would help me out for a bit. You kind of owe me for walking out on me."

Kain pinched the bridge of his nose and counted to ten. He couldn't beat him; it would be a waste of time.

"I don't think that's such a good idea."

"Why the hell not?"

"I have mates of my own, and they don't like you."

"I don't give a damn what they like! We are bonded for eternity. Not even death can break what we have. You will do this for me, and

I won't kill you."

"You won't kill me—we both know it's true. Besides, you couldn't anyway. You tried it once, and I'm still here. Come in you giant pain in my ass."

"Help me with my mates. Do you have somewhere I can keep them where they won't be able to escape?"

Kain glanced over at the two unconscious humans. This was not how he wanted to spend his day when he got out of bed this morning.

"Why are your mates unconscious, James?"

"Funny story," James laughed.

"You know what, I don't even want to know. We can take them to the guest room with the bars on the windows and doubled padlocked iron door. Be nice to my mates."

James stumbled back in shock.

"I'm always nice!"

Kain looked at him without saying a word. He knew James better than he knew himself. He was never nice except to him, and he hadn't been nice to him in a long time.

"Fine! I won't say a word to the little manipulative she-bitches."

"James!"

"All right!"

"Don't make me regret this."

James followed Kain into The Oracle's home. He hated those little cunts, but he didn't have many options at the moment. They didn't fool him, either. Not by a long shot. He had plans to expose them as soon as it was beneficial. If they thought that Kain was their happily-ever-after, they were sadly mistaken. Kain only belonged to one person, and neither of them was it. Kain was his and would always be his. They would find out soon enough, but for now James would let them continue to live in their little fantasy world where they believed they called all the shots. They thought they were playing them all like puppets, but James wasn't so easily fooled. He was surprised they'd managed to fool Kain for so long, but he was probably misinterpreting what he'd seen. Believing it to be something it wasn't, but James saw all. As soon as The Oracle was no longer useful, he would remove them from what was his. James didn't share his toys, and Kain was his first.

"They've been missing for weeks. Where the fuck are they?" Alexander shouted.

"If I knew, we wouldn't be having this discussion," Derrick said calmly.

"We need to find Isobelle! I won't have another child taken from me," Derrick Jr. said.

"Samuel's death was necessary at the time. Now that Alexander and Isobelle are both missing, it's time we pay him a little visit, don't you think, Alexander?"

"See that it's done. Whatever it takes. I want them found days ago."

"Derrick, come take a little ride with your father."

CHAPTER 20

Taylor got out of bed. Finally. Jackson and Jenny had been up for hours, but Taylor was still trying to figure things out. He needed to talk to both of them and voice his concerns. Sitting on the information wouldn't help in identifying the problems.

He made himself presentable, "presentable" meaning some sweats and a t-shirt, after taking care of basic necessities in the bathroom. Once he was done, he made his way downstairs. He found both his mates in the kitchen.

"Ooh, bacon! Gimme!" Taylor exclaimed.

He snatched several strips off Jackson's plate, 'cause even he wasn't dumb enough to steal food from a pregnant woman.

"Mmm, so good," Taylor said around a mouthful of bacon.

"Seriously Tay, you act like you haven't eaten in days. Stay away from my plate and fix your own," Jackson said.

"But your bacon tastes better," Taylor said flashing a grin.

He listened to Jackson mumble something about biting off his fingers and started laughing.

"You wouldn't dare. Anyway, we all need to talk," Taylor said.

"About what? The fact that my daughter's gone completely off the reservation?" Jennifer asked.

"Not at the moment. Krista's issues can wait. We need to talk about the changes I've been noticing since we all mated," Taylor said.

"What do you mean, 'changes?'" Jennifer asked.

Jennifer dropped her fork and felt her heart race. *What the hell was going on?* Mating with them had changed them somehow. Something that would probably get them killed.

"Jennifer, please calm down," Taylor said. "It's nothing bad. It's just, well, I can do things I couldn't really do before. Like, shock people. I think. I feel little currents flowing along my skin sometimes when I'm angry or annoyed. I'm not one hundred percent sure yet what it means, but something is happening. And I'm faster. I mean I've always been fast, but I'm even faster now."

"Is this what's been bothering you?" Jackson asked.

"Yes, but I thought I was imagining things at first, and then I had to figure out how to explain what I meant," Taylor said.

Jennifer looked at Jackson.

"Has this been happening to you as well?"

"Now that we're talking about it out loud, yes, I've noticed a few changes as well. Sometimes I even think I hear you in my head, and I know we couldn't do that at first. It was only strong emotions I would feel, but now there is a buzzing, a kind of static. From time to time, your voice becomes jumbled," Jackson said.

"I hear that, too. Is there anyone who would know what's happening to us?" Taylor asked.

Jennifer thought about it for a moment then had to shake her head.

"Probably not. I don't think we've ever been with anyone outside our species. Our mating and Krista's mating are the only exceptions I've ever heard of. Most of the different species usually stick to their own kind, and if anyone has mated outside their species, they aren't shouting it from the rooftops. As a last ditch effort we could ask The Oracle, but I don't want to deal with them at the moment," Jennifer said.

"Let's just think on it awhile," Jackson said. "I'll get a whiteboard later and put it up in one of the offices. As we notice new things, we'll just write it down. Then if we can't figure things out on our own, we'll ask The Oracle, or you could try to get in touch with that Seer you used to know."

"Okay, sounds like a plan," Taylor said.

"Agreed, but if you start noticing any negative side effects, we don't wait to find an answer," Jennifer said.

She watched as Jackson and Taylor nodded their agreements then went back to eating breakfast. It was always one thing or another lately. Jennifer wanted her peace and quiet back. She hoped whatever the hell was going on would be resolved before her baby was born, but even as she thought the words she knew they were unlikely. A shit storm was coming, and all the people she held dear were right in the fucking middle of it. All she could do was gather her strength for the upcoming battle and prepare herself to do what she had to do to protect not only herself but the ones she loved.

"So, have you figured out a way to get rid of your father yet?" Nathan asked.

He was tired of waiting around. He needed to start making shit happen.

"We keep letting him believe that we are going along with his wishes," Krista responded. "I get him to slowly trust me, and when his guard is down I'll rip his throat out. For now, I'm not strong enough, but once I start training and using my Mystic powers and learning to control them better, I'll be unstoppable. I mean I am supposed to be able to destroy the entire world, right?"

"Well, while you're figuring out how to kill us all, I need to go speak to Jackson about putting together the ceremony to formally hand the pack over to him," Taser said.

"Okay, give me a minute to get ready," Krista said.

Taser snorted and said, "Do you really think you're coming with me? You will be torn apart on sight. They don't want to see you, and I can't say I blame them. You went full villain on your mother and unborn sibling. Jackson and Taylor won't let you anywhere near their mate and child willingly. I will go alone. You find us a decent place to stay. I'll be back once I get every detail sorted. Nathan, you might want to call your family. You did vanish without so much as a 'by your leave', and I'm sure your mother is foaming at the mouth about her precious son going missing."

Nathan just growled, but he knew Taser was right.

"You can't go alone!" Krista yelled.

"Why the hell not? I haven't murdered anyone in coldblood lately. That was all you," Taser said.

"The Mooyers are out there. How long do you think it will be before they notice two of their own missing? They will start an all-out war," Krista said.

"Don't be ridiculous," Taser laughed. "They don't want us exposed any more than we do. Exposure means panic, and the Mooyers like being in charge of their ridiculous mission to wipe us all from the planet. More than likely they will plan their attacks carefully. They don't know if Alexander and Isobelle are alive or dead, and Alexander is a Carvanis, so they will tread lightly. They'll want him unharmed, and going on a vengeance spree won't get them the answers they seek. No, they are sneakier than that and a tad bit smarter. They won't go around just snatching people off the streets to try to figure out if they are non-human or not. Now, if you'll excuse me, I have to go. I'll call to check in," Taser said.

He could hear Krista's furious screams as he walked out of the warehouse. But he didn't care. She didn't get to tell him what to do, and she knew better than to try to control him again. The next time she tried, his wolf would forget they were mates and rip her throat out. Then again, the beast hadn't complained the first time. Stupid fucking wolf.

Taser knocked on the door and waited for an answer. He knew someone was home, as he could hear movement from inside. A few moments later the door was opened.

"What are you doing here?" Taylor asked.

Taser noted the tight set of Taylor's lips pressed together and the barely controlled rage in his eyes, but he refused to back down. He was still an Alpha, dammit, even if he was giving up his pack. Another thing he needed to remember to thank Krista for.

"I didn't come to fight, and I'm alone. I need to talk to Jackson about the formal ceremony to give up the pack," Taser said.

Taser waited in silence as Taylor just stared at him as if playing a scene in his head.

"Fine, come in. But if that mate of yours pops in here, we won't be held responsible for our actions," Taylor said.

"I assure you she will not be coming," Taser said.

Taser followed Taylor into his home and was escorted to the living room. Jennifer was curled up on the couch with a book, while

Jackson napped next to her with his hand on her stomach. The moment Taser stepped into the room, Jackson's eyes shot open and pinned him to his spot.

"Taser, to what do we owe the pleasure? Come to give your blessing in your mate's execution?" Jackson growled.

"As much as I'd like to agree with you, sadly I cannot. She's still my mate, and her death would cause me great pain. I've come to discuss the ceremony," Taser said.

"What ceremony?" Jennifer asked.

"The formal ceremony to relinquish control of the pack to Jackson and Taylor, and you of course," Taser said.

"You were serious about that?" Jennifer asked.

"Yes. Krista can't be taken back there. The pack would try to murder her in her sleep, and then I'd have to kill them all," Taser said.

"Okay..." Jennifer said.

"So when do you want to do this?" Jackson asked.

"Tomorrow if we could," Taser said.

"We'll gather the pack. I'll call the triplets and they'll see it done. Meet us at the pack house at noon tomorrow," Jackson said.

"Nathan and I will be there. Krista will stay home," Taser said.

"Good," Jackson replied.

Taser said his goodbyes and called his mates to let them know he was on his way back to the warehouse after he stopped for food. They relayed their orders, then Taser hung up. Taser started the jog to the restaurant because the quicker he got there, the quicker he could make his way back to his mates to plan their next moves.

CHAPTER 21

Isobelle woke up with a massive headache. Where the hell was she, and what the hell had happened the night before? She couldn't remember a thing.

"Ah good, you're awake," James said.

Then it all came crashing back to her. She knew that voice. She winced when she moved her head. It felt like she'd been hit with a bag of bricks.

"What the hell did you do to me, you son of a bitch? And where is Alexander?" Isobelle asked.

The groan to her right caught her attention. It was Alex, and he was stirring as well.

"Just knocked you unconscious for a little while. The two of you were being quite unreasonable," James said.

Isobelle realized he was being completely serious. The psycho believed every word he was saying.

"You're insane," Isobelle accused.

"Guilty!" James exclaimed, throwing his hands up in mock surrender.

"Isobelle, don't talk to him. You have no idea what he's capable of," Alexander said. "The books you've read only scratched the surface."

"There are books about little old me?" James laughed. "How delightful! I must read these or you must tell me what they say."

"What do you want with us?" Isobelle snarled.

"It seems fate has decided that the both of you are mine," James

said.

"What do you mean by 'yours?'" Alexander asked.

"Well—" James was cut off by Isobelle.

"Don't you dare say it! It is impossible. I won't allow it," Isobelle said.

"Isobelle, don't be rude. I don't like rude. Now as I was saying, you're my mates. This is going to be so much fun!" James said.

Isobelle watched as he clapped his hands together like a child and knew she was going to regret the next few years of her life. She was under no such illusions of escaping or being rescued.

"You can't keep us locked in here forever," Alexander said.

"I can't take you around my daughter at the moment, because for one, she's uncontrollable in her thirst for virgin blood"—James looked pointedly at Isobelle—"and for two, she has to find us a suitable place to live. That abandoned warehouse she's holed up in will not do."

"You don't have a house, preferably one without bars?" Alexander asked.

"I have no desire to go back there. I went briefly while you were both unconscious to gather some belongings. Which reminds me, your things are in the cage with you. For now you will stay here in my old lover's basement until I figure out what I'm going to do with you," James said.

"Will you at least feed us?" Isobelle asked.

"I'll see what I can do," James said.

Isobelle watched James' back as he walked away. She wanted to rage and throw things but decided it was best to conserve her energy.

"We need to get out of here," Isobelle said.

"Unless you can teleport, we aren't going anywhere," Alexander said.

"Then what are we supposed to do?"

"We wait for now and when the moment comes, we take it," Alexander said.

Isobelle knew he was right but that didn't mean she had to like it.

James listened to his mates from the top of the stairs and barely contained his laughter. They thought they could slip away from him. It was never going to happen. He searched for Kain and asked him to help him prepare a meal for his mates. He was already in the kitchen, his mates nowhere to be found. James stopped in the doorway to take in the sight of his first love for a moment. He'd been away from him for so long but could still feel the touch of his skin next to his. If he had been the weeping type, surely he'd be in a sea of tears right now.

"Why are you staring at me like that?" Kain asked.

James smiled because Kain hadn't even looked up from his food prep.

"Just admiring the view," James said.

"Yeah, or plotting my death again," Kain said.

"That was one time!" James said.

He threw up his hands in frustration. Kain was never going to let it go.

"It should have been no time," Kain said.

"I would have brought you back had I succeeded."

"Sadly, that does nothing to comfort me."

"It's not like you didn't blast me as well. It took me weeks to recover from the heartache."

"I bet it did. Did you want something or are you just tormenting me?"

"Seems my mates need food."

"Well, they've been unconscious for days. I'm sure they are not only hungry but thirsty as well. Help me make more sandwiches. I was working on feeding my mates as well. They get into their Oracle stuff and forget to take care of themselves."

James just grunted. He didn't trust those bitches, and coming from him that was saying a lot.

"What was that for?"

"Nothing, I promised I'd behave."

"And since when have you ever behaved?"

James smiled. "Never, but I need you to help me contain my mates for now. So I'll hold my tongue."

"No, I want to hear what you have to say."

James thought about it and in the end decided what the hell. The Oracle's power held no power over his. He liked to let them think it did.

"Fine. But you asked for it. I don't trust them, and I think they are lying to everyone. They have an endgame, I'm just not sure what at the moment."

"That's ridiculous. I believe you're just jealous."

"Jealous? That's rich. Make no mistake, Kain O'Grady. You belong to me—heart, body, and soul. I'm inside you in ways no one else will ever be. No one will ever have you the way I've had you."

"We both have our own mates. Whatever we had is done."

"Is it?"

James slammed Kain's body into the far wall, pinning it with his. He ran his nose along the crook of Kain's neck and chuckled at the moan the action evoked. He barely ran his fangs along the path his nose had taken and gently pressed down. Not enough to break the skin but enough to remind Kain that his words, no matter how much he didn't want them to be, were true.

"Don't," Kain whined.

"Why not?"

"Because," Kain whispered.

James reluctantly pulled back, diffusing the energy in the room. He straightened himself out before returning to the sandwiches he had been preparing. His conflicting emotions were causing him to think unclearly, and if he wanted to be five steps ahead of everyone else, he would need his head in the game. He couldn't afford to let anything distract him, especially Kain.

Kiateya gathered her family in her office. She'd still not heard from Nathan, and she was ready to call in the Chowder, but she needed to make sure the rest of the family hadn't heard from him either. She looked at her husband, Nathan Sr., her two sons, Declan and Race, and her only daughter, Kisty. She looked each and every one of them in the eyes before she spoke.

"Your brother is missing, and I'm ready to go to war with whoever has him. I don't care how many people we piss off in the process," Kiateya said.

"Now, now, Mother, no need for dramatics." A familiar voice from the doorway drew Kiateya's attention. Nathan had returned.

"I'm hardly missing and even if I was, I'm a grown man who doesn't need his mother fighting his battles."

"Where the fuck have you been? I've been trying to reach you for days!"

"I needed to clear my head and talk with my mates."

"You mean that demon spawn! No, absolutely not. I forbid it."

"You forbid it. You don't get to forbid anything to me."

"You are still a part of this Chowder, and I am still your Alpha. You will do as I say or suffer the consequences."

"Father, Declan, Race, Kisty, if you should ever need anything from me, you know my number. I have to go before I murder our mother."

"Don't you turn your back on me, Nathan Brimming Jr. If you walk out that door—" Kiateya started.

"What, Mother? If I walk out of this door then what? You'll disown me? You forget your place if you think you can command me. The men allow the women to believe they are in control, but we all know who the real Alphas of a Chowder are. You are just put in front for show. I have to go. My mate has a big day tomorrow, and I need to be there to support him."

Kiateya watched as her firstborn turned his back on his family for two people that weren't even the same species. Her heart broke.

"That little shit. How dare he?"

"Give it a rest, Mother," Declan said. "He's big enough to make his own decisions. I have to go as well. I have things to do today."

"Agreed," Race said.

"Sorry, Mama," Kisty said.

Kiateya watched as her children filed out of her office. Unbelievable. Was she the only one who cared about the choices Nathan was making?

"Those ungrateful little bastards," Kiateya growled.

"Don't stress yourself, dear," her husband said. "His first loyalties are now to his mates, as they should be. He's alive and well, so just let him be."

But she couldn't just let it be. She had a duty to her children. If they wouldn't protect themselves, she'd do it for them. Besides, mama always knew best, and in this case, she was sure that girl was going to be the death of her son, and she couldn't allow that. Not while there was breath still in her body.

CHAPTER 22

"How angry do you believe he's going to be?" Derrick asked his father.

"Knowing him, extremely angry for several reasons. But we need him to find Isobelle and Alexander."

Derrick and his son walked up to the modest one-story house they'd known so well over the years. It was Samuel's mother's house—the Dylia, Avery Lynn. Not many members knew that some of the Legacy members were encouraged to breed with the things they hunted, but alliances had to be made. Everyone at one point in his or her life signed a deal with the Devil, and The Mooyer Society was no different. It was for the survival of the Legacies and the strength to go up against those that could kill them quicker than they could blink. They needed an edge, and Callisto Carvanis, may she rest in peace, had orchestrated a way. Didn't matter that she'd gone against everything they'd been taught—that girl had greater plans for The Society, and she only trusted a select few who in turn passed it down to the worthiest of successors.

Derrick Sr. rang the doorbell and waited. The sight that greeted the two men was exactly the same as the first day they'd met her. She still had brown eyes that were capable of swallowing a man whole, and her jet-black hair didn't have a single grey strand in it. If Derrick had been able to, he'd have given her a son, but it wouldn't have looked right since he was in line for head of the family. So the task fell to Derrick Jr.

"I'm surprised to see you two. Y'all haven't been 'round since y'all dropped my son off, beaten and broken," Avery said.

Derrick could practically feel the malice coming off her in waves. The clawed hands and elongated canines were also a good indicator.

"Cut it out, Avery, and let us in," Derrick Jr. snapped.

"Why the hell should I? My boy doesn't want to see either of y'all. Go away and leave us alone. I mean it's what y'all are good for, ain't it?"

"Alexander is missing," Derrick Jr. blurted.

Derrick just looked at his idiot son and shook his head. The boy couldn't hold water.

"Mama, what did he just say?" a voice yelled from inside the house.

Derrick Sr. watched as Avery sighed. She would let them in.

"I guess y'all better come in off the porch," Avery said. "I ain't condoning this visit, just so we're clear."

They were led to the living room where a familiar figure was sprawled over the couch sipping sweet tea.

Samuel. Healthy and alive. And still in fighting shape, apparently. He looked as if he'd healed nicely from the run in with that crazy Mystic.

"You seem to be doing quite well, Samuel," Derrick Sr. said.

"Considering I'm 'dead?' Yeah. But rain still causes my knee to flare up, and I have a permanent limp. You said something about Alexander going missing? Was he on a mission?" Samuel asked.

"Well, not quite. He'd taken a week off unexpectedly and then never showed back up. His partner is missing as well. We sent a team to their residences and a few choice items were missing. We also found remnants of their IDs, credit cards, and cell phones in Alexander's home incinerator," Derrick Jr. said.

"Maybe they decided to run away together, ever think of that?" Samuel asked.

"Don't be absurd! Alexander would never do such a thing. Something or someone has taken them," Derrick Sr. said.

"But why? Why them and not someone else? Unless... are they not the only ones missing?" Samuel asked.

"No one else is missing that we know of," Derrick Jr. said.

"Then why are you here telling me this?" Samuel asked.

"Because you might be the only one able to find him! You have connections we don't because of how close you are to supernaturals,"

Derrick Sr. said.

"They kind of frown on killing your own kind, regardless of whether they were bringing unwanted attention to themselves," Samuel said. "Besides, you turned your backs on me. Not the other way around. You banished me from The Society and left without a word, and I know you told Alexander I died. So why the fuck should I help you?"

"You would be helping Alexander and Isobelle, your sister," Derrick Jr. said.

"Sister? What are you talking about? There was no Isobelle, I would have remembered."

"We only found her recently," Derrick Jr. said.

They waited for Samuel to digest all the information they'd given him.

"Fine, I'll help but I'll do it my way. I'll call you if I hear something."

"Wait, what? We need you to come back to The Society," Derrick Sr. said.

"Not a chance in hell. I'm going to have a hard enough time getting Alexander to forgive me when I find him, and I want no part of your little Society ever again. Get out."

"But—" Derrick Sr. started.

"You heard him. Go on and get!" Avery yelled.

Reluctantly, they left and got back in their car. They hoped Samuel knew what he was doing and they needed to locate Alexander and Isobelle before the rest of The Society found out they were missing, especially Misha, Alexander's oldest brother. He'd tear the world apart looking for his baby brother, if they couldn't find him first.

Jackson waited with his mates for Nathan and Taser to show up. They had roughly thirty minutes left before noon. He wondered what was taking them so long.

"What time did he say again?" Billy asked.

"Noon," Taylor answered.

Billy looked down at his watch. "It's eleven-thirty right now. The pack is getting restless."

"And as the new betas, it's your brothers and your job to settle them down," Jackson said.

"You're the boss," Billy said.

Jackson watched as he walked over to his brothers and said something. He didn't hear what it was, but it got them moving. They approached the rest of the pack and said something else, and then there was silence. Good, Jackson was getting a headache from all that damn chatter. He looked up when Taylor elbowed him and pointed his head toward the road. He could see two figures walking up to the gate which promptly opened for them. Taser must have punched in the override code. It didn't take them long to walk up to the house.

"You sure you want to do this?" Jackson asked in greeting.

"It's what must be done. Doesn't matter what I want," Taser grimaced.

Jackson sighed.

"Fine, let's get this over with then."

Jackson watched as Taz climbed up to the podium with Nathan right behind him. He adjusted the microphone and cleared his throat before addressing the pack.

"I've gathered you all here today to bear witness to the transfer of leadership of the pack to Jackson, Taylor, and their mate Jennifer. It isn't a choice you have to agree with, and once the ceremony is over and you want to challenge them for the position, that is your right. But for now the ceremony will start," Taser said.

Jackson, Taylor, and Jennifer stood beside Taser and Nathan on the stage.

"I, Taser Jameson, step down as Alpha and relinquish responsibility to the pack to Jackson Dawls, Taylor Durham, and Jennifer Johnston," Taser said.

"I, Nathan Brimming, step down as Alpha-mate and relinquish responsibility to the pack to Jackson Dawls, Taylor Durham, and Jennifer Johnston," Nathan said.

"I, Jackson Dawls, accept your resignation and take responsibility of the pack," Jackson said.

"I, Taylor Durham, accept your resignation and take responsibility of the pack," Taylor said.

I, Jennifer Johnston, accept your resignation and take responsibility of the pack," Jennifer said.

"So we have spoken, so let it be done," Taser said. "I give to you your new Alphas!"

The pack howled their acceptance, and once they'd quieted down, Jackson spoke.

"I hereby appoint Billy, Bane, and Brian as Betas of the pack. Do you formally accept?" Jackson asked.

"We do," the triplets said.

The pack could be heard howling for a second time, the bonds that had been pulling away from each other snapping back together. The pack was as it should be.

"We have to go. See you around," Taser said.

Jackson and Taylor shook Taser and Nathan's hands, but Jennifer stopped them.

"Take care of my girl. Try to keep her out of trouble. And just so you know, I'll be coming for her once I'm able. It won't end well," Jennifer warned.

"We are well aware of what's to come," Taser said.

Jackson watched as the pair left the pack lands. He lifted his head back and howled, his pack mates joining in his sorrow for not only the loss of their former Alpha but their friend.

Taser clenched his fists as the howls from the pack threatened to overwhelm him. He'd give anything to be able to join them in song, but they were no longer his. They were taken from him. He didn't know if he'd ever be able to forgive his mate for causing him to become a lone wolf. He wondered how long before the madness started to creep in. Wolves weren't solitary creatures. They needed a pack, and sadly his mates didn't make a pack. Dylias needed to be around other Dylias. Had any of his mates been the same species, he would have been able to cope, but now he was sure he was on a slow ride to his ultimate death. A lone wolf was usually put down because the loneliness caused it to go insane. They would wreak terror and despair wherever they went. Killing without thought or care. He'd seen a lone wolf or two put down by Jackson's father when he was younger. It hadn't been a pretty sight, and he had no intention of becoming one of those monsters.

He would have to figure out a way to become a part of a pack again. He was sure he had a few years before the madness started to set in. He wasn't quite sure how long it took, being as it was different for each Dylia. But Taser was strong. He was an Alpha for fuck's sake. Madness would not claim him, at least not without one hell of a fight. Taser Jameson didn't know how to quit. He'd never been a quitter, and he wasn't going to start now.

CHAPTER 23

A FEW MONTHS LATER, 2014

Jennifer was trying her hardest to pull herself out of bed. She had just reached one year of being pregnant, and she was ready to have this baby months ago. She'd forgotten how miserable it was for a Mystic to be pregnant. She had hoped with the baby being part Dylia, the length of time before birth would have been shorter. Seems she was having no such luck. She was hungry, and moving around was becoming unbearably annoying. So she did what any woman in her situation would do.

"Someone, anyone, come quick!" Jennifer yelled.

Several footsteps could be heard running up the stairs, the perks of moving into the pack house with a bunch of Dylias with amazing hearing.

"Jennifer, is it the baby?" Jackson asked.

Taylor and the triplets were right on his heels.

"Jennifer, what's wrong?" Taylor huffed.

"I'm hungry," Jennifer whined.

"Hungry! Are you kidding me? You screamed like a banshee because you were hungry?" Jackson growled.

"Don't you growl at me, asshole! I'm the pregnant one here. Now find me food and don't come back without at least enough to feed a small army. And all my favorites better be included."

Jennifer watched the men blink at her in surprise before filing out of the bedroom to do her bidding. Taylor was the only one to stay.

He walked over and climbed in the bed next to her.

"That was a low blow," Taylor said, laughing.

"You carry around a little person in your uterus, and then we'll talk," Jennifer smirked.

Jennifer laughed right along with Taylor and snuggled up next to him as she waited for her food to be served up to her on a silver platter. Maybe this whole pregnancy thing wasn't so bad after all.

James teleported himself inside the cage that held his mates and laughed when Isobelle screamed and pushed him into the bars.

"Why do you do that?" Isobelle asked.

James wiped the tears from his eyes before he spoke.

"Because it's hilarious," James said.

"Laugh it up, asshole," Isobelle huffed.

"I don't know why you encourage him," Alexander said.

"I think she enjoys our times of bonding," James said.

"You know what I would enjoy more? Being let out of this cage. I'm not an animal," Isobelle said.

"But you cage up my kind like we are?" James asked.

"That's because you are animals!" Isobelle exclaimed.

"Really? Let me tell you a little story about Seers, sweetie. Humans can't have visions like they do," James said.

He let that statement sink in for a moment, then delighted when the truth registered not only on Isobelle's face but on Alexander's as well.

"Impossible! I would know if I weren't human. My parents are both human," Isobelle said.

James could practically see the steam rolling off her in waves. Her clenched fists and gritted teeth were adorable.

"One day I'll tell you the entire story and a few secrets about The Mooyer Society. But for now, I'll say this: a human can only be born a Seer or Oracle if they have supernatural blood somewhere in their bloodline, and you, my dear, have a supernatural bloodline. I can smell it on you, and I'm sure I could taste it too, once I bit you. Alexander does as well."

"That's a lie! No Carvanis would ever sleep with a creature such as you and have children with it," Alexander spat. "I read some crazy things in the old journals, but nothing like you're implying."

"Oh, but they did and still do. You think your Society is so pure and noble in its righteous war of eradicating supernaturals, but we will never be killed off because without us they wouldn't be as strong as they are. Your own relative, Nathaniel, is a Seer, is he not? I know more about The Mooyer Society than you'll ever know."

"You lie," Alexander said.

"And my parents have never even dealt with supernaturals. They aren't aware of their existence," Isobelle said.

"Cassidy Mina is not your father. Derrick Casey Jr. is," James said.

He let out one more fit of laughter before abruptly disappearing into thin air, teleporting out of the cage and to the warehouse where his stupid daughter was still dwelling. He needed to find out what was taking her so long to find another place.

When Samuel was told where his contact could be found, he'd thought the Hyjia was mistaken. But no, he was standing outside an abandoned warehouse that had definitely seen better days. He was getting sick just thinking about all the infection and disease that was properly riddled inside the walls of the place. Nevertheless, he needed some answers, and the cat had said this was where Nathan Brimming was located and that he'd recently started hanging out with other supernaturals.

Samuel approached the warehouse entrance, and before he could knock or shout, the heavy metal loading gate rose, revealing a very angry Dylia.

"Who are you and how did you find us, mutt?" Taser growled.

"Ahh, you must be Taser, mate of Nathan. The Hyjia who told me where to find him said he was mated to a Dylia. I didn't much believe him until now. I am Samuel, and I need to speak to him," Samuel said.

"What do you want with my mate?"

"I'm told he might be able to help me locate an old friend of mine."

"Let him in, Taser," Nathan said.

"He could be lying," Taser said.

"You would know if he were lying Taz," Nathan said.

"Fine, but you try anything and I'll rip your insides from your body," Taser said.

"Duly noted," Samuel said.

Samuel looked around the warehouse and cringed. How the hell anybody could live like this was beyond him. He didn't like to judge, but holy shit.

"Is there a reason y'all are in this shithole?" Samuel asked.

"Trust me, we're trying to remedy the situation as soon as possible. Nathan Brimming Jr."

"Samuel Casey, please to make you acquaintance."

"Casey, as in The Mooyer Society? I'm confused. You're a wolf," Nathan said.

"It's complicated."

"I bet it is. What can I do for you?"

"I'm looking for my friend and his partner. You might know them. Alexander Carvanis and Isobelle Mina. I was told they were missing by my father. Told him I'd put a few feelers out and see what I could find."

"Alexander doesn't seem like the type to hang around with a Dylia," Krista chimed in. "I'm Krista by the way. Their other mate."

"Ma'am. Alexander doesn't know that I am a mix, and I just found out that Isobelle is my sister. Now I don't give a damn about The Society, I just want to find my best friend and my little sister."

"That may prove to be a difficult task," Nathan said.

"And why is that?"

"Because, you see," Krista said, "they are the mates of my father. Perhaps you've heard of him, James Johnston."

Samuel closed his eyes and prayed that he'd misheard her.

"Come again?" Samuel stuttered.

"I said my father has them, and he has no intention of ever giving them back, regardless of if he wanted them or not," Krista said.

"That's what I thought you'd said. I am so fucked."

Isobelle sat on the little twin bed that was hers in shock. None of it was true. It was all lies. He was a liar.

"He's a lying son of a bitch," Isobelle murmured.

"More likely he's not. James Johnston has been called a lot of things in the books, but a liar has never been one of them," Alexander said. "Maybe he's just mistaken.

"But he seemed so sure of himself. It doesn't make sense. None of it makes sense. I need concrete answers," Isobelle said.

"If it's the truth, the day of your ceremony would make sense," Alexander said.

"What do you mean?"

"You know, that little speech Derrick made and the fact that his father is so protective of you. Derrick has a lot of bastards, and he's always welcomed them with open arms. His father, too. He must have only recently found out you were his or else he'd have brought you in a long time ago. He's done it many times. One thing he's not is a bad father. He loves all his children equally."

"But why wouldn't they tell me? I deserve to know the truth."

"Maybe they didn't want to hurt you. I mean, you were twenty-two when you were brought in."

"Yes, but Derrick Sr. knew me before then. He was at my high school graduation. He had a private conversation with my mother. My mother, oh my god! She's always hated him, and it had to do with whatever he said to her at my high school graduation. Maybe he told her he knew what she'd done. But why would she do it? She loves my father? I don't understand any of this. I need to talk to my mother."

"Do you really think our resident lunatic is going to let you have one phone call?"

"Dammit! This is getting out of control. He can't keep us locked up forever. We need to have a rational discussion with him."

Isobelle gave Alexander a dirty look when he snorted.

"You really think that's going to work? I wouldn't count on it."

"Of course it will work. We just have to get him to trust us."

"Really? And how are we supposed to do that? First chance I get, I'm going for his throat."

"No, you will never be able to kill him. I can feel the power rolling off of him and besides, we have no idea what his Mystic powers are."

"I'm not mating with that monster."

"What choice do we have?"

"Isobelle, are you listening to yourself? You want to walk into the devil's lair and offer yourself to him on a platter. I think you've been in this basement a little too long."

"You can very well do what you want, Alex, but I'm tired of being caged. Besides, if what he says is true, we aren't far from monsters ourselves. At least this way we'll have one of the scariest of them all watching our backs. And don't think for one second that The Society won't kill us for the things we know and can do if they were to ever find out. Derrick may know my secret, but that doesn't mean the others will let me live if they knew it too, and nothing Derrick could say would keep them at bay."

"The man is evil, Isobelle! He's part of the reason The Society was created in the first place."

"Is he? How do we know The Society didn't lie about that too? They could be lying about a lot of things, and we just blindly follow where they lead. I'm not sure about you, Alexander, but I'm tired of being a sheep. I'm talking to him when he comes back. You can do whatever you want."

Isobelle turned over in her bed with her back to Alexander and closed her eyes. So many secrets, so many lies. She wasn't sure what to believe anymore, but for some reason, she believed every word James had said to her. True, he didn't have to be so snobby about it, but he'd been the only person so far who'd never lied to her. Even Alexander hadn't told her the truth. He'd plotted behind her back and tried to destroy her. Until James gave her a reason not to trust him, she had no other choice. It was time she started taking responsibility for her own life, starting with James Johnston, her supposed mate.

CHAPTER 24

James could hear the Dylia talking with his daughter and her mates. He hissed when he heard his mates' names mentioned. He strolled over to the stranger and picked him up by the neck and bared his fangs. The Dylia's hands turned into claws and his canines extended, but James didn't fucking care. He could eat the pup for breakfast; he was so young, just over thirty, barely.

"What do you want with my mates, and who sent you?" James hissed.

"Here we go," Krista said.

"I'm waiting!" James shouted.

"Maybe if you stopped choking him, Father," Krista pointed out.

James growled at his daughter, so she took a step back. He looked back at the wolf he had picked up and shook him a little, then let him drop to the floor. He watched in boredom as the little shit coughed and clutched at his throat.

"Why do you need my mates?" James asked again.

"People are looking for them, and they won't stop until they find them. And whatever reason Alexander had for leaving must have been a good one. They think he's been taken, but I know Alex better than anyone. He wouldn't leave without a fight, and his apartment didn't have a thing out of place," Samuel said.

"How does a Dylia know so much about a Mooyer?" James asked.

"Because I was one, and so is everyone on my father's side."

"Who is your father?"

"Derrick Casey Jr."

"Ah, I see. Come, I will take you to see them, but they will not be returning with you."

"That's fine, I just want to make sure they are okay. They are, aren't they? You didn't do anything to them?"

James was offended. He had never hurt anyone just for the hell of it. Okay, that wasn't entirely true, but they were his mates, and even if he didn't believe that sort of thing, he felt they were his, just like he felt Kain was his.

"I would never hurt them," James hissed.

"You hurt me, and I'm your daughter," Krista said.

"Shut up before I hurt you again. And find us a place to stay so I can take my mates out of that damn cage in Kain's basement!" James bellowed. "And why aren't you training?"

"The Mystic you sent for hasn't shown up yet," Krista said.

"When he does, remind him that my time is precious and the next time he decides to waste it I'll kill him," James said.

"Your time? You're not even here most times. And it's *my* time he's wasting," Krista said.

"Don't poke the bear, dear," Taser said.

"Your time is *my* time, little girl," James growled. "Everything about you is mine! Stop fooling around and get to work on controlling and utilizing your powers before you get yourself killed. How do you expect to take over the world when you don't even know the full extent of your capabilities? You disappoint me. Come, wolf, we have some place to be."

James grabbed the boy and teleported him back to the basement. Upon seeing him, Alexander looked like he'd seen a ghost. Isobelle was sleeping. Good, he'd sprung a lot of information on her earlier. She would need her rest and her strength for what was yet to come.

"Samuel?" Alexander stammered, unsure of what he was seeing before him.

"Hey, Alex. It's been a long time," Samuel said.

"They—they told me you were killed. How are you here? How are you not dead? What's going on around here, dammit?"

His shouting startled Isobelle awake and she fell off her bed. James winced when she hit the ground and so did Alexander and Samuel.

"Sorry, Isobelle," Alexander murmured.

"What the hell are you screaming about?" Isobelle demanded.

"Well, I've just seen a ghost or my father's been lying to me for twelve years."

Isobelle looked up and saw a stranger that vaguely resembled her and definitely resembled Derrick Jr.

"Who is this man, Alexander?" she asked.

"Samuel Casey. Your brother, if what James told us is true, and my best friend growing up. I'm a little surprised to see him, though, because my father and his grandfather told me he'd died on our first solo mission together as partners."

"Well, shit."

Now that Samuel was face-to-face with not only Alex but his long lost sister, he was at a loss for words. How to explain what had happened that day and what he was?

"Well, I guess I should start with the fact that I'm not completely human. My mother is a Dylia," Samuel said.

He waited for the fallout, but he was met with silence. He was sitting on Alexander's bed across from Isobelle's, facing Isobelle and Alexander. James had pulled the seat from outside the cage inside and left the door open. None of them said a word.

"Well, aren't you going to say something, Alex?" Samuel asked.

The suspense was killing him, and he couldn't take the waiting any longer. He needed to know what was going on in Alexander's head.

"I—" Alexander began. "I have no words. I need you to explain this to me like I'm a child."

"Well, basically a lot of what you hear about The Mooyer Society is complete and utter bullshit. There is a secret society within the secret society. Coincidentally, it was one of your ancestors who started it. You know the one, Callisto Carvanis. That girl was something else. She had more Mystic tendencies than a full-fledged Mystic and the sadistic nature of one as well. That girl didn't pull any punches."

"I don't think I want to know any more right now. Just tell me how you're not dead."

"It's the Dylia in me. Had I been completely human I would have died. As it were, she messed me up pretty badly. Took me months to recover, and I ain't been the same sense. Only reason you recovered as well as you did is because she didn't slam you as hard as she'd slammed me. By the time she would have, she'd been distracted. Instead of healing up right alongside you, your father believed being friends with me was making you soft. He didn't approve of our growing closeness and sent me away to live with my mama for good. Said it was for the best. Said they would tell you I died so you wouldn't come looking for me. I was disowned and threatened. Told if I ever came looking for you they'd kill my mama. That was what your daddy told me. My family let him get away with it, and now here we are."

"I'll come back to all this later but if they threatened your mother, why are you here now?" Alexander asked.

"Because you and Little Missy here went missing, and my father and grandfather knew I was the best shot they had of finding y'all. I told them I would deal with it myself and call them with an update. I'm not calling shit, but I figured I'd try to find you anyway. I knew if you'd disappeared, more than likely you wanted it that way. What I didn't account for was you being kidnapped from a safe house by your mate and locked in a cage."

"It's a temporary precaution," James defended.

"Whatever you say," Samuel said.

Samuel wrote his number on a piece of paper and gave it to Alex.

"Here, you call me when you're ready to talk. Now that I know you ain't dead, I got to get back home."

"I see you haven't lost that damn accent."

"Nope, it's only gotten worse."

"What are you going to tell The Society?"

"Depends. Is there something you want me to tell them?"

"Yes," Isobelle interrupted. "Tell them we know all about their fucking lies, and we're done. Tell them to stop looking for us or they won't like what they find."

"What she said," Alexander responded. "I'll call you in a few days. I just need time to get my thoughts together."

"Fair enough. James, could you teleport me back to my car please?" Samuel asked.

"I suppose. I'll return shortly with food, and we'll get you two showered," James said.

"We need to have a sit-down and talk when you get back as well,"

Isobelle said.

James only managed to hide his surprise from years of practice.

"I won't be long."

James teleported Samuel back to his awaiting car, then teleported himself to Kain's kitchen and started to prepare food for his mates. He wondered what they needed to speak to him about. Nothing good probably, but it would be amusing nonetheless. He placed the food on a tray and teleported straight inside the cage. He watched as his mates ate, and once they were finished, he escorted them to the bathroom and drew them a bath. Once the water was how he wanted it, he motioned for them to get inside.

James took great delight in watching them undress, but something had changed. Isobelle didn't seem as distressed about undressing in front of two men. He squinted his eyes at his mates and probed their thoughts, then scrunched up his nose in confusion. He wasn't picking up any negative thoughts; hell, he was hardly picking up any thoughts at all. It was like they'd gone numb. This was not good, not good at all. Once they were in the bath, James placed a barrier spell on the door before going to find Kain. They were plotting something, and he just couldn't figure out what.

Samuel got into his car and pulled out his cell phone. He dialed his father's number and waited for him to pick up the phone. Once he did, he didn't tell him what Isobelle and Alexander said. In fact, he didn't even tell him he'd found them. He did to his father what his father had done to Alexander—lie.

"They were killed," Samuel said.

"Excuse me?" Derrick Jr. gasped.

"They are dead. They were on a personal mission tracking a rogue group of Dylia, and they were killed. I don't know what group it was because no one knew their identities. They were scouting them and gathering information when they were scented by one of the wolves coming back to the hideout. He warned the others, and they ambushed them. They never stood a chance, and once they ripped them apart they burned the bodies until there was nothing left. I'm sorry, Father," Samuel said.

"Alexander's father nor your grandfather are going to be happy with this news. What the hell were they thinking?"

"I don't know, Father. Maybe they wanted to make sure there was something before they brought in the rest of The Society."

"Keep your eyes and ears open. Alexander is going to want to find the ones who did this and make them pay. We won't even discuss what will happen when Misha finds out. Now I have to find a way to tell Isobelle's mother she's dead. Thanks for looking into this, Samuel. I love you, son."

"Yeah, sure you do."

Samuel disconnected the phone before his father could speak again. Fuck him and the entire Mooyer Society, especially Alexander Carvanis Sr.

CHAPTER 25

"I called this special meeting of the Council to inform you that after speaking with a credible source, I've found out what happened to Alexander and Isobelle," Derrick Jr. said.

"Well fucking spit it out!" Alexander shouted.

"They're dead."

It was like the calm before the storm. Everything had gone still and then just as suddenly, chaos.

"Bullshit! My son is not dead. Where the hell is he? Who's taken him?" Alexander screamed.

"I told you, they're dead. My source wouldn't lie to me."

"Is he sure?" Derrick Sr. asked.

"Positive."

The Council was silent, too silent. Nothing good was going to come from this.

"I want them all dead. Every last one of them," Alexander said.

"Come again?" Derrick Jr. asked.

"You heard me! Anyone with even an eighth of supernatural blood is to be hunted down and killed. Round up all The Society members that fit into the category. That includes your children as well. Their lives are all forfeit," Alexander raged.

He'd finally lost his shit, but he was sadly mistaken if he thought the members whose children carried more than an eighth of the paranormal creatures they hunted would stand by and let their offspring be slain. He didn't know them as well as he'd thought.

"I'd think very carefully about what you're saying," Derrick Sr.

said.

"Nothing to think about," Alexander said. "I want it done, and I want it done now."

"Too fucking bad what you want," Bailey Connelly, head of the Connelly family, said. "You think our mission stops because of one child? You're delusional. I don't care who you believe yourself to be, but the rest of us won't sit by while you murder members of our families, especially when we know that by some miracle all your little secret abomination children will miraculously survive. We will not compromise all we've worked to accomplish because your child was killed. We've all lost children. Yours are not fucking special. You act out aggressively toward our families, and we'll all ban together to wipe out yours. If you don't believe me, try it, asshole, and see."

"I think it's fair to say that the rest of us agree with Bailey's assessment," Derrick Sr. said. "My Isobelle was killed too, and we won't even discuss what you forced us to do to Samuel. Your tyranny ends now, Alexander. If you want to declare vengeance on the ones responsible for their deaths, be my guest, but you will not take it out on The Society. This meeting is dismissed."

Derrick Jr. watched as the Council members filed out of the meeting room. The last thing he saw before he followed them was the sparks of rage and madness in Alexander's eyes. This was not over, not even close.

James rushed to find Kain. He was in the living room reading through The Book Of Mystics. James had taken it from the warehouse, and when Kain saw he had it, he'd asked to read through it. He was hoping something important dwelled in its pages. He'd only glanced at it when he'd first received it and was kicking himself now for not committing it to memory all those centuries ago.

"Kain, I think my mates are sick!" James exclaimed.

He watched Kain's eyes widen in shock before he closed the book and gently sat it on the table in front of him.

"You've had them caged for months against their will, and now you're worried about the impact of your actions?" Kain asked.

James waved his statement away with his hand.

"This has nothing to do with what's going on now. It's like they are catatonic. They made no objections while I watched them undress for the bath, and Isobelle said they wanted to talk."

James put the word *talk* in mock-quotations and had a slight frown on his face when the word escaped his lips. As if talking was the worst thing in the world to do. He was even more annoyed with Kain when he started laughing uncontrollably. The moment it became so bad he fell off the couch, James walked away. He'd forgotten how much of an asshole his mate could be sometimes.

"I wonder what that was about," Isobelle said, pointing to the door and James's retreating back.

"Who knows? Probably the fact we aren't yelling at him about peeping while we take a bath has him confused," Alexander said. "Or the fact that we aren't making a big deal out of him making us bathe together like always."

"I just can't muster up the energy to care anymore, plus this hot water is doing much to soothe away the craziness of today. I don't even recall how long we've been living like this anymore."

"I don't want to recall it. If I do, I'm bound to kill myself just because."

"Don't be so melodramatic."

Isobelle rolled her eyes at Alex. He was so morbid sometimes.

"I'm just being honest. How did this become my life? Kidnapped after attempting to run away from everything I've ever known?"

"The luck of the Irish?"

"Ha, ha. Very funny."

"It was a little funny."

"So what are we going to do now?"

"Exactly what I said before. We adapt and see what this mate business is about, and try to come to an understanding with our captor. I for one am tired of living in a cage, even if he's made sure we're comfortable."

"I guess you're right. It's just going to take me some time to wrap my head around it. You don't suppose he's going to want to have sex with us, do you?"

Isobelle opened her mouth then closed it. She'd never thought about it. Guess she'd have to add that to the talk they needed to have.

"I guess we're just going to have to ask him."

"Ask me what?" James said.

Isobelle shrieked, and Alexander cursed.

"Why must you do that? Make some noise when you move!" Alexander shouted, hand on his chest to try to calm his raging heart.

"Force of habit and a part of my nature. So what did you want to ask me?"

Isobelle swallowed hard. Now that he was standing there being fairly reasonable, she was a bit intimidated. She was about to speak, but no words came out.

"I think what Isobelle is trying to say is she wants to talk about our relationship. Where is it going, and are you going to want to have sex with us?" Alexander stated.

They watched as James' eyes nearly popped out of their sockets. He started to back up out of the doorway. Isobelle found her voice at the sight.

"Wait! Don't leave. We just want to talk. No decisions need to be made right away."

"Please tell me you're not serious. You want to talk about a potential relationship between the three of us?" James asked.

"Well, yeah. You said we're your mates right? We aren't so stupid we don't know what that means," Isobelle said.

"No one in their right mind wants to mate with me, well besides Kain when we were together," James muttered.

"Timeout! We're staying in your ex's place? Seriously!" Isobelle shouted.

"Are you angry?" James asked, confused.

"I can't talk to him right now. Alexander, you talk to him. I'm going back to my relaxing bath. Men are so stupid."

"Explain this to me, Alexander," James demanded.

"You don't move potential lovers into your old lover's home. It's not an ideal situation," Alexander said.

"Still don't understand it."

"Okay let's try this: you're dating someone, and they used to date someone else, and you both need a place to stay. Your new lover moves you both in with their old lover, how would you feel?" Alexander asked.

James thought about what he said and let it sink in. It soon registered, and he could feel his body starting to heat up. His Mystic powers begging to be unleashed and destroy everything in its path.

"I see, but I must tell you both that even though you are my mates I've loved Kain since we were in our twenties. We were together well past one thousand years and love like that doesn't go away. Ever. He will be mine again and so will the two of you. Think about it and figure out a way to accept it."

"Um, serious question. Doesn't he have his own set of mates?" Isobelle asked.

James's laughter confused her.

"Not everything is as it seems, but all will be revealed in time."

"Are you sure you're not a Seer?" Isobelle asked.

"No, just really old. And I've absorbed a lot of power over the centuries. Finish your baths, and then I'll take you to the kitchen to get something to eat and introduce you to Kain."

Isobelle watched him go. She sat back into the hot water and closed her eyes.

"What do you think?" Alexander asked.

"I think if we're as honest with him as he is with us, we'll be fine."

"And the Kain thing?"

"One step at a time, Alexander. We're in new territory, and it's better to get all the facts first before making a move."

"You're in charge this time. I'll just sit back and follow your lead."

"That's a first."

"I'm trying to turn over a new leaf."

"I call bullshit."

"Possibly. We'll see how long it lasts.

They sat in silence, both lost in their own thoughts. Could they do it? Forget everything they knew and had been taught and make their own assumptions? It wouldn't be easy, but it was worth a shot. Not much they could lose anyway. Besides their lives. But honestly, were they ever really theirs to begin with?

CHAPTER 26

Krista was getting her ass handed to her. These Mystics weren't fucking around. She was nowhere near their league and wouldn't be for a while yet. Her training sessions were getting bloodier every day. Nathan and Taz looked on in pity at her pathetic attempts at defending herself.

"Krista, you are going to have to do much better than that. They aren't even breaking a sweat!" Nathan yelled.

"Do you want to take a water break?" Taser asked.

Krista flipped them both the bird and wheezed out, "Fuck off!"

Her cheeks burned with embarrassment as she heard their combined laughter. *Way to support the team.* She put her focus back on blocking the attack of the two Mystics she was currently training with. They were throwing blasts of energy toward her, and she was doing her best to dodge their blows while also sending out her own blasts. Her father made this shit look easy, but it was far from it. It took a great deal of effort and concentration, and at her age, it should be an afterthought. She growled in frustration when she was hit with another blast in the chest.

"That's fucking it! I'm done for the day."

"Your father won't like it," one of the Mystics said.

"Too damn bad what my father doesn't like. I'm no use at the moment. I'm like a bone the two of you are playing over. I need a few days to gather my strength and practice throwing blasts. Come back next week same time, and we'll jump back to it."

"As you wish. If your father asks, we won't lie to him," the other

Mystic said.

"Yeah, yeah."

Krista limped toward her mates. Taz had a bottle of water held out for her, and Nathan had a wet cloth. She greedily took the water and downed it as fast as she could as Nathan started rubbing her down with the towel. She was feeling much better now that she wasn't getting the shit beat out of her.

"So what's the deal with the sudden change of hearts?" Kain asked over dinner.

His mates were in their meditation room as always so it was just James, Isobelle, Alexander, and Kain.

"Well, out of everyone we've known so far, it seems James is the only one who's been truthful from the beginning," Isobelle said. "No secrets or hidden agendas and no games. He's the only one brave enough to wear his true face regardless of how anyone else feels about his actions. He wants what he wants and doesn't sugarcoat or pussyfoot around the issues."

"I have no reason to lie. Lying takes too much time. Eventually, lies can be forgotten, and you end up caught up in a web of deceit. I just like to lay all my cards out on the table regardless of the consequences," James said.

"I'm still not sure how you know the things you know, especially about who someone's parents are, but I believe every word you're saying," Isobelle said.

"I've lived a long time, and I've acquired quite an assortment of abilities like the one that allows me to see the threads of someone's life, beginning with their lineage. I can even look as far back as the beginning of several ancestors spanning a good hundred years. I can see the threads of your conception, Isobelle, and it leads to Bethany and Derrick, not Cassidy. The same with you, Alexander."

Alexander frowned over his meal.

"What do you mean? I know who my parents are, unlike Isobelle. I wasn't lied to about that at least," Alexander said.

"Actually, yes you were. If you think about your family and how they act toward each other, which person always stood out as unique?

You know how your siblings are, and although they respect and tolerate each other, it only goes so far. Which one is different, especially where you are concerned?" James asked.

"I—I don't think I understand what you're trying to imply," Alexander said.

"Fine, I'll spell it out for you. Alexander is your grandfather, not your father. Misha is more than just your older brother. You are his son. Don't ask me how it happened as I don't know the particulars, but your thread leads back to him and your mother, not Alexander. In order to get the entire story you'd have to ask one of them, but I can tell you this, Alexander Sr. doesn't know because if he did you wouldn't be alive to know the difference," James said.

They all watched Alexander, anticipating the moment when everything processed in his head and his cord snapped. It never came, though. He just picked up his fork and continued eating his meal as if his world hadn't just been flipped on its axis.

"Alex," Isobelle said tentatively.

"I think I'd like to sleep in a proper bed tonight, James, if you don't mind. I'm sure you could place a barrier, but I assure you I won't be tempted to escape."

"James, the room you're using is big enough for the three of you," Kain said. "It's time you take them out of that ridiculous cage anyway."

"Fine, let's finish dinner, and I'll take you both to my room," James said.

James drew in a deep breath and slowly let it out. They were going to be in the same room as him, in his bed. Was he ready for something like that? He'd not shared a bed with anyone since Kain left him, and he definitely didn't know how to share a bed with a woman. The only one he'd ever been with was Jennifer, and everyone knew how that turned out. He was starting to believe he'd made a horrible decision, but he wasn't one to run from a challenge. He faced them head on with fangs bared and claws unfurled. This would be no different.

CHAPTER 27

James shifted awkwardly around the room as his mates got ready for bed. What had he gotten himself into? And how the hell were they all going to fit in this bed?

"Maybe I should get Kain to find me another bedroom," James said.

"I think we should all mate," Isobelle said.

"Excuse me?" Alexander asked.

"You want to what?" James added.

"Isn't that the point of being mates? To share some kind of bond? What are we waiting for? Let's do this thing," Isobelle said.

"Um, don't you want to wait a while before we do that?" Alexander asked.

"Wait for what? The apocalypse? If you don't want to that's fine, but I figured we'd get it out of the way," Isobelle shrugged.

"You and I are basically human; we can't mate with each other," Alexander said, confused.

"By mating with both of you, it mates you to each other," James said.

"Then let's do this. Do we need to be naked?"

"Not necessarily," James said.

"Then what needs to happen?" Isobelle asked.

"I bite you both, then you drink my blood and a bit of each other's," James said.

"Okay, I'm ready," she said, removing her shirt.

"Wait, dammit! Shouldn't we discuss this first?" Alexander asked.

"What's to discuss?" Isobelle asked.

"You're still a virgin, and the only female James has been with is his niece—whom he raped!"

"Well, you have all the experience. Show us how it's supposed to be done," Isobelle challenged.

"Well, well, well, I do believe this should be very educational," James said.

"You're not helping," Alexander said. He threw a glare at James for good measure.

"What do I do first?" Isobelle asked.

"Put this on her," James said to Alexander.

Alexander took the blindfold from James and stared at it.

"Really?" Alexander asked.

"What? I'm adventurous with my sex," James said.

"Whatever. Come here, Isobelle," Alexander said.

Once Isobelle stood in front of him, Alexander placed the blindfold around her eyes then walked around her so that his chest was facing her back. All the while James just watched from the corner of the room. Alexander moved his hands to the waist of Isobelle's pajama pants, tugged them down her legs, and helped her to step out of them. Once she was in nothing but her panties, he led her to the bed and helped her lie on her back. He couldn't help but remember the day when he nearly had sex with her in the empty room. He'd regretted his decision to walk away ever since, but he would do more than make up for it now.

Alexander started by rubbing his hands up Isobelle's legs, then moving to her breasts. He gently massaged each mound until all that could be heard was Isobelle's moans and the heavy breathing of James and himself. He leaned his head down and took one of Isobelle's nipples into his mouth and sucked and nipped slowly but with firm pressure. He did the same with its twin. Suddenly he felt hands at his pants. He looked behind him and saw James. He didn't even hear him move. His heart increased in tempo at the sudden closeness because he'd never once been attracted to a man. But his body was betraying him at the moment. He kept his focus on Isobelle as he felt James' hand begin to stroke him from root to tip. A deep, rumbling groan was pulled from the depths of his soul. It felt amazing.

"What's happening?" Isobelle whispered.

"Nothing you need to concern yourself with right now," James murmured. "Just enjoy what's happening to you."

Alexander heard her growl in frustration, but she didn't say another word of protest. He lifted up to assist James in removing his sweats and scooted down to remove Isobelle's lace panties. He felt James slide beneath him, trying desperately to control his rising anxiety. He shouted a curse at the nip that James placed just above his hipbone. He was going to be the death of him. Alexander gently blew on the little nub peeking out between Isobelle's legs. He licked and teased it so that it would come out to play. It didn't take long before Isobelle was pushing his head down and lifting her hips up. He grabbed her hands and pinned them to her sides. He was in charge at the moment, not her.

He moaned deeply at the sudden heat that engulfed his shaft all the way to his balls. Nothing had ever felt so good in his life. He was going to shoot his load as quickly as a boy going through the beginning stages of puberty. He tried to pull back from James' mouth, but he wouldn't have it. James just slowly bobbed his head up and down in slow strokes, driving Alexander insane. He started to take his frustrations out on Isobelle and sucked and licked for all he was worth. He then slowly worked two fingers inside her and crooked his fingers to rub against that place that was guaranteed to make her scream. He didn't have to wait long and as soon as she was coming he felt a prick in his thigh, and he was going over the edge right along with her. Alexander lay there limp, halfway on top of Isobelle, and barely felt James move from under him. He felt the bed dip slightly and then heard a moan come from Isobelle. He looked up to see James' fangs embedded in her throat. Then he saw James bite into his own wrist and shove it toward her mouth. The old Mystic then offered his wrist to Alexander, who hesitated for just a second before latching on as well.

The sweet taste was the first thing his tongue registered once he started to drink. He could feel a stirring in his body and a buzzing in his blood. Then James pulled his wrist back and bit into Isobelle's and offered it to Alexander. He drank the blood, which had a stubbier sweetness to it, and James licked the wounds and they disappeared. He did the same thing with Alexander's wrist for Isobelle. A few moments later Alexander felt a rumbling in his body.

"What's happening?" Alexander asked.

"My blood is starting to change you. Over the new few weeks, months, and years, you'll start noticing more and more changes. I'm not sure exactly what you'll be able to do, but you'll be able to do a lot of damage in a few years, and you'll age differently and heal quicker than normal. Rest now next to Isobelle. I'll be back to check on your both later."

"Where are you going?" Isobelle asked.

"To check on a few things. I'll be back soon."

Alexander crawled up the bed to snuggle behind Isobelle and drifted off to sleep. He didn't know what they'd done, but it was too late to turn back now. They'd aligned themselves with the Devil, and now they had to prepare to march into Hell at his side.

"What did you do?" Kain asked.

James paused in the doorway of the kitchen. No one had been able to sneak up on him for centuries. He was losing his touch.

"Kain, I didn't see you there," James said.

"Don't play games with me. You did something. I felt it. What was it?"

"If you must know, I mated. Not that you care."

"You did what?" Kain asked softly.

"I claimed my mates."

"Did you not think of how it would make me feel?"

"I don't understand what you mean. You have your own mates, do you not?"

"Yes, but I haven't mated them!"

"No need to shout. Why are you so angry?"

"Because we are bonded for eternity, regardless of being mates."

"Who says that has to change? I'll tell you like I told Isobelle and Alexander. You are mine, do you hear me? Mine! Make no mistake about it. Now I'll let that sink in for you. I'm going to bed. Strange things are taking shape, and I need to be prepared."

Kain watched James disappear around the corner. God, he wanted to choke him out. How could he hate and love one person so much? It was insanity.

Kain found his mates in his office where they had been spending more and more time lately. It was time he claimed them to show James he was done messing around with him.

"I need to claim you both, now," Kain said.

At first, he didn't think they'd heard him, but then their eyes opened and looked him right in the face.

"Why the sudden interest?" Angeline asked.

"Sudden interest? You're my mates, and when mates find each other, they claim each other."

"Be that as it may, we cannot afford the distraction of a mating," Fatima said.

"Distraction? Our mating is a distraction," Kain whined.

"You are overreacting. What is really going on?" Angeline asked.

"You know what? Never mind. I'm going to bed."

They watched their mate storm out of the office. They couldn't mate with him for several reasons, the most important being that they weren't really his mates. Their mothers had performed a spell on them when they were born and made it so Kain would believe they were when he saw them. Couple that with the visions they'd given him, and all the ducks were lining up in a row. The Oracle may be a lot of things, but they would not force a bond on someone just for the hell of it. They had some sort of standards. They would just have to deal with his anger, which was nothing compared with their parents. No, they had a mission to fulfill. Everything else was just a distraction they didn't need.

CHAPTER 28

A FEW MONTHS LATER, OCTOBER 2014

Nathaniel had been looking for months, and he had no idea where his brother could be. He was never any good at the whole witch blood shit anyway. Alas, he had no choice but to visit The Oracle. The thought of it made his skin crawl. He didn't understand why they were doing it, but he needed their help. He would let it go for now, but he sure as hell didn't want to. Didn't matter anyway, the events would unfold as they were meant to. He drove to the twins and Kain's house in deep thought. Where the hell could Malik have gone so fast?

He stopped the car and parked it. The door had opened before he had even unbuckled his seatbelt. It was Kain at the door.

"I need to see them," Nathaniel said.

"Not today, they are preparing," Kain replied.

"I need to see them now."

"Not today."

"I don't have time for this shit! I need to find my brother, and they are going to help me do it."

"I said—" Kain was interrupted by twin voices.

"We don't know where he is," The Oracle said.

"Bullshit! I see right through the both of you," Nathaniel said.

"Careful how you talk to my mates, human. You will respect them," Kain threatened.

"It is you who should be careful of the company he keeps. Tell me where he is, or you won't like the outcome of my wrath," Nathaniel addressed The Oracle.

The twins stiffened at the implication. They still had plans to make, destinies to mold. They had no choice. They had not seen this outcome coming.

"What riddles do you speak of, Oracle?" Kain thundered. His power swirled around him like the exchanging positions of the moon and the sun.

"All in due time," Nathaniel evaded. "Are you going to tell me what I want to know, or do I have to speak of things you wish left unspoken?"

Angeline and Fatima bit back twin growls. Nathaniel could be a problem. A very big one, especially if he found his brother. But they had no choice. At least for now they didn't. They showed him in his mind where his brother was.

Nathaniel dipped his head in thanks and left to find his brother. He needed to hurry before irreparable damage was done. Already, things were out of alignment. Fates changed and distorted. He needed to be at his strongest. He needed his brother. It was time they fully became an Oracle. They also needed to find their mates. He didn't know how much more time was left to reverse the chain of events already set into motion, but he would know soon enough.

"What things didn't you want him to speak of?" Kain asked The Oracle.

"Nothing. He was being an asshole," The Oracle said dismissively.

"No, it didn't sound like 'nothing' to me. Tell me what you know."

"It is not meant to be spoken of right now."

"Bullshit! Nathaniel didn't seem like he would have had a hard time saying whatever it is had you not told him what he wanted to know."

"He was being overly dramatic," The Oracle sighed out.

"Stop keeping fucking secrets from me."

With those words Kain stormed out of the house.

"How long do you think it will be before he no longer relents so easily?" Angeline asked.

"We just have to be more careful. Time is growing shorter, and the window is getting smaller. We don't have any time to waste. We must stay the course. Don't get weak on me now!" Fatima exclaimed.

"Weak! I'm no such thing. This is our parents' doing. They insisted on The Old One becoming our mate. I would have never willingly let us be a part of this situation. Now is not a good time to have found a mate, especially one that isn't even really ours. I will NOT let him ruin this. We have worked too hard to steer these events perfectly, and no one will stand in our way."

"You would kill him, sister?" Fatima asked with an eyebrow raised. "James would make sure there was nothing left of us."

"I will do whatever it takes. It's not as if Mystics rely on the fact of even finding a mate. We weren't raised to believe we would even have one."

"Very well. We will wait and see. We will have to be careful. No more uninvited guests, especially Nathaniel. Lucky for him, he's weaker than us. Even with finding his brother. He will never see everything fast enough to stop what we have ensured is in motion. Come, sister, we must meditate."

Fatima didn't need these kinds of setbacks right now. Everything was important. Any small thing could make or break their plans. They had been working toward this for centuries, and it was almost a reality. They needed to go into a deep sighting and possibly reevaluate their plan of attack. They would have to be careful around Kain and possibly James. They were going to have to tell them a few half-truths to get them over their suspicions and questions. Fatima knew the perfect distraction for her mate: James. She knew James had some tricks up his sleeve. He had no idea that they were aware of all of his plans. But for now, they would let him play his little games. Games he wouldn't win.

"So I think I've finally found the perfect place for us to hole up, and it's not a condemned warehouse this time," Krista said.

"And it only took you several months," Taser teased.

Krista threw her hands up in surrender.

"Excuse the hell out of me! I've only been searching for a place, plus training with Mystics that my father sends this way. I can't do everything. The two of you could have been looking."

"I've been busy turning the pack over to Jackson and Taylor," Taser said.

They both looked at Nathan, who just shrugged.

"It's your fault we're in this hellhole. Only seems fair you're the one to get us out of it," Nathan said.

"You're an ass," Krista said.

"And you're the daughter of the Sevil's right hand, but here we all are."

"Now, now children. Let's not fight among ourselves. When do we leave?" Taser asked.

"Immediately," Krista said.

They weren't bringing any of the trash from the warehouse, so she grabbed both their arms and teleported to the nice little four-bedroom house she'd purchased with her father's money. Sure, she could have used her own, but her father was a dick, and she'd gotten greater pleasure from using his bank account instead. Plus, the look on his face when she stopped by The Oracle's house to tell him first was priceless.

The best part, though, was when he said they could move in without him for the time being. He and his mates were going to stay at Kain's a little while longer. She had no idea what her father had up his sleeves, but his absence meant she'd have more time to work on her plans for getting away from him for good. She hadn't forgotten the torment he'd put her through since she found out he was her father. She had every intention of paying him back double what he'd bestowed upon her. She just needed a little more time to prepare herself for what was to come.

CHAPTER 29

After several hours of driving and more than a dozen stops in between, Nathaniel had finally found the cabin his brother was supposed to be residing in. What he was doing all the way the hell out here, was anyone's guess. Nathaniel got his bag out of the car and walked to the front door. He rang the bell and waited. It didn't take long.

"How did you find me, little brother?" Malik asked.

"I have my sources. Now are you going to let me in or do I have to stand out on the porch all day?" Nathaniel asked.

"You weren't invited so why should I?"

"Don't annoy me right now! I'm tired, dirty, and hungry. Step aside before I bowl you over."

"Well if you're going to get snippy," Malik huffed.

Nathaniel walked into the cabin and looked around. The place was very nice. It reminded him of his old cabin before Malik found him and forced him to flee.

"We need to talk, but first I need a shower and some food."

"Fine, I'll show you to the spare room and bath, and I'll start supper. Come down to the kitchen after you've finished."

Nathaniel followed Malik up the stairs to a freshly painted room. It had a full-size bed, a few pieces of furniture, and its own bathroom. Malik showed him were the towels and toiletries were and left him to get himself together. Nathaniel hoped Malik didn't leave while he was up here; he had no desire to chase him all around the world.

Forty-five minutes later, Nathaniel was showered, shaved, and freshly dressed. He felt one hundred times better, and he could smell the stew cooking from downstairs. His stomach grumbled fiercely, and he patted it. He made his way downstairs where his brother waited.

"Something smells good. Is that Mom's beef stew?" Nathaniel asked.

"Yes, but I'm sure it's not as good as hers or yours for that matter. It won't be done for at least another hour so you might as well say what you have to say so you can eat, get a few hours rest, then be on your way," Malik said.

Nathaniel pursed his lips. He didn't know why his brother was making things so difficult.

"You know why I'm here. We need to merge as brothers and be who we were born to be."

"It's not right."

"It doesn't matter. Our blood isn't purely human, and now we have to live with the consequences of our ancestors' actions. Something is coming, and it's threatening to destroy everyone, human and non-human alike. If we want even a chance to stop it, we need to become a proper Oracle. The Oracle that's currently passing out information is giving false claims and steering things to their benefit. They need to be stopped before it's too late. You know what I'm saying is right."

"I didn't ask for this, and neither did you. When did it fall on us to save the world?"

"When the very first paranormals managed to infiltrate The Society and reproduce within it. Add to the fact that crazy little Callisto decided to take it a step further in defiance to her bitch of a mother, Reagan, for trying to control her fate. All that equals disaster and other people cleaning up the mess that's left behind."

"How much time do we have?"

"A month, maybe two before this Oracle starts to play its hand."

Malik dragged his hand down his face and sighed. He didn't want any part of this catastrophe, but it seemed he had no choice. That wasn't true—he had a choice, but could he live with the fallout if he did nothing while the world crumbled around him? He just wanted to be normal, but as always, someone decided that was too much to ask for and made him into the thing he hunted and killed.

"Fine. We can start in the morning. Come and eat. I'm sure the food is ready by now."

Nathaniel silently cheered. They wouldn't be fully prepared when the Mystic Oracle twins struck, but they wouldn't be totally helpless either. It seemed the games were beginning, and he had no intention of being on the losing side.

CHAPTER 30

"I've decided we need to speed up our plan. Nathaniel will be a problem, especially once he finds his brother," Angeline said.

"Then why did we tell him where he was?" Fatima asked.

"Because we had no choice. He would have exposed us, and we are too close to our goals. Already, we don't have much time, especially with James being here."

"What the hell do you suggest we do then? This entire thing was your bright idea."

"No, it was our parents' idea. They gave him the vision long before we were born. They started this, and it seems we must finish it and quickly."

"I don't want to do this anymore!"

"It doesn't matter what we want. It is what must be done."

"Then what do you suggest, Angeline?"

"Christmas will be here shortly. I think it's time to have a party."

The Oracle looked over the Christmas party invitations and smiled. This was going to be one of the best parties ever. The guest list included Jennifer, Jackson, Taylor, Krista, Nathan, Taser, Nathaniel, Billy, Brian, Bane, James, Alexander, and Isobelle. To say the shit was about to hit the fan would be an understatement. The Oracle smiled.

It was going to be perfect. They got up and put the invitations in the mail just as the mailman was coming. They made sure to put a little spell on each envelope to make sure they reached their intended party wherever they happened to be staying. The party was set for a week and a half from today on Christmas Eve, and they couldn't wait to see the looks on all the guests' faces. They had to make sure to put up cameras to capture this rare moment.

"What are the two of you so happy about?" Kain asked.

"Oh, you know—just getting in the Christmas spirit," The Oracle said innocently.

"Why do I have the feeling that you are up to no good? You know what they say about naughty girls? Do I have to put lumps of coal in your stockings this year?" Kain said, cocking an eyebrow.

"We have no idea what you're talking about," The Oracle said.

"Fine, don't tell me."

"We won't. Besides, you will find out soon enough."

ONE WEEK LATER

"Our guests should be rolling in any minute, sister," Angeline said.

"Great! Hopefully, they remember the rules of engagement. The cameras are discreetly placed and shouldn't be noticed at all," Fatima said.

"Let's get this party started, shall we?"

They heard the doorbell ring but had long felt the approaching presence of Jennifer, Jackson, Taylor, and the Cole triplets. They were buzzed with anticipation for the havoc this little Christmas party was about to cause. Angeline opened the door and smiled.

"Welcome to our home. Please come in and make yourselves comfortable. The rest of our guests should be arriving shortly," Angeline said.

Just as she was about to close the door, she felt the presence of Krista, Nathan, and Taser arriving. She held the door open for them to come inside as well.

"What the hell is this?" Jackson exploded. "What the fuck, what are they doing here?"

"They were invited, of course," Fatima said with a frown.

"We're leaving," Jennifer said.

The group began to walk out but found that they couldn't. Some sort of barrier was placed upon it.

"What the hell is this shit? Let us out of here!" Jennifer demanded.

"Sorry, dear, once you cross the threshold you can't leave until the party is over. Which is for the next several hours. So I suggest you deal with it," The Oracle said.

"That isn't going to work for me. Let us out now," Jennifer said.

"I would calm myself if I were you. We wouldn't want you to go into labor early," The Oracle smirked.

"Why you little bitches," Taylor growled.

Before The Oracle could respond, Kain came up from the hallway with James, Alexander, and Isobelle.

When Jennifer saw James, she freaked. "You have got to be fucking kidding me! Please, someone, tell me this is some sort of sick joke. That bastard is dead! I killed him. He should never be able to resurrect again."

Her breaths were coming in short, chopped pants. This wasn't happening. How the hell was this happening?

"Jennifer! How I've missed you. Have you met my mates?" James asked.

"Stay away from me, you animal!" Jennifer shouted.

"That's no way to talk to your favorite uncle. Besides, what would our daughter think?" James asked with his eyes wide in mock shock.

He was such an asshole, and he couldn't bring himself to care.

"What is going on here?" Kain asked. "Angeline, Fatima, did you do this on purpose?"

Kain knew he should have looked into their little party more. He wasn't sure what games they were playing, but he had no intentions of being a part of them.

"This is the way it must be," The Oracle said.

"Bullshit!" Kain replied. "This isn't a game. You don't get to play around with people's lives just to see their reactions. Jennifer, I didn't know they were going to do this. Yes, I was aware that James had returned, but I did not have anything to do with this spectacle."

"Do not under mind us! We are The Oracle!"

"No, you are two little, spoiled manipulators. You forget I spent the better part of nearly two millennium with the biggest manipulator of all time. You two have nothing on James. I'm not buying this, "We are The Oracle" bullshit. Now let these people leave if they so desire."

"The little bitches put a barrier on the doors," Billy said.

"You did what?" Kain asked.

The electricity had started to spark from every part of his body as his temperature rose. How could he have not seen it before?

"Oh, excuse me. Another of our guests is here, and it looks like he brought a friend," Fatima said.

She opened the door to let Nathaniel and Malik in. She ushered them inside before anyone could warn them not to enter. They knew once their mate found out what was going on he would be angry, but it had to be done. They had things they needed to do, and they couldn't discuss or seek his approval in order to do them. He would get over it in time after he saw that everything was for the best.

"I think we have been deceived, brother," Malik said.

"So it seems," Nathaniel said. "Seems I was right in my assessment of you, Oracle."

"We are doing what's best—"

"For you," Isobelle broke in. "This is all some sort of chess game to the two of you. You are moving us all around like pieces on a board. You use your gifts for your own purposes. You fabricate visions and speak them as if they are truth."

"Silence, human, you don't speak to us," The Oracle said.

"Oh but I do. You see I've had much time to process a lot of things since a deranged psychopath held me captive in his dungeon. I've had time to attune myself with my gifts, and I've seen much."

"Shut up!"

The Oracle shot a combined blast of energy toward Isobelle, but James caught the fireball with one of his own before they could even blink. The combined blast reverted back to The Oracle, and they fell to the floor.

"Hands off my merchandise. Only I can cause her pain or pleasure. You are not afforded the luxury," James said.

Everyone watched as The Oracle wiggled around the floor in agony. It was quite amusing. Even Kain didn't go to their aid. They had played him for a fool as well.

"Well, what will we all do now?" Nathan asked. "We can't leave so we might as well make the best of it."

"How were you able to return?" Jennifer asked.

"Our daughter, of course. I taught her how to counter the spell," James said.

Jennifer looked at Krista. She looked at her with the hurt and betrayal that was cutting her to her soul.

"How could you do this?"

"Do you think I wanted to? I was forced that hand, and the only thing I could have done was play it," Krista said.

"You could have come to me!"

"He would have had me killed!"

"He was already dead!"

"And what?" Krista screamed. "You don't think he could have done it, even in death? He appeared to me when he shouldn't have been able to. You know nothing of our species. The things we are capable of. I've been reading the book written by his grandfather, Constantine, and the things we can do are limitless. You are a fool, Mother, and you raised me to be one as well."

Everyone watched the heated exchange in silence—everyone but James, of course. He was amused, to say the least.

"You know what he did to me," Jennifer said softly.

"I also know what he did to me, and I was not going to live through it again. Yes, he raped you, but the things he did to me were far worse. He took away my beliefs and replaced them with something foreign. I couldn't recognize myself in the mirror anymore. I have no idea what this thing is I've become. I was not prepared for the savagery that being the daughter of James Johnston would do to me. You left me weak and vulnerable to his attacks."

"I thought he was dead."

"Even still, I was not prepared for a true Mystic regardless. Any of our kind could have killed me at any moment. I only knew what you told me, and it was not enough."

The accusations were too great for Jennifer to abide. The shock and stress of her circumstances caused her to cry out in pain. The baby was coming and far too soon. She should have had at least a few more months. She put her hand out to the wall to steady herself. She needed to get out of here.

"We need to leave. Now. Lift the fucking barrier, Oracle, or I'll put both your heads on spikes."

Jennifer looked to where The Oracle lay on the floor, unmoving. Damn James. His blast had knocked them unconscious.

"Let me help," Krista said. "They won't be awaking for some time. I speak from experience."

"Stay away from me."

"Don't be stupid. I can still do my job. I've delivered thousands."

"Just let her look. We are right beside you," Taylor said.

Jennifer let her mates hold her as her daughter pushed on her stomach.

"We need to get you to a bed, and I need to look and see what's going on. Kain, is there a place we can put my mother?" Krista asked.

"Of course. Follow me to the spare room," Kain said.

Jackson picked up Jennifer and rushed behind Kain. Krista and her mates remained close on his tail.

"Well, this should be a great story to tell the children," Alexander deadpanned.

"Where did our ray of sunshine go?" Isobelle asked.

"James? Who knows? Probably to torment his niece some more."

"Alexander, I would like you to meet my twin, Malik Carvanis," Nathaniel said.

"Pleasure," Alexander replied. "I see you've briefly had the pleasure of meeting our mate, whatever the hell that means."

"It means he will kill anyone who harms you, regardless of if he wants to or not," Brian said.

"And you know this how?" Alexander asked.

"Because it's the same feeling we have right now for these twins before us," Bane said.

"Mm, well that's great and all, boys, but we have much to do and no time to entertain abominations," Malik said.

"Malik! Apologize at once," Nathaniel scolded.

"I will not!"

"Please excuse my brother," Nathaniel said.

"Don't you apologize for me."

"Someone has to."

"I will not be mated to animals or men."

"We will discuss this later, and as far as the animal comment, you know as well as I do what our blood is mixed with."

"Um, yes—the lies and secrets held by the inner circle of The Mooyer Society," Alexander said.

"We have much to discuss about the families of The Mooyer Society," Nathaniel said. "But not now."

"I hate to interrupt this lovely conversation, but shouldn't we pick those two up off the floor?" Isobelle asked.

"No, serves them right for all the shit they've done in organizing this little party," Billy said.

"Touché."

"If you would excuse us, Isobelle and Alexander, we would like to talk to our mates in private," Brian said.

"Of course. Isobelle, let's see what we have in the kitchen. We've not had much free reign in months. Might as well take advantage of our limited freedom before James is back to hovering," Alexander said.

"Works for me. Have fun, kids."

The Oracle woke up in the place between the living and the dead. What the hell had happened? This was not going as they had planned. The only thing they could do now was hope the cameras caught what they were missing. Until then they were alone in this place that they didn't belong.

"Hello, children. What have you done to screw up this time?"

"Mothers and Father? How is this possible?" The Oracle asked.

"Would you believe it was a Christmas miracle?"

This was not good. Not good at all. They'd been dead for decades, and showing up like this now didn't bode well for either of them.

CHAPTER 31

Misha nearly ripped his father's office door off its hinges. He didn't even flinch when he heard the crack of it slamming into the wall from the force of his anger.

"What are you doing to find Alexander?" Misha roared.

His hands were balled up into fists, and he slammed them both down on his father's desk, causing papers to scatter and tiny figurines to fall to the floor. He wanted him found, and he wanted it done now.

"Have you lost your mind?" Alexander screamed. "Alexander is dead, and as far as the people who've killed him, there have been no leads."

"Bullshit! You know as well as I do that Alexander isn't dead. I won't believe it until I see a fucking body. If you don't do anything to find him, I will."

Misha stalked out of his father's office and barely stopped himself from slamming the door behind him. He found his mother in the hallway but didn't want to deal with her either. He walked right past her, but he could hear her footsteps following quickly behind him.

"Misha, you must calm down," Cassandra harshly whispered.

"Why are you whispering, Mother?" Misha asked, bored.

"Will you stop so I can speak with you?"

Misha wheeled around to face his mother so fast that she nearly fell coming to such an abrupt stop.

"What do you want?"

"You have to calm yourself. You don't want to incur your father's wrath. You know how he gets."

"Calm myself? My son is missing, and you want me to calm myself?"

"Shhhhh! Do you want your father to hear you? He'll kill us both!"

"He could try to kill me, but he'd be unsuccessful. You, on the other hand, wouldn't fair too well. Besides, it was you who manipulated a child into giving you what you wanted. I was an innocent victim. You knew Father didn't want another child, and you made sure to get yourself pregnant anyway. I was prepared to let you keep your secrets, but now my son is missing, and all bets are off the table. I will do whatever it takes to bring him home, and that includes throwing your sorry carcass to the wolves. Now get out of my way."

Misha left his mother standing in the middle of the hallway. He had to find Alexander, and when he did he was going to tell him the truth. It didn't matter if he wanted to hear it or not.

Jackson placed Jennifer on the bed and reluctantly stepped aside to allow Krista to be next to her. He didn't trust her, not for a second.

"I'm watching you. One wrong twitch and you'll regret it for the rest of your life," James warned.

"Just move out of my way. I've been delivering babies for years, long before I ever knew you existed," Krista said. "I need you to get undressed from the waist down, and I need everyone that's not her mate to give us some privacy."

"But I'm family," James whined.

"Get out before I kill you just for fun!" Jennifer screamed.

"You don't have to get all bitchy about it. I need to check on my mates anyway," James huffed.

Jackson watched as everyone left the room but Taylor, who was helping Jennifer get her pants off. He turned to Krista.

"Are you sure you know what you're doing, and are you able to control yourself?" Jackson asked.

"I'm perfectly capable. Now I need someone to find me some gloves, a lot of towels, and you might want to get a few face towels and a bowl of cool water for when she starts getting too hot. This is going to be a long night," Krista said.

Jackson exited the room and found Nathan and Taser outside, pacing back and forth. Good, he could have one of them look for the things he needed.

"Krista says she needs gloves, towels, washcloths, and a bowl of cool water," Jackson said.

"And rubbing alcohol if you can find it!" Krista yelled from inside.

"I'm sure you heard the last part," Jackson said.

"Sure, we'll be right back. We'll ask Kain if he knows where that stuff is," Nathan said.

"Please hurry," Jackson said.

He went back into the room and closed the door behind him, then watched as Krista's head bobbed under the blanket between Jennifer's legs.

"What is she doing?" Jackson asked Taylor.

"Something about checking dilation. Sounds disgusting to me," Taylor said.

They watched as Krista's head came back into view.

"It means I'm seeing if the baby's head is visible yet," Krista explained. "We're going to have to wait until she's opened enough to allow for safe passage through her birthing canal."

Jackson held up a hand to stop whatever else she was going to say.

"You know what, spare me the details. Jennifer, do you need anything?" Jackson asked.

"Drugs!"

"Sorry, Mom, my medical bag with all the good stuff's at the house. You're going to have to do this the old-fashioned way again."

"This is bullshit! What's the point of giving birth in the modern world if you still can't have drugs?"

"And so the fun begins," Krista murmured. "You guys may want to take a seat. We're going to be here for a very long time. She's only two centimeters, and we can't do anything until she gets to ten, which could take minutes or hours."

"Ah dammit," Taylor sighed.

"Exactly," Jackson agreed.

"Kain, Krista needs a few things for the birth," Nathan said.

"Let me look and see what we have in the back. Give me a moment," Kain said.

"So how's she doing?" Isobelle asked over a mouthful of food.

"Really, dear, talking with your mouth full?" James admonished.

Isobelle just looked at him and went back to her sandwich.

"I think she's doing as well as can be expected being locked in the same house with the psycho who tormented not only her but her daughter as well," Taser replied.

"So I've heard. Well, if Krista needs a second pair of hands, I'm available," Isobelle said.

"I'll let her know," Nathan replied.

They all looked to the hallway Kain was coming from with a medium sized medical bag.

"Hopefully this has everything she'll need, and I'll bring some towels in," Kain said.

"Could you bring a bowl of water as well?" Taser asked.

"Coming right—" Kain stopped mid-sentence when he felt his grandfather's presence.

"Kain, do you feel that?" James asked.

"I believe so. Is that who I think it is?" Kain asked.

Before James could reply, both of their grandfathers had popped into the living room.

"Who the hell put spells around the house? We almost weren't able to get in," Constantine said.

No one said a word, too shocked by their sudden appearance.

"Well! Someone answer me, dammit! James?" Constantine asked.

"The Oracle," James said slowly, and then added, "What are the two of you doing here?"

"I should have known those two idiots were up to no good. Their mothers and father were the worst. And I'm here because my newest Oracle granddaughter and grandson are about to be born," Constantine said.

"That's impossible. All Oracles are identical," Kain said.

"Ah, but something wicked this way comes. Fates are changing, and destinies have been altered," Rory said.

"Nathan, Taser, take these things to Krista before she sends a search party. We'll fill you in on the rest later," Kain said.

"Oh, we all need to gather together, Constantine said. "I need to tell a story and I only want to tell it once. Jennifer will be in labor for quite a while. We have time. Lock The Oracle downstairs in the cage, Kain."

"I know they've done questionable things, but you want me to lock my mates in a cage?" Kain asked.

"Boy, those girls are not your mates," Rory growled. "James and his two sidekicks are. You've always known James was yours, and you couldn't figure out the rest because The Oracle's mothers put a spell on you. We just discovered this not long ago. Now we'll need to undo it, but it will take a bit of time. But we'll worry about that later."

So many fucking lies and secrets. How many more were there? Kain was getting tired of all the bullshit.

"You know what, I can't deal with this right now," Kain said. "James, help me lock them up. We'll meet everyone else in the spare room. Someone find the triplets and the other Oracle."

"Oh the mostly human ones, yes, good. I'm glad they are here as well," Constantine said.

Isobelle and Alexander stared at one another.

"Well, at least we'll never be bored," Isobelle said to Alexander in passing.

"And that more than anything frightens me," Alexander replied.

They'd finally found their mates only to have one of them hate them. Brian was tired of all the hate. He just wanted an uncomplicated life, but it seemed that was too much to fucking ask for.

"I'm not mating anyone, especially three men who can turn into wolves," Malik said.

"They are much more than wolves, aren't you?" Nathaniel asked.

"You already know the answer to that question," Billy said.

"Yes, but I want to hear it from one of you," Nathaniel replied.

"What the hell are you two blabbering about?" Malik asked.

"Can you not feel the dual nature of them?" Nathaniel asked.

"Not paying close enough attention I guess," Malik said.

"Or old age is starting to slow you down," Nathaniel muttered.

"Can we please focus on the issue?" Bane asked.

"What issue? There is no issue. I already told you people, I'm not mating with wolves. And even if you weren't wolves, you are men. MEN!" Malik said.

"So you're homophobic?" Billy asked.

"No, I don't like men. Not wanting to have a sexual relationship with another man doesn't make me homophobic. And secondly, I've been killing paranormals for a very, very long time. My brother was lucky to drag me to this bullshit event in the first place. I'm barely tolerating my need to kill every last one of you just for shits and giggles. But I refuse to acknowledge your ridiculous notion that we're in any way, shape, or fashion, mates. Now if you'll excuse me—" Malik started.

"Um, I hate to interrupt, but we are all having a meeting in the spare bedroom. Apparently, there's more shit that needs to hit the fan," Alexander said. "So come on and grab a seat. I managed to find some popcorn and a bottle of Jack. I have a feeling we're going to need more than the one bottle, though, before everything's said and done."

"For fuck's sake! What the hell is it now?" Brian asked. "This conversation isn't over either."

"The hell you say," Malik replied.

All five men reluctantly followed Alexander to hear about these newest developments for this shit show that was slowly playing out.

CHAPTER 32

Misha's hands gripped the steering wheel tighter. He couldn't believe months had gone by without any kind of lead on Alexander. It was as if he'd disappeared from the fucking earth. It was unacceptable. Someone had to know where he was, and he'd bet all his money that this someone was Samuel Casey. Sam had always had Alexander's best interests at heart so it wouldn't surprise Misha if he lied to his father about knowing where Alexander and Isobelle were. In fact, he'd bet his life he knew exactly where they were.

Misha pried his hands off the wheel and got out of the car. He walked up to the house of Avery Lynn, rang the doorbell, and waited.

"May I help you?" Avery asked.

"I need to speak with your son, please. My name's Misha Carvanis, and I need him to tell me where my son is."

"How would my boy know where your son is? He ain't seen nobody from that little secret society y'all been running since they dropped my boy off beaten and broken."

"I'm not calling you a liar, ma'am, but I know he knows where Alexander is, and he's going to tell me."

"And if he doesn't?"

Misha moved so fast that the thought to move had hardly registered. He had his knife out and held to Avery's throat before she could say uncle.

"Then one of his immediate family members is going to go missing for every week that I don't know where my son is."

Misha heard the unmistakable sound of a shotgun being pumped and looked up to see a double barrel pointing right at his head.

"Youse bes' back away from my mama, boy, 'for I blow your fucking head off," Samuel said calmly. "And don't think I'll miss, cuz I won't. Then old man Carvanis will be short two sons, the oldest and the youngest. How's about them odds?"

Misha held up both hands and took several steps back. Avery rushed behind her son, her eyes glowering with rage.

"Tell me where he is."

"I'll tell you like I told my daddy. Alex is dead and so is Isobelle. Now get the fuck off my property."

"Fair warning, Samuel, I'll tear this fucking world apart looking for my son, and I don't give a damn who I have to go through to find him."

"Do what you gotta do, and I'll do what I gotta do."

"You and me, we're not finished."

"From where I'm standing I'd say we was done. Now go on, get."

Misha turned on his heels and returned to his car. It seemed he was going to have to play hardball after all. No matter, he did this type of shit for fun.

"Now that we've all gathered in one place, where should I begin?" Constantine said.

"How about the beginning?" James asked. He gave his grandfather a look that let him know he was bored and wanted him to hurry up with his old man ramblings.

"Don't make me send you to your parents," Constantine threatened. "Better yet, do you want me to have them resurrected for a little while?"

"You wouldn't dare!" James exclaimed.

"All right, you two. Cut that shit out right now!" Jennifer yelled. "I don't need this stress so either tell the fucking story, Grandpa, or move it along."

"So rude, just like my Marcella was," Constantine said in resignation. "Fine, I'll start from the beginning. I hope you all are comfortable. This is going to take a few hours. Now let's see... which storyline to start with first? Ah, yes, that stupid 'Prophecy' I had when I was just a boy."

"Time out," Krista said. "You are the original prophet?"

"I was just starting to come into my powers, really, and I kind of misspoke," Constantine confessed.

"Misspoke!" Krista yelled.

"Hey, who's telling this story, girl? Me or you?"

Krista huffed but didn't say another word.

"Now, if my family is done interrupting me, let's begin with that 'Prophecy'. It can be interpreted several different ways. But there is only one correct way. Krista could very well destroy the world as we know it, but it doesn't necessarily have to be."

"Explain," James said, then thought better of it and added, "Please."

Constantine seemed pleased with that gesture. "Basically, had I never uttered that prophecy out loud, then it wouldn't have meant anything. A Seer's powers are a little different from an Oracle's. For a Seer's reading of a person to be absolute, they must say the words out loud. If they just think them, then the outcome could go either way. The vision will either come true or not. For an Oracle, regardless of whether they speak a reading out loud or think it, it will still be true."

"I don't understand. I had a vision of a friend dying weeks before she did and it happened, but I never spoke about it out loud," Isobelle said.

"Ah, you saw a vision of the future, which is much different from deliberately trying to see a person's future. When I spoke the words of 'The Prophecy,' I was trying to see into my own future for my family. That was what was shown, and because I gave power to it by saying it out loud, it made it truth."

"So you cursed us," Jennifer said between contractions.

"In theory, that's exactly what I did. Had I not pushed for answers, things that came to pass may have not."

"As fascinating as that is, there is always this thing called 'free will'," Alexander began. "James chose to force himself upon Jennifer, Jennifer decided to carry the child to term and raise her, Krista decided to bring her father back to life after her mother had ensured his death, and Krista decided to go ape-shit crazy. So ultimately, if she's going to destroy the entire world and everyone in it, it's her decision. She can either decide to fuck everybody over or take responsibility for her actions and get her shit together!" Constantine shook his head, but Alexander continued regardless. "Everyone is in charge of his or her own fate. Not Seers or Oracles but individual people. Isobelle and I decided to run from The Society, which led to our kidnapping and mating. We could have easily gone back to The Society and demanded answers."

"You have no idea what it's like!" Krista shouted. "The constant drive to hurt and torture everyone around me."

"Cry me a fucking river, princess. Seems like you were spoiled and not taught how to properly control your urges," Alexander said.

"Excuse me?" Jennifer screamed, breathless.

"You fucking heard me," Alexander said. "You raised her knowing she was a monster, yet you tried to make her out to be something that she wasn't. You're the reason why she is so weak and why she couldn't even come close to being a challenge for her father."

"I thought he was dead," Jennifer said.

"Thinking and knowing are two different things. You left her wide open and defenseless. Had she run across a Mooyer worth their reputation, she would have stood no chance. Knowing how to fight and knowing how to utilize all your abilities are two different things. Most of the supernaturals that ever escaped a Mooyer did so because they knew how to use their natural gifts, not because they tried to stay and fight. Had they tried they would have lost every time. The Society is the real fucking deal, and apparently, that's because they come from the same bloodline as you creatures. We aren't completely human after all. Although they like to still lead us to believe we are."

"I did what I thought was best!" Jennifer shouted.

"For who, you or your daughter? I'm sure everyone knows the answer to that question so no need to provide one."

"That's enough out of you," Jackson growled.

"What? The truth too hard to swallow?" Alexander asked.

"You have no idea what you're talking about," Jackson said. "You weren't there, and you aren't her."

"I know enough to know that she was part of the problem and not the solution. Sugarcoat the shit all you want, but the actions of many overrule the few. We are all paying for the sins of our fathers. Constantine, could you please explain how The Society was infused with paranormal blood without them knowing?"

"Of course. Let's take a small ten-minute break to regroup and meet back here. I think it's a good time for Krista to check Jennifer's progression as well."

Everyone left the room to give Krista privacy to check Jennifer's vitals and to think about what they'd been told so far. It was getting heavy with all the lies and secrets being revealed. Tempers were rising, and high blame was being passed around like a joint at a stoner's party. Kain foresaw several more outbursts in the next few hours. He started down the basement steps to check on the Oracle and see if they'd woken. He had a thing or two he wanted to say to them when they did.

"Mothers' and Father, how can this be? Where have you taken us?" Angeline asked.

"Silence, stupid girl," the Oracle said. "You've disappointed us greatly. Did we not set the stage perfectly? Did we not give you all the tools needed to accomplish your tasks? Did we not make clear your fucking mission?"

Angeline knew better than to speak when their parents got like this, but Fatima wasn't always so quick.

"Screw you! You think it's been easy using our gifts for anything besides their intended purpose? You believe you can do a better job? Oh yeah, that's right, you're fucking dead! Oh, and how did you die? I'm glad you asked. You died from an ambush by The Mooyer Society that you didn't see coming. The all and powerful Oracle, the one who was called upon to teach Oracles from the world over, didn't even see their own deaths coming for them. But yet you judge us! We've accomplished things you can't even begin to imagine. You've been dead for over a century so you have no idea about anything, you miserable old bitches!" Fatima shouted.

Angeline tried to reach her sister first, but she was too slow. She was always too slow. The sounds of bones snapping were loud in the empty space they'd somehow occupied. She saw their father even wince at the sounds.

"Mothers, please," Angeline begged. "She didn't mean it."

"She meant every word, the little ungrateful slut. We gave you everything you could have ever wanted, and this is how you repay us," their mothers said.

Angeline pleaded with their father with her eyes, but he only turned his head away. She should have known. He never defied the will of their mothers.

"We are doing what you wanted. Everything was coming together, but then Krista brought James back," Angeline said.

She slowly made her way to her sister. If she moved any faster, her mothers would notice and keep her from reaching Fatima. If only she could touch her sister, they could remove themselves from this place and get far away from their parents' wrath.

"You should have known what she was doing ahead of time and planned for it," their mothers said. "Instead, you allowed Kain to give her a vial of his blood!"

Angeline didn't even bother to answer. She'd finally reached her sister. She touched her and thought of another place, any place, but the one they were currently in.

"NO!" their mothers shouted.

But it was too late. They were always too late, and if Angeline had anything to say about it, they'd never see them again.

CHAPTER 33

Kain checked the cage, but the twins were still unmoving. James must have pushed quite a bit of power into them for them to still be unconscious. Knowing James, he stopped seconds from killing them completely so it could be days before they regained consciousness. The conversation they needed to have was going to have to wait. That was fine with him, and it gave him more time to get his thoughts together. How could he have been fooled so badly, by basically children, no less? He didn't have time to dwell on the answers as the ten-minute break was nearly up. Besides, he wanted to grab a bite to eat before heading back to the spare room. He started back up the stairs and took a detour to the kitchen before returning to the gathering.

Krista checked her mother's dilation progress and groaned when she realized she was only at four centimeters, only a two-centimeter difference from hours ago. She was used to human births, and they moved far quicker than this. If this were the norm for Mystics, she'd never become pregnant if she could help it. She was just finishing up when everyone started to file back into the room.

"How far?" Jennifer asked.

"Only four," Krista replied.

"Dammit. I'd forgotten how long Mystic births could take. I'd thought it wouldn't be as bad since they aren't full blood, but I guess I was wrong."

"The pain and discomfort will be worth it once our son or daughter is born," Taylor said.

"Easy for you to say. You're not the one giving birth," Jennifer said with a weak smile.

"Here, drink this," Jackson said.

Krista watched as her mother greedily gulped down the water. She again had the thought of securing effective birth control as soon as possible. There was no way she was enduring this form of torture.

"All right, everyone, now for the story you all really want to know. It's a fairly long one so get comfortable," Constantine said. "Rory will start, and I will finish."

"It all began when Gregori Carvanis thought it would be a good idea to start interrogating the paranormals instead of just killing them," Rory explained. "They would capture them, torture them for information, then kill them. The first paranormal to be captured was Thaddeus Brimming. He was in captivity for only a day when he escaped their little holding cell and took out several members of the village during his breakout. He took a few hits but nothing he didn't survive. His mother, Selene Brimming, was furious as he was her only surviving child and she couldn't have anymore. She'd already lost so many, and at the thought of having lost the only child that lived to adulthood, she wanted retribution."

"I think I've heard parts of this story," Nathan said. "At least the part where he was captured and then escaped, but that's pretty much the version they have passed down in the Brimming family."

"Yes, but there is much, much more that has never been revealed. Representatives from the Dylia wolves were there as well, Dawls, Durham, and Jameson. But ultimately it was Selene's idea to breed with humans until the perfect paranormals of each species were created and could blend in. We all know the half-breed Hyjias and Dylias can't pass, as they are stuck between shifted form and human, but the children's, children's, children's, children of them can blend perfectly. After several failed attempts and deaths, four centuries after we'd originally agreed to the plan, we'd finally found where The Mooyers were hiding and had perfected the human/paranormal blend. We sent in six children, two of each species, to seek refuge with the hunters and ingrain themselves into the village. It worked perfectly, but what none of us could have foreseen was how Mystic-like Reagan had become. It seems she inherited all the vile parts of a Mystic and the human blood did nothing to counter her moods. She convinced the rest of the children to abandon the mission they were bred to carry out and instead use The Society for vengeance of what she saw as a betrayal by her own kind. She believed we'd left them to be slaughtered in the event that they couldn't convince the village of their intentions," Rory said.

"Reagan, did she give birth to Callisto?" Alexander asked.

"Indeed she did," Constantine said. "And she was the beginning of the end."

"How so?" Nathaniel asked.

"On Callisto's thirteenth birthday, Reagan shared with her the origin of her heritage. Before then, Callisto was consumed with her legacy as not only a Carvanis but also a Mooyer. She couldn't wait to join the family business, even though women weren't allowed directly into The Society at the time. Her mother sharing the fact that she had Mystic blood in her veins devastated her and warped her mind. Although Callisto was the youngest, she held the spark of power that her mother recognized in herself, so she believed she would do her bidding and be honored. It backfired on her and Callisto, along with her cousin/lover Christian and a few of their cousins when they decided they would incorporate more Mystic and paranormal blood into The Society. Thus, a secret club inside the secret club was born. I don't think it would have been so bad had her mother not forced her to kill her baby by Christian. At the time, Reagan and Gabriel, Christian's father, wouldn't take the risk. They forbade them to be intimate together ever again and forced them to marry someone else. They still saw each other in secret, of course, but that is another story for another time," Constantine said.

"The main point is that by wanting to tear The Mooyer Society apart from the inside out, Selene's plan only succeeded in making them stronger. It gave them the strength and cunning needed to go toe-to-toe with their distant relatives," Rory said.

"So you're telling me our bloodlines were polluted because of the kidnapping and torture of one person?" Malik asked.

"That's exactly what we're telling you," Constantine said.

"And that a Carvanis is to blame for the secrets within The Society and the fact that our mission statement is a big joke?"

Alexander asked.

"Callisto was extreme," James said.

"You've met the lunatic?" Isobelle asked.

"A time or two. I mean she is a Johnston after all," James said.

"What the hell do you mean?" Billy asked. "She was alive how many centuries ago, and she wasn't a Seer or Oracle. So am I missing something?"

"Who said she wasn't a Seer?" Kain asked.

"You know her as well?" Bane asked.

"Not firsthand, but I've seen her in a few dreams," Kain said.

"So is she dead or alive?" Brian asked.

"She's not dead… in fact, she's still very much hands-on in The Society. She just goes by a different name," Constantine said.

"Name? What name?" Alexander asked.

"Are you sure you wish to know the answer to that question?" Rory asked.

"Oh please don't tell me she's masquerading around as one of my aunts or cousins," Alexander pleaded.

"I can say with a straight face that she is not your aunt or cousin," Constantine said.

"Then who the hell is she?"

"She's your mother," Constantine said.

CHAPTER 34

Misha strung up one of Samuel's wolf cousins by his ankles. He hated resorting to this kind of behavior, but he was given no choice. This was the result of backing a man into a corner and lying to his face. The people you loved suffered the consequences of your actions. All Samuel had to do was tell him where his son was and he'd have taken care of the rest. But no. So now Misha had to resort to extreme measures to get the answers he sought.

"I'm only going to ask this once, and your answers will determine if you live or die, do you understand me?" Misha asked.

"Fuck you!" the wolf snarled.

"Don't say I didn't warn you," Misha murmured.

Misha got his whip ready and began the interrogation. He didn't have time to waste.

"What do you know about a wolf pack killing two Mooyer members?" Misha asked.

"Go to hell!"

Misha pulled his arm back and brought it down while also flicking his wrist. The crack of the whip was accompanied by the howl of the wolf.

"Same question as before. If I were you, I'd tell me what I want to know."

"Samuel will hear of this," the wolf growled.

"Samuel had his chance to talk. By refusing, he has sealed his family's fate. I warned him, but he did not listen. Now give me a name."

"There is no name! Had a wolf pack killed two Mooyer members, they wouldn't have been able to hold the secret. Word would have traveled fast, and no such story has been told. I answered your question. Now let me go."

"Who said that's all I intended to ask? We are going to be here for quite some time. It will go quicker with your full cooperation, or I could use the whip again. Either way is fine with me."

"You're insane!"

"Well, I am related to monsters, so what did you expect?"

"Where are we?" Fatima asked.

"The place that only exists to you and me," Angeline answered.

"I'm not healing properly."

"That's because you aren't really hurt. Not in real time, anyway. We need to find a way to wake up. Who knows what they've done with us?"

"What if we can't wake up? What if we're dead?"

"We're not."

"And how do you know? James isn't known for pulling back."

"He will want answers, and you can't get those from a dead body. Plus, bringing us back to life would require more energy than he's willing to expend at the moment. He brought us to this place just before death. It will take a few days to wake up."

"What are we supposed to do in the meantime?"

"Regroup and re-strategize. We have work to do regardless of what others think. We're doing what must be done. The world must end and take all the human trash with it. Paranormals should be the only creatures to walk the earth. It will be as it was always meant to be before humans were created."

"Are you sure we are doing the right thing, sister?"

"You're having second thoughts?"

"I don't know. I'm tired, and I just want to be done with this. We will be met with resistance now that they know part of our plans."

"We are an Oracle. We hold sway over a lot of power that we normally wouldn't. They can try, but they will not succeed. It would take one much older than James or Kain to stop us, and there are none."

"If you say so. I'm going to rest and restore my strength. We will need every ounce once we awaken."

"Sleep, Fatima, and I will watch over you."

Angeline comforted her sister with Fatima's head in her lap. She would die before she'd let anyone hurt her. They would see this mission through and be done with it. Eventually, the other supernaturals would see it was for the best.

CHAPTER 35

"I'm sorry, I could have sworn you said that my mother was some centuries-old psychopath," Alexander laughed. "This is not my life. First, James tells me that my brother is also my father, and now you're saying my mother, Cassandra Carvanis, is really Callisto Carvanis. It's impossible. She is a Singer," Alexander said.

"Is she? How much do you really know about your mother? And there are no pictures of Callisto or even recollections of what she looked like. You've studied the journals, along with Nathaniel and Malik, and have either of you ever read what she looked like? You've read what she's done, but you have no idea what she looked like," Constantine said.

"Is that all or are there more lies from my childhood that you wish to expose?" Alexander asked.

"That is all, for now," Constantine said. "There is nothing more to be done at the moment. Although I wish to speak to Isobelle about her powers a bit more in private. We must all leave this room now. The babies are coming."

"You want to talk now?" Isobelle asked.

"Yes, it won't take long," Constantine said.

"Lead the way then," Isobelle said.

Everyone started to file out of the room besides Jennifer, Jackson, Taylor, and Krista. Nathan and Taser stood just outside the door while everyone else migrated to the living room. Krista checked her mother once the door was closed. Ten centimeters, perfect. She was ready.

"Okay, Mom, when I say push, push," Krista said.

"Just hurry up, would you? I just want to sleep for a day or two after this," Jennifer said.

"One of you get the blanket ready," Krista said to Taylor and Jackson.

"I got it right here," Taylor said.

"Good. Okay, Mom, push!"

"Ahhhhhhh," Jennifer screamed.

"You're doing great, Mom, I can see the head. Give me another push."

"Oh my god! I forgot how much pushing a person out of your body hurt. Pull it out already, Krista!"

"You're worse than the human women. One more big push to get past the shoulders."

"Both of you are getting fixed immediately!"

"Don't be absurd!" Jackson growled.

"Don't even think about it," Taylor added.

They were interrupted by the high-pitched cries of their baby.

"What is it? A boy or a girl?" Jennifer asked.

"It's a boy. Bring the blanket, Taylor," Krista said.

Krista wrapped the baby in the blanket and handed it back to Taylor. It was a boy, and he was adorable. Her mother's screams forced her attention away from her baby brother.

"What? What's wrong?" Krista asked.

"I don't know!"

Krista looked down and saw the beginning of another baby head.

"Oh shit! There's another one."

"Another what?" Jackson asked.

"Get another blanket. Quickly," Krista said to no one in particular.

She coached her mother through a few more pushes and out popped a little girl this time. A sister.

"It's a girl," Krista said, shocked.

She wrapped her in the blanket that Jackson handed to her. She then carefully handed the baby back to him. The door was suddenly thrust open.

"We need to go, right now," Nathan said. "Teleport them all home, Krista, then meet us at the house."

"What happened?" Jackson said.

"Constantine did something to Isobelle after she snapped at him. I don't know all the details at the moment. Also, congrats. Now let's move it. We'll fill you in later once we know more."

"You guys ready?" Krista asked.

"The barrier's been lifted?" Taylor asked.

"I think Constantine and Rory broke it when they forced their way in," Krista said.

"Then let's go," Jackson said.

They huddled together, and once everyone was touching, Krista teleported them to the pack lands. They would be safer there for the time being. The rules of the game were changing, and Krista was no longer familiar with all the players. Now that she'd laid eyes on her siblings, she'd kill anyone or anything that threatened them. Even herself.

"The boys will call with any news. They are beautiful children," Krista said.

She took one last look at her mother and teleported home.

"What's so important?" Isobelle asked.

Constantine looked up to find James and Alexander right behind her. They were in the kitchen while everyone else was either in the living room, spare bedroom, or outside the spare room in the hallway.

"I remember saying I wanted to speak to her privately," Constantine said.

"Rory's still here," James pointed out.

Constantine watched Kain come into the kitchen as well.

"And that means exactly…?"

"If Rory can stay, so can we," James said. "We're her mates, after all."

"So I take it you will all be mating with my grandson soon?" Rory asked.

"He's already mine," James said.

"Yes, but he needs to become theirs as well," Rory said.

"It will happen," James said.

"Fine, I'll leave it alone for now," Rory said.

"I guess she'd probably tell you all what was said in here anyway."

"Probably," Alexander said.

"Isobelle, you are the only one who can stop 'The Prophecy'."

"Come again?" Isobelle said.

"A Seer spoke the original curse and only another Seer can counter it."

"Why me? Why not an Oracle?"

An Oracle can only shape and manipulate a curse uttered by a Seer, not stop it completely. That is what the Caprice twins were doing, molding it to their will. While Nathaniel and Malik can try to steer it in another direction, only you can actually stop it."

"Again I ask, why me? I'm sure I'm not the only Seer in the world."

"No you aren't, but you are mated to James, who is a direct descendent of me and one of the actors in 'The Prophecy.' Your link to him links you to me, the Seer who created it."

"This is bullshit! I don't want to be responsible for the fate of the fucking planet!"

"It's your destiny," Constantine said.

"What were you saying earlier, Alexander, about choices?" Isobelle asked.

"They are ours to make," Alexander said.

"Exactly. And I choose to sit on the sidelines with a bag of popcorn and watch this shit burn. You fucked up, Constantine. You fix it. I'm not your cleaning lady."

Isobelle felt every nerve in her body scream. She was on fucking fire. It hurt to the point where she couldn't even scream.

"Grandfather, stop it right now!" James yelled.

"I will not be spoken to in that manner ever again. I don't care who she is to you. I have no problem killing her. I suggest you have a little chat with your mate. Call out to me in a few days, and we will talk again. Come, Rory, we've stayed long enough.

James watched as the two men teleported out of the house. He hoped that meant the barrier spell had been lifted. They couldn't stay here anymore, none of them could.

"We need to leave this place at once, James said. "Kain, go get the twins from the basement and take them to my new home. Secure them in the basement there. Alexander, inform one of Krista's mates that we're leaving. I'll take Isobelle and let the triplets and the male twins know."

The boys rushed to do as James had instructed. James needed to get Isobelle in a healing tub at once. She would have no lasting damage, but his grandfather could be a right prick when he wanted to. He'd forgotten that about the old man, a mistake he wouldn't make again.

CHAPTER 36

"Should we revisit our talk about being mates?" Bane asked.

"I wouldn't," Malik said. "Too much talk has been done today. I don't want to hear anything else right now. I just want to go home and rest."

"Here, take my number. Give it a few days and call," Nathaniel said.

They didn't like it, but they had no choice. Brian took the offered card and put it in his wallet. He looked up as James came rushing in with an unconscious Isobelle.

"What the hell happened to her?" Billy asked.

"My grandfather. We all need to leave this house at once. It's not safe here. Go home, we'll call you in a few days to regroup," James said. "The barrier is no longer active. You wolves should go back to the pack lands. Your Alphas should be there by now. Nathaniel and Malik, you should come with us."

"Give me the address. We'll meet you there," Malik said.

James nodded and sent the information telepathically.

"Alexander, come! We must go," James said.

"I'm here, I'm here. Krista just teleported back and got Nathan and Taser. I'm ready," Alexander said.

Alexander watched as the triplets and twins walked out the front door to their cars. He trusted they would get where they needed to go. James held out his hand to Alexander and teleported as soon as he touched it. He needed to talk to Kain, and they needed to wake up the Oracle. They had questions that needing answering.

After Misha had called the cleanup crew, he dialed his father's number. He'd gotten the answers he needed but sadly at the expense of that poor wolf's life. It was Samuel's fault, really. All he had to do was tell Misha what he wanted to know and it wouldn't have been an issue.

"Father, they've been kidnapped by James Johnston. The Mystic. I'm not sure where he's hiding them, but we will find them. Samuel lied. I just tortured one of his cousins. I'm on my way home now. Yes, it appears that war is inevitable. We've been betrayed by our own. I don't care; an example needs to be made, a big one at that. I'll talk to you when I get home."

Misha hung up, then gathered his things and left the warehouse. He changed into a clean pair of clothes and washed as much blood off his hands and face as he could. He tossed his soiled clothes into the warehouse, then got in his rental car and headed to the airport. He'd buy a ticket once he got there—he wasn't worried about availability. Money opened many doors.

It didn't take long to arrive at the airport. He dropped the rental car off and headed to the ticket lanes. An hour and a half later he was on a non-stop flight home. It was time to clean house, starting with the Caseys.

"Derrick, new information has been extracted. Samuel lied. Alexander and Isobelle are very much alive, and they've been kidnapped by James Johnston," Alexander said.

There was a long pause over the phone before Derrick spoke.

"I see. Samuel will have to be dealt with," Derrick said.

"See that you do, because if not, Misha will."

"Understood."

Alexander hung up the phone and found his wife inside the doorway of his study.

"What the hell are you doing eavesdropping on my

conversations?" Alexander demanded.

"Oh, will you shut up with your ridiculous whining? Where is my son?" Cassandra asked.

"How dare you talk to me that way?"

"I'll talk to you any way I want from now on. You have no idea who you're fucking with. I was content to sit on the sidelines while you ran this family, but then you went and lost my pride and joy. So now I'll be taking over from here. I'll keep Misha updated on my progress. You can go fuck yourself for all I care. Now if you'll excuse me, I need to have a little chat with an old relative."

Alexander was convinced his wife had finally abandoned ship. He should have had her committed years ago. He'd pawn her off on Misha when he returned. He was the only one who could ever make her see reason.

CHAPTER 37

Derrick and his father pulled up to the Mina residence and got out of the car. This was not going to go over well, but Derrick was done with the niceties. His daughter was missing, and he planned to get her back. But first, he needed to right a wrong.

"Are you sure you want to do this?" Derrick Sr. asked.

"Absolutely. I want to see the look on the lying, manipulative bitch's face when she sees me."

"After you, then. This is your show," Derrick Sr. said.

Derrick rang the doorbell and waited for Bethany to come to the door.

"Can I help—" Bethany's words caught in her throat.

"We need to talk," Derrick said.

"Honey, who is it?" Cassidy called.

Bethany found her voice at the sound of her husband.

"No one. Seems they have the wrong address," Bethany said.

"Bullshit!"

Derrick pushed his way past the front door, and his father quietly followed behind him.

"You can't just barge in here. Get out of my house before I call the police!" Bethany shouted.

"Beth, what's going on? Who are these men?" Cassidy asked.

"Hello, Cassidy, I'm Derrick Casey Jr., Isobelle's real father."

"What is he talking about, Beth? Who is this man?" Cassidy asked again.

"I'm so sorry, Cas," Bethany sobbed.

"You didn't," Cassidy said.

"She did. She lied to you, and she used and lied to me," Derrick said. "I just came to let her know our daughter is missing, and I plan to find her, whatever the cost."

"Mama, I need you to go with the rest of the pack and find safety. A war is brewing, and I need you safe," Samuel said.

"And where will you go?" Avery asked.

"I'm going to call Alexander. He will watch my back like he used to."

"How do you know he won't stab you in it?"

"He mated the Mystic."

"Fine, but you bes call me every day. If not I'm gone rip this world apart looking for you."

"I'll be fine, now go before The Society comes."

Samuel was going to rip Misha Carvanis' throat out the next time he saw him. He could already taste the blood in his mouth. How dare he torture and kill one of his family members? He'd started something that he wouldn't be able to finish.

Cassandra teleported to the house James was holding her son in.

"James, cousin, you're getting harder and harder to pin down. Now tell me, where is my baby boy?" Cassandra asked.

"Callisto, it's nice to see you again," James said.

"Liar, you wished I had died when Christian did, and please call me Cassandra. I stopped going by Callisto centuries ago."

"Mother?" Alexander asked.

"There you are! Come, let Mother look at you. Out of all my children, and there have been many, you are my favorite aside from Misha."

"Is it true?" Alexander demanded.

"Is what true, dear?"

"That you're really Callisto Carvanis and Misha is not only my brother but my father as well?"

"I'm afraid so."

"How could you? You seduced your own son!"

"You say that like it's a bad thing? It's a family tradition, passed on from generation to generation in Mystic culture."

"We never slept with our children," James supplied.

"Silence!"

"I believe you forget yourself, Callisto. You may be a power within The Society, but here with us real supernaturals you are nothing," James said.

James saw the rage in her eyes, but she knew he spoke the truth.

"I've just come for my son. Let him leave with me now and his father won't go on a rampage, slaughtering everything in his path," Cassandra said.

"He's mine. Besides, he has no intention of returning to any of you."

"You can't take him from me!"

"He came willingly. Now leave this place and never return."

"This is far from over. You will regret your actions here today."

"Oh how little you frighten me, Callisto. Go away before I send you to be with your lost lover."

As quickly as she'd appeared she was gone.

"Well, that was unexpected. How did she find you, James?" Alexander asked.

"Like calls to like," Kain explained. "All Mystics worth their salt can seek out their family through their blood unless the family member they are trying to reach is blocking them somehow. You must be blocking your family, so she reached out to James. But I'm curious to know how she knew you were with him."

James' phone rang in the silence. It was Samuel.

"Here, Alexander. It's Samuel."

"Hello," Alexander said.

"Alex! I need your help. Send someone to get me. Your crazy brother killed one of my cousins for information on your whereabouts. They didn't believe me when I told them y'all was dead. He'll come for me," Sam said.

"Where are you? I'll send Kain. Here, Kain, find out where he is and go get him," Alexander said.

Alexander watched as Kain spoke with Samuel, then disappeared.

He was back in less than ten seconds, with Samuel in tow.

"Sam, what the hell happened?" Alexander asked.

"Your family is insane, that's what happened. Misha threatened my mama and family, so I put a shotgun to his head. I guess he didn't like that either, so he kidnapped and tortured one of my cousins. My whole pack had to move. I didn't go with them because I figured they'd be safer. Which reminds me I need to call my mama. Give me a minute."

"Maybe I should just call Misha and tell him to stop looking for me," Alexander said.

"Knowing your brother, do you honestly think it will work?" Kain asked.

Alexander thought about it for a moment and realized that no, it wouldn't. Misha would never stop until he brought Alexander back home.

"Doesn't matter. I'm not going back. What do we do now?" Alexander asked.

"We get Isobelle healed up, finish our mating, and then we pool every resource we have together to get ready for war," James said. "This ends once and for all. The Mooyer Society has been allowed to survive for far too long. Kain, show Samuel to a spare room, then meet me in the basement. Alexander, you stay here with Isobelle. We won't be long."

James made his way to the basement where The Oracle was being held. He needed to wake them up. He couldn't wait for them to come out of their coma on their own anymore. With as much power as he could gather safely without killing them, he shocked them awake. Their combined screams were music to his ears.

"Good then, you're awake," James said.

CHAPTER 38

Jennifer could feel the power gathering around her children. An Oracle. It was unheard of. Oracles had always been identical. She didn't know what this meant for her children, and she wasn't sure she wanted to know. She didn't know anything anymore. She'd seen a spark of her old Krista today, and it only served to break her heart. She didn't know if she could kill her. She'd had no problem killing the rest of her family, but this was her child—her firstborn at that. Maybe she could reason with her. Didn't she owe it to not only herself but also to Krista to try?

"What are you thinking about so hard?" Jackson asked. "You think of names yet?"

"Just thinking of everything that's happened in the past twenty-four hours."

"Yeah, I hear ya. It's been some weird shit going on, that's for sure."

"How are my little wolf pups?" Taylor asked.

As soon as he said wolf pups, both babies shifted into little wolves.

"Um, are they supposed to be able to do that at their age?" Jennifer asked.

"No. They should have had another thirteen years before that was possible," Jackson said.

"I thought so," Jennifer said.

"So who's all freaking out right now?" Taylor asked.

They all raised their hands in the air.

"Maybe ask them to shift back?" Jackson suggested.

"Good idea," Jennifer said.

"Hey pups, why don't you shift back? You're freaking your parents out," Taylor said.

Jackson punched him in the arm.

"What was that for?" Taylor asked.

"Don't tell them stuff like that," Jackson said.

"Hey, it worked," Jennifer said.

They looked down and the babies were back to being babies.

"I'll be damned! Our babies are geniuses. They take after me that way," Taylor puffed.

"Get over yourself," Jennifer said. "Get out of here, you two, so we can get some rest."

"Wait, baby names, woman!" Jackson said.

"Oh yeah, right. Let me think for a moment," Jennifer said.

Jennifer thought about names for her babies. They had to have their parents' last names, of course, so they just needed first and middle names.

"Katarina Bristol Johnston Durham Dawls and Kili Bastiaan Johnston Durham Dawls," Jennifer said.

"They're perfect," Jackson said.

"What do you think, little pups? Like your new names?" Taylor asked.

Little wolf howls came from human throats so they took it as a yes.

"Okay, now go away so we can rest," Jennifer said.

"Fine, but you don't get to hog them all the time," Taylor pouted.

"You say that now, but just wait until they start screaming and throwing things," Jennifer said.

"Wolf pups don't throw things," Jackson said.

"We'll see," Jennifer said.

After Jackson and Taylor had kissed her and the children, Jennifer snuggled down with her little bugs and fell asleep.

"So what are we going to do now?" Nathan asked Krista.

"What do you mean?" Krista asked.

"I mean things are different now. Everything we thought we knew, we had no idea."

"The plan hasn't changed," Krista said.

"You can't be serious," Taz interjected.

"What? You think I should back down?"

"I think there are bigger things in play, and we are going to need your father to defeat whatever those things are," Taz said.

"I don't care."

"What do you mean you don't care? We are going to need all hands on deck for this, whatever this is," Nathan said.

"He isn't allowed to get away with what he did. I was named the destroyer of this world, and I plan on doing just that, destroying it," Krista said.

"Okay then… you destroy the entire world and everyone in it. What does that accomplish? What about your siblings? You feel good knowing you're going to sacrifice them?" Nathan asked.

"That's not fair!" Krista screamed.

"Oh, and killing them along with all the world because you were tortured by your father is?" Taz asked.

"So what? I just give him a pass?" Krista asked.

"You know what, you heard Alexander's speech about choices. Do what you want, Krista, you will anyway," Nathan said. "Come on, Taz, I'm hungry, and I'm sure everyone else is, too.

CHAPTER 39

Alexander looked around at the Council and members within The Society. It was time a few changes were made. They'd allowed certain things to go on for far too long.

"I'm sure most of you are wondering why this meeting has been called," Alexander began. "I assure you it's for nothing good. It is with a heavy heart that I'm suspending operation of the secret, secret society at once. We've been betrayed by one of our own. We've been lied to and led to believe that two of our members were murdered when, in fact, they are still alive and have been kidnapped. We know who took them, and we know who lied to us. Both situations will be dealt with swiftly, but the matter of shutting down an operation that's been in practice for centuries will take time. Some will even have to be put down as well, to make an example out of them. We must be united on this, as we can no longer afford to be divided in our intentions. Our mission statement is simple, and it is time we got back to our roots."

"So we are to just sit back while you kill members of our family, Legacy members at that?" the head of the Connelly family asked.

"You are either with us or against us. If you are against us, you are easily replaced. We've inbred ourselves too closely to our enemies. I don't know what Callisto was thinking when she was alive, but she overreacted, as I heard was the cause with a lot of things she did. It's no wonder she met her end so quickly. She is the reason we've strayed so far from our path, but it's time we fix the sins of our mothers and fathers before us. Those who object, voice your opinions quickly because the quicker you speak up, the quicker you can be made to choke on your own blood. I'll put it to a vote only once. Yes or no?"

"Yes," Derrick said.

"Yes," the Connelly head said.

"Yes," the Singer head said.

"Yes," the Mason head said.

"Yes," the O'Brien head said.

"Great choice, gentlemen. Now, you have two weeks to bring me names, and then we go hunting. Dismissed!"

Alexander was done with the passive bullshit. He should have put an end to the outside breeding when he first took over as head of the Carvanis family. It was a mistake he was paying for now. His son was going through who only knew what, and he wasn't sure how much longer he had before he'd be finding his body discarded like a piece of trash on the side of the road. No, he would not sit around and wait any longer for action to be taken. He'd be ruthless in his hunt for his youngest son. He was going to have to go back to the days of his most successful hunts. He would show no mercy, not even to his own family. After all, it was his family that started this, and his family would end it. Callisto was lucky he wasn't alive during her reign, or he'd have put her down like the rabid dog she was. Then he wouldn't have to deal with the aftermath of her idiotic plans.

Malik and Nathaniel concentrated as hard as they could, but they still couldn't access the full extent of their powers. Maybe they weren't trying hard enough, or they were trying too hard. Whatever the case, they needed to figure it out and fast.

"We aren't doing something right!" Nathaniel exclaimed.

"Maybe we are just trying too hard. Let's take a break, I'm starving, and I smell food in the kitchen."

"Okay, but one more time. Then we can eat," Nathaniel pleaded.

"Yes, now close your eyes and concentrate."

Malik and Nathaniel faced each other and held their palms out, touching each other. Nathaniel started a low hum in his throat, and Malik followed his lead shortly thereafter. They swayed to the tune from side to side and concentrated on seeing the future of the world. Malik was just about ready to give up, but a tingle had formed at the base of his back. It traveled up his spine and along his arms until it reached his fingertips. He knew that moment his power met his brother's because he saw The Mooyer Society as clear as if he were standing outside the compound at that moment. Alexander had gathered the Council and the secret, secret members and basically declared war on all paranormals and even members of their own families. He was planning a massacre. They couldn't let it come to pass. Spilling that much blood would cause a stain upon the earth, a stain that would call to a greater evil. Before the seeing ended, one word was whispered unto them: Venefica.

"We must warn everyone at once. We are running out of time," Malik said.

"I thought for sure we'd have more. We need to ask James who the Venefica are but later. Tonight we have time, and I just want to eat and rest," Nathaniel said.

"I agree. Besides, they still haven't gotten all the answers from The Oracle yet. Let's go downstairs and see what's being served for dinner.

CHAPTER 40

"What did I miss?" Kain asked James.

"Nothing yet. Our guests have just woken up.

"Good, I'll just pull up a chair and let you do what you do best."

James had really missed this side of Kain. The side that was so full of rage he didn't care what happened. He rarely got to see this side of his lover, but when he did, all he wanted to do was lock them in a room and not leave for days. But that would have to wait. They had work to do.

"Did you enjoy your nap, Oracle?" James asked.

"Let us out of the cage, and we'll show you," Angeline taunted.

"What? You're speaking independently now?" James mocked.

"Go back to Hell!" Fatima shouted.

"Ladies first, but before I reunite you with your parents, I have a few questions I need answers to. It should be stated that I'm prepared to get said answers by any means I see fit."

"Kain, you're going to let him do this to us? We are your mates," Angeline pleaded.

The electric current traveling along Kain's skin was enough to make James hard. He'd missed that particular power of Kain's. He'd done some wicked things to James with that power, but as pleasurable as it was, James also knew how deadly it could be.

"You are nothing but filthy liars. My grandfather removed whatever curse your mothers put on me, and I now see you for what you truly are. If James doesn't end up killing you, make no mistake—I will. Speak to me again, and I'll have your tongue cut out," Kain

said.

The electric current leapt from his skin and skated along the bars of the cell. The twins took several steps back. James didn't blame them. He knew there was enough current flowing out of Kain to kill forty men, so two Mystics considerably younger than both of them would be no problem. They didn't possess even half the powers their mothers had.

"I suggest you make this easy on yourselves and tell us what we need to know voluntarily," James said. "If I have to ask questions, I'll get cranky, and I get power happy when I'm cranky."

"Do your worst, there hasn't been a cage built that would keep us captive for long," Angeline spat. "Do what you will, but we will not break. We will be free of these bars, and when we are, we'll make sure everything you hold dear will suffer. Don't worry, we'll save you front row seats."

"Does your sister speak for you?" James asked Fatima.

"Always."

"Don't say I didn't warn you."

Hours later James could still hear their screams echoing in his ears. They hadn't said a word. If James wasn't so annoyed, he might have been impressed. As it was, he was tired, hungry, and anxious to complete his mating. He stopped at the kitchen with Kain right behind him and fixed himself a plate. He did the same for Isobelle, while Kain fixed Alexander and himself one. He wasn't sure who had done the cooking, but his mouth watered at the sight of spaghetti and garlic bread. He put two drinks in his pocket and did the same with Kain. They headed upstairs to eat and complete their foursome. James had a feeling that tonight would be the last bit of quiet before all hell broke loose. They would need to break The Oracle. They needed to know exactly what they had planned and what they'd already put in motion. The survival of the entire planet rested on those answers, and James had every intention of getting them before the week was over.

"We can't tell them, we can never tell them," Fatima sobbed.

Angeline didn't know how she had the strength to even talk.

Actually, she did know. Angeline had taken the brunt of the torture. Had she not, her sister would have squealed hours ago. She wasn't as strong as Angeline because she was second born. So it was up to Angeline to keep them on track. She couldn't even speak to comfort her sister; she was in that much pain. James was worse than their mothers. She thought she'd known what pain was growing up in that house, but she was so very wrong. And it was only the beginning of their torment. James enjoyed causing them pain. Got off on it.

"Do you hear me, sister?" Fatima asked.

Still, Angeline couldn't muster the energy to talk or even send a wave of energy to her sister. Several of her bones were broken, including her neck. She would take at least a few days to heal from her injuries. She just hoped James waited that long before coming back down for answers, but unfortunately she knew that he would not. The last thing she felt was her sister crawling behind her and wrapping her arms around her and sobbing. She was going to have to find her strength somewhere because if she did not, her sister was going to tell them exactly what they wanted to know, and Angeline couldn't let her do it.

Alexander rubbed the cool cloth along Isobelle's body to help soothe the burning pain. She'd stopped screaming and occasionally let out a whimper or two. Constantine was an asshole and a powerful one at that. For all his talk about her being the chosen one, he had no problem almost killing her. All because she had no intention of fixing the mistake he so foolishly made in his youth. It pissed Alexander off that he cared so little for her welfare, but who was he fooling? No one but himself. He knew what these monsters were capable of.

Could he even call them that anymore, seeing as he was one of them? Yes, he could. He didn't hurt people just for the sake of it or because they didn't agree with him. He'd done a job, and he didn't relish the kill. He didn't savor it for days and think upon it days later. He wasn't a monster, but he'd allowed himself to be mated to one. Isobelle as well. He could have stopped it. Hell, he probably should have stopped it. But he wasn't sure about anything anymore, and as long as James didn't hurt Isobelle or him, he'd ignore everything else.

Then there was Kain. He didn't know what to think of the fact that he was also their mate, although James had made it clear from the beginning that he intended for Kain to be a part of their lives. The only consolation was that Kain wasn't as violent as James. Yes, he'd killed Eli's sons, but it was more out of grief and love, not cold-blooded malice. It took years to finally learn the name of the creature that had been responsible for the start of The Mooyer Society. It was Callisto, his mother, who actually put it in the journals. She must have learned it from James.

Alexander still couldn't get over his fucked up family tree. He couldn't imagine his mother as the bloodthirsty girl described in those journals. She'd been nothing like that while he was growing up. She'd been attentive and loving, in the way that she knew how to love. She'd favored him more than any of his other siblings besides Misha, and now he knew why. It was making perfect sense. He was brought out of his musing by the sound of Isobelle's soft whisper.

"What happened? Where are we?" Isobelle asked.

"We are at the house Krista found. James brought most of us here after Constantine fried all your nerves."

"What an ass. I can't believe he did that because he wasn't getting his way. I see where James got it from."

Alexander chuckled at her assessment. He could see it a little.

"Speaking of James, where is he?" Isobelle asked.

"I'm here and I come bearing rations," James said.

Alexander helped Isobelle sit up so she could eat. The four of them piled on the bed and started to eat their food. The spaghetti and garlic bread was some of the best he'd ever had.

"Whoever cooked this needs to make it a weekly thing. This is delicious," Alexander said between bites.

"Would you like to be alone with your food?" Isobelle teased.

"Possibly," Alexander said.

They all laughed at his excitement over the pasta.

"Did you get anything out of The Oracle, James?" Alexander asked.

"No, but one is weaker than the other. We'll go in again tomorrow. It shouldn't take long since I've worn down the stronger one. Now I just need to work on the other. She'll be spilling all their secrets in no time," James said.

"Good, the quicker we know what they know, the quicker we'll know what we're dealing with. We need to get everyone together to gather as much information as we can. Isobelle and I also need to start training again. We've gone too long without sparring."

"I can train with you both. James doesn't need my help to get the information he needs, and frankly, if I have to lay eyes on either of them again I'm liable to kill them before they tell us anything," Kain said.

"I think that's a good idea," Isobelle said. "We can't send them to their maker just yet. Now are we going to address the elephant in the room or do I need to just come out and say it again?"

"Can we at least finish our meal before you talk about the mating?" Alexander asked.

"We will have to do more than just drink blood this time. We will have to consummate it," Isobelle explained.

"Consum—" Alexander started. "Can't you just say sex?"

"I'm trying to make everyone comfortable is all," Isobelle said.

"Children, behave," James said.

"We have plenty of time to discuss our mating," Kain said.

"Actually we don't. I had a little vision when I was out of commission. We need to have sex and mate fully tonight. We can't wait any longer. So eat up boys and freshen up. We have work to do."

"You make it sound so cold and clinical," Alexander said.

"What? You want chocolates and flowers? I'm the one losing my virginity to three guys at once, so I get to make it sound however I want."

"Touché," Alexander said.

They ate the rest of their meal in silence. Kain took the dirty plates back downstairs, and Isobelle took a shower. Twenty minutes later they were all showered and sitting on the bed in their pajamas, the men in just the bottoms and Isobelle in a tank and shorts.

"So how are we supposed to do this?" Isobelle asked.

No one said a word or moved for that matter.

"Okay, I'll start," Isobelle said.

Isobelle pulled her shirt over her head and took off her shorts. She wasn't wearing any panties so it didn't take long before she was standing in front of the three men, naked. She heard their sharp intakes of breaths and considered it a good sign. It was as if a spell had been cast. All at once, three pairs of hands were touching every inch of her body. She closed her eyes to get the full feel of every touch, every lick, and every nip. She was lowered to the bed, but by who she couldn't tell. Not yet anyway, but one day she would know the distinct caressing of each individual man. Today she would just enjoy the sensations they were producing together.

She gasped when she felt one set of lips on each breast and the last set at her core. It was a triple assault, and she could barely catch her breath from it all. She was in sensory overload and couldn't figure out which way was up. She didn't know if she wanted to move her hips, push down on the heads at her breasts, or just scream to the heavens. Had she known sex could feel this good, she would have given it up a long time ago. Okay, that was a lie, she'd only ever wanted to have sex with one person before James imprisoned them in his dungeon. Having three men on her at once was almost too much to bear.

"I can't...I don't...oh my god!"

She couldn't even produce words properly. She heard a chuckle to her left and growled in response. It wasn't funny. Her brain was turning into mush. Isobelle let out a sound she'd never heard before when two fingers were shoved inside her roughly along with the pull/push of her clitoris. It was hot... she was so damn hot. It felt nothing like the first time between Alex, James, and her. This time was a million times more intense. Was it because they were finally complete? She didn't know, but she wasn't ready for any of these feelings to stop.

She groaned in protest when the sucking on her clit abruptly stopped.

"Patience," a voice that sounded suspiciously like Alexander's muttered.

He was first. He was going first. Isobelle almost came right then and there. She'd waited so long, years in fact, for this day to come. Now that it was finally here, she was about to be done before he'd even slipped the tip in. She had to distract herself, but she could barely string coherent thoughts together. Thankfully, she didn't have to wait long before he was sliding home with a groan of his own.

Isobelle let out a shriek when the thin barrier inside her was broken, but she quickly forgot about the pain when he started to thrust. And oh did he thrust. He filled up every available inch of space she had, and it felt incredible. The sucking on her breasts became full-on bites as fangs pierced her flesh, sending her pleasure to another level. Honestly, she believed she blacked out for a moment. When she could feel again, she was coming, and she didn't think she would stop anytime soon.

A bloody wrist was shoved into her mouth, and she knew from the taste that it wasn't James or Alex's blood. It was Kain's. It was a bit sweeter than James but still just as strong. She heard a shout from Alex followed by spurts of warmth. He pulled himself out of her and switched places with one of her other mates. She thought it was Kain, but she couldn't be sure. Whoever it was, the man wasted no time in filling her to capacity again. She let out a purr when her sweet spot was tapped and tried her best to arch her back with the weight of her other two mates pressed against her chest. One abandoned her breast for her mouth, and she moaned into it. It had to be Alexander because she felt fangs in her breast again. She once again floated into that place between being awake and being unconscious.

She held it in just as long as the first time she came, until she was sent back into another body numbing orgasm. She didn't know how much more she could take. She'd lost count already. She just had to last until James got a turn. She could feel the strings that tied them all together grow tighter. The only thing missing was Kain biting Alex, which Isobelle hoped would transpire soon. She felt Kain go still against her before he bellowed his completion and eased his way out of her. She could feel the semen leaking out of her and pooling beneath. It made it easy for James to slide quickly inside her. She felt Kain and Alexander shift to the side of the bed, then James had his fangs embedded in her throat as he pounded her for all she was worth. It felt fantastic.

Without removing himself from her core or his fangs from her neck, he'd managed to pick her up and set her on top of him. He never once stopped pumping inside her, and for the twentieth time she was coming and screaming and coming again. She could feel sleep lulling her in, but before it was able to claim her completely, she felt the final string of their bonds snap into place. Needless to say, she fell asleep with a smile on her face. As far as losing one's virginity went, she had no complaints at all.

CHAPTER 41

Constantine sat in his bed and sighed. He was getting too old for this world. He'd been among the first children born to the supernaturals. Maybe it was time to call it a day and join the rest of his family in Hell. It wasn't a particularly bad place to be. It was just like Earth but without all the damn drama.

"What's wrong with you?" Rory asked from the bed beside him.

"Tired. Maybe we should have joined our wives after they were killed a few centuries ago," Constantine said.

"Don't be foolish. After all these millennium, we can finally be together without worrying what anyone would say. Or is that the problem? You're still ashamed all these centuries later?"

"Of course not. We're old, too old, for wars and fighting."

"Who says we have to fight? Being old has its advantages. You let the young fight the battles while you sit on the sidelines and cheer."

"Perhaps. But you know as well as I do, they will need our strength. They can't fight more than one enemy at a time, and I have a feeling they will have to battle not only the Mystic Oracle, but Krista, the Venefica, and The Society as well."

"The Venefica? They are of no concern. They hide out in the shadows and never leave their little mountain unless they've been kicked out. And when they are they don't last long before they are killed. The Venefica don't scare me," Rory scoffed.

"I wouldn't dismiss them just yet."

"And that's why you're stressed, worried about things that shouldn't even register on your radar."

"Just be glad you aren't a Seer."

"I've killed and absorbed enough Mystic powers that I'm as good as one."

"Indeed you have. Tell me then what you have seen."

"The usual: death, ruin, and destruction. Some won't make it, while others will barely be able to hold on."

"Sounds about right."

Rory watched as his lover's eyes went white. He was having a vision. He hated Constantine's visions. They always left him incapacitated for several days. He did the only thing he could do in this situation: make him comfortable on the bed. Once that was done, he gathered all the things he would need to assist Constantine once the visions let him go. He hated what the visions did to him. Hated how weak they made him afterward. He wouldn't be able to take care of himself for days. He didn't care what Constantine said; he was glad both of their wives had perished. They were in the way anyway, and he hated to see Maria's hands on what belonged to him. Every time he witnessed her hands on him he wanted to rip her apart. The happiest day in his life was hearing she'd passed alongside Regal in a village uprising. Served them both right.

He wasn't ashamed to admit that he had lost no love for either of them. The only thing useful they had done was produce their children to carry on the family names. He'd gladly go another two or three thousand years without seeing either one of them again. It was his time to be with Constantine, and he wasn't quite ready to give him up, if ever. He lay next to his lover and prepared himself to ride out the storm. Whatever it was he was seeing, they would deal with it together.

Cassandra, or Callisto, as she'd once been called, sulked in the shadows. She would give anything to be running The Society again. She could barely contain her rage at her current husband planning to undo all her hard work with a war they didn't need. They should be fighting the full bloods, not each other. She'd incorporated more supernatural blood into The Society as a way for them to have an advantage, and now they were throwing centuries of work out the window. She was half tempted to march in there and kill them all, but that would expose her hand too soon. So she watched and waited, two things she did best, and when the time was right, she would show them all why she was so feared during her reign.

She had preparations to make before she revealed her true identity. She couldn't wait to see the look on her current husband's face when he realized who she really was. He would die by her hand just as every husband before him had. She would take out the pain of losing her lover on everyone until the day she no longer drew breath and was sent to join him. But it wasn't yet time for her goodbyes. She needed to ensure her legacy wasn't destroyed. She'd worked too hard to mold The Society to her plan, and she'd be damned if she'd let Alexander Carvanis fuck them all up.

She was a Carvanis long before he existed, and she was sure she'd be one long after he was dead and buried. She needed to find Misha. At the moment, he was the only one she could trust of all her children. For all his talk, he knew as well as she did what his father would do to him if he found out Alexander was his son. He'd keep their secret if he knew what was good for him. Her son was a lot of things, but stupid had never been one of them.

Kiateya felt the shift in the winds. A storm was coming, but she didn't know when and she didn't know why. She would need to gather her Chowder and make preparations to evacuate and take shelter in their other compound, the one with better security. The one they were in now could easily be breached, and she couldn't take the chance. She called her husband on the phone and told him her thoughts.

He agreed and said he would start gathering the families and prepare for the long journey. Kiateya texted her children and told them to gather only what they would need and to be ready to leave at first light. She texted Nathan Jr. and told him they were going to the other compound. He thought it was a great idea. She asked him what he knew, and he responded that he would talk to her in a few days. He was still gathering information and wanted to relay it all at once. She texted her goodbyes and went to gather things from her office then to find her husband. They had to move quickly—Kiateya feared that waiting until first light would be too late. They needed to leave in the next few hours.

She found her family and let them know about the change of plans. Two hours later their compound was deserted, and they were on their way up into the mountains. Kiateya wouldn't settle down until they arrived at their destination.

"We can't find the Dylia pack or the Chowder of Hyjias. It looks as if both groups left in rather a hurry. Many items were left behind, and everything is in disarray. We have no idea which way they headed either," Daniel Carvanis told his father, Alexander.

"They couldn't have gone far. Send out search teams. I want them found. Someone knows something, and I want to know what they know. I want that information as soon as you have it. Lives depend on it. Do you hear me?" Alexander said.

"Yes, Father. It will be done."

Daniel hung up and looked at his sisters, Samantha and Veronica.

"He's not happy. He wants search teams, and he's out for blood. At this point, I don't think it matters whose it is if he doesn't get Alexander back soon."

"Unbelievable!" Samantha screamed. "He didn't even want him when he found out Mom was pregnant again, now he doesn't care how many of us are sacrificed to find him."

"He's lost his mind along with Mother and Misha. We just need to make sure we don't get caught in the crossfire. I have no desire to die for any of them," Veronica said.

"I don't believe we have a choice in the matter," Daniel said gravely. "All three of them will gladly offer us up for a trade-off to have Alex back. How do we know he didn't leave on his own? I don't like any of this. I haven't for months. I don't know about the two of you, but I plan to do a bit of investigating of my own."

"Lead the way, little brother," Samantha said.

"I'm right behind you," Veronica said.

"Good, let's start with this compound. Maybe the cats left something of use behind."

EPILOGUE

After walking forever with only a few breaks in between, Sy and her husband, Jamie, had finally made it to Massachusetts. They were exhausted but determined to get to the place she had felt the presence of her brothers. The tiny pull from the spell was still working, and they found a back road that would have been impossible to spot. They forced their legs to move until they came upon an iron gate.

Sy looked around and found a little machine attached to the gate. She pressed the button with the telephone icon on it.

"Well, here goes nothing," Sy said to Jamie.

A few moments later a gruff voice came through the speaker.

"What?" the voice said sternly.

"Um, excuse me, but is there a Billy, Bane, or Brian available?" Sy asked.

"Who the hell wants to know?" the voice answered.

Sy looked around nervously. Would they remember her?

"Um, their little sister," Sy said.

There was a long pause on the line.

"What is your name?" a different voice boomed.

"Sy," Sy squeaked out.

After several moments the iron gates creaked opened.

"Come to the front door," the second voice said as the speaker clicked off.

"Well, here goes nothing," Sy said, breathless. "You ready, Jamie? Get your power ready in case they try anything crazy. We don't know who else is here."

"Got it," Jamie said.

They walked through the gates, and Sy saw a few wolves to her right, staring at them. Oh crap! Why were their wolves just roaming about? Sy grabbed Jamie's hand and picked up the pace. The door was already opened when they arrived at the front porch, and three sets of identical faces with golden eyes were staring at her. Sy stopped abruptly and let fire dance in her hand.

"Put your fire away, little sister. My name is Brian," Brian said.

So that was the voice yelling at her through the speaker.

"Yes, unless you want us to drown you with water," the first voice said. "By the way, I'm Bane."

"So I take it you must be Billy," Sy said to the last face.

"Correct," Billy said. "What are you doing here? Were you banished?"

"Not exactly," Sy said.

Brian smirked.

"Really? How about you tell us exactly what happened? Come in," Brian said.

Sy pulled Jamie behind her as they followed after her older brothers. They led her to a huge sitting room. Once she sat down, her story just spilled out of her mouth. She could see the array of emotions that simultaneously adorned their faces as she recounted every little detail. Once she was finished, she sat back and waited. She didn't have to wait long.

"Before this goes any further, you need to know the truth," Billy said.

"The truth? What truth is that?" Sy asked.

"That our mother and Elder Julie are liars. We are half Dylia—werewolves. That's why we were banished. Not the ridiculous story that the cursed Elder Julie's mother came up with. Not because we didn't pass our stupid Rumspringa. We passed that with flying colors. Our mother didn't want your father to know she had been unfaithful with our father. Venefica never have triplets. If everyone didn't have their heads up their asses they would have realized the problem," Billy explained.

"Yes. We don't know how the current Elders found out what was going on, but they did. Our mother and Julie put on a great show, though. They are more than just good friends. They are in love and sneak around all the time when they think no one will notice. The Venefica aren't all good and holy, as everyone seems to believe. They want people to believe that. It's why they isolate themselves so much. They don't want people to see them for who they really are," Brian added.

"But you have been through enough," Bane said. "We can finish this later. For now, you need rest and a damn bath." He cocked his head to one side like a wolf. "Did you two marry?"

"She's mine," Jamie spoke up for the first time.

"We didn't have the ceremony, but we've looked out for each other these last six months. Why?" Sy asked.

"No reason. I guess you two can share a room," Bane said.

The triplets showed them to a fairly large room that also had a bathroom attached to it. They called it a suite. Well, it was certainly sweet. They didn't have things like this in their Amish-like village. They showed them how to work some of the basic things and left them to it and said they would catch up later.

She and Jamie cleaned up and got ready for bed. As she lay next to him, she couldn't help but nudge him before he fell asleep.

"Jamie," Sy said.

"Mm," Jamie mumbled.

"I think we are going to love it here."

And with that Sy fell asleep, nestled under Jamie's arm.

The triplets knocked on the open front door and waited for someone to allow them in.

"What do you boys need?" Jackson asked.

"It's more of what we need to tell you," Billy said.

"Okay, we're listening," Taylor said.

"We aren't full Dylia," Bane said.

"I'm not sure what you mean," Jackson said. "You smell like a wolf, and you can change like the rest of us. Besides, I don't smell anything else."

"That's because we are half Venefica, and we can twist a spell or two," Brian said.

"I'm sorry, Venefica? As in the elusive cult of supernaturals that no one has seen for pretty much ever?" Taylor said.

"Exactly," Billy said.

"And why have you decided to tell us this now?" Jackson asked.

"We have decided to wage war against our coven," Brian responded.

Fire leaped from Brian's hands, denoting the rage burning inside of him. Taylor took a few steps back with his hands up.

"And what is that?" Taylor asked.

"Oh, it's his Adducere element," Bane explained. "Most Venefica have a lead element that's better than the others, but we can still manipulate them all."

"I see. Seems we need to have a long, long conversation, boys. Have a seat—this might take a while," Jackson said.

"We need to find her before she finds them. If she gets to them before we do, they will come for us. You remember what they said, don't you?" Harper asked.

"Shut up, you idiot," Julie snapped. "This is all your doing. You just couldn't do as you were told, and now we have to clean up your mess, one that should have been dealt with long ago. We must gather the coven and prepare for war. It's time Billy, Bane, and Brian Cole were put to death for their treason."

"I told you to convince your mother not to banish them. All you had to do was tell her not to, and she'd have done it."

"So this is *my* fault?"

"You could have tried harder is all I'm saying," Harper said.

"And you could have kept your legs shut, but you don't see me throwing that around in your face, do you?"

"You just did."

"I have no time for you. Let's go. We have a score to settle."

To be continued…

CALL TO ACTION

The author thanks you for buying a genuine edition of this book by complying with the author's copyright.

Your feedback in providing an honest review would be appreciated, but in no way is expected. Losing yourself in this story for a few hours is one of the author's rewards.

If you want to stay informed on other stories by the author, you can sign up for the author's [http://www.authorshakuitajohnson.com/newsletter] newsletter to receive updates, bonus content and more.

OTHER WORKS FROM THIS AUTHOR

DARK INDISCRETIONS SERIES

Dark Indiscretions Book 0.5 - *Now Available*
Dark Indiscretions Book 1 - *Now Available (FREE)*
Dark Indiscretions: Monster Unleashed Book 2 - *Now Available*
Dark Indiscretions: Seer Destined Book 3 - *Now Available*
Rumspringa Book 3.5 (Same world as Dark Indiscretions) - *Now Available*
Dark Indiscretions: Triple Cursed Book 4 – *Now Available*
Dark Indiscretions: Past Hunted Book 5 - *Coming Soon*

COLLECTION OF POEMS

Inside The Heart Of My Soul - *Now Available*
Days To Come - *Now Available*
Heart Speak: Complete Works of Inside The Heart Of My Soul and Days To Come (Paperback and Audio) - *Now Available*

STAND ALONE

And So She Waited - *Now Available*

THE DARK INDISCRETIONS CHRONICLES

Callisto Carvanis: And A Legacy Was Born - *Now Available*

SHAKUITA JOHNSON

KISS AND TELL: ENCOUNTERS OF A PROSTITUTE

Vixen - *Now Available*
Diamond - *Now Available*
Candy - *Now Available*
Madeline - *Now Available*
Star - *Now Available*
Asterisk - *Now Available*
Complete Box Set Vol. 1-6 - *Now Available*

Wanton Secrets

Wanton Secrets – Currently featured in SMUT... Coming Soon

NON-FICTION

Letters To Kyle - Now Available

NEXT INSTALLMENT
RUMSPRINGA

Set in the same world as Dark Indiscretions comes a story about love, sacrifice, perseverance, and magic.

What would you do for love? Would you sit by and let it pass you by, or would you grab onto it no matter the cost? Would you break the rules and leave everyone else behind so guarantee your own happiness?

Sy Cole wants what all sixteen-year-old girls in her coven want. To master one of the four elements, move out of her parents' home, and into her new one with her chosen husband. It seemed all that was within her grasp, when it was brutally snatched away.

Instead of sitting by and letting her life be dictated, she acted. When faced with having to choose family over love, she chose love. She took control of her life and went on a journey that would turn all she knew and was always told upside down.

On the run and looking over her shoulder Sy, along with her love Jamie, look for the only people she believes can help them now…her brothers.

Join Sy as she undergoes the ceremony that changes her life forever. Whether it's for good or bad is still to be determined.

PROLOGUE

MIDDLE OF NOWHERE, RHODE ISLAND, 1999

Billy, Bane, and Brian Cole, identical triplets, looked at the bulletin board in the old barn for the tenth time in two days. Their sixteenth birthday was in another week, and then their Rumspringa would begin. Up to four days of elemental magic trials—air, water, earth, and fire. They couldn't wait; they were each hoping for something different. Even though they weren't full Venefica—Sorcerers, they could still create elemental magic. No one but their mother and her best friend knew they were also Dylia—werewolves. Not even their "father". They were made to swear not to ever say anything and to never shift around anyone no matter what.

If they did, they would be killed and so would their mother. It was taboo in the Venefica to intermix with species. Their mother made a 'mistake', as she liked to call it, by sleeping with their father. Seems their mother made many 'mistakes' that she didn't want people knowing about. Whatever, they didn't really care. As long as their Rumspringa was a success. They weren't thrilled about the getting married part but whatever. They didn't like keeping their hair as long as a girl's either, but sacrifices had to be made.

This was their home. They were safe here and had two baby sisters to protect. They were pretty sure they would have an Adducere—lead element, even though they were half werewolf. They began reading the board again. Something about it just didn't sit right with them.

LAWS OF THE VENEFICA

1. *Absolutely no inter-species mating of any kind. You marry who the Elders tell you.*
2. *Absolutely no same-sex anything of any kind. If you are caught you will be beaten. NO questions asked. NO explanations.*
3. *The Elders word is LAW. ALWAYS. To oppose them is treason.*
4. *The Rumspringa is our most scared and time-honored tradition. Those who don't take it seriously will be punished harshly.*
5. *Anyone who violates any of these laws will be put to death immediately along with their entire family (after being beaten or punished).*

THE RULES OF THE RUMSPRINGA

1. *Those who don't master an Adducere will be banished*
2. *There will be up to four days of trials*
3. *Once the trials are over, there will be a completion ceremony*
4. *The Elders will announce who you will marry and when*
5. *Loss of control of your Adducere will not warrant banishment, you will just have to be taught harshly*

"This is craziness," Billy whispered to his brothers. "Why do we want to stay here again?"

"Because anything less will be getting our whole family killed. Think of our sisters," Bane reasoned.

"Yes, now let's stop talking about it before someone hears. We better go get to work on the farm before father starts looking for us," Brian said.

They made their way home and got to their chores before it was time for their afternoon school lessons with their mother.

***

The week passed fairly quickly. The boys dressed in their black ceremonial robes and met their father downstairs so they could eat breakfast and go down to the clearing. Their mother and sisters where at her best friend Julie's house, and they wouldn't see them until the completion ceremony on the fifth day. It was another one of the Veneficas ridiculous traditions.

They ate quickly and rinsed out their bowls. They followed their father and went outside. The Rumspringa went by quickly. Billy and

Bane's Adduceres were water. Brian didn't find his until the last day and it was fire. They were happy enough with the outcomes. At least they all found an Adducere and wouldn't be getting banished. One the day of the completion ceremony Brian had a bad feeling, but his brothers told him it was just nerves.

"Don't worry, Bri, we made it," Bane said.

"Oh course, you're right. I'm just a little nervous. Let's go before father has to come up here," Brian said.

They went downstairs and ate in relative silence. Their father broke it when he spoke.

"I'm very proud of you boys. It's unheard of for triplets to be born. I feel so lucky, and you all passed your Rumspringas," their father said.

The boys shifted around uncomfortably. Even though they loved him like their father, they felt bad that he didn't know he wasn't their birth father. Brian spoke for all of them, as he usually did.

"Thanks, Father. It means a lot to us," he said.

"Very well, let's go. Don't want to be late," their father replied.

They were barely on time for the ceremony. They made their way to the stage and got ready for the arrival of the Elders.

"Welcome to yet another successful Rumspringa," the Elder said. "It's amazing every six months that we do these. It takes me back to my own. Now before we proceed, we have an announcement to make. After careful consideration, my wife and I have come to a much-needed conclusion. We shouldn't have let it go on for this long."

What the hell was this about? The triplets gave each other confused looks. Never had a completion ceremony started this way.

"As you know, never in Venefica history have triplets been born. It's unheard of. There must be some kind of curse. We were hoping they would fail the Rumspringa, but sadly they didn't. It gives us no pleasure but Billy, Bane, and Brian Cole, you are banished. You have two hours to collect your things and say your goodbyes," the Elder announced.

What. The. Hell. This couldn't be happening. Before Brian could fully process the Elder's words, both his brothers had shifted. This was so not good. Panic broke out over the entire barn.

"Abominations!" the Elder's wife screamed. "Helen Cole, what is the meaning of this? I was there when you birthed these things. You have broken our laws."

"I was raped!" Helen sobbed. "I was so ashamed. I had no idea what their father was. If I had of know I would have killed them myself in the womb."

That lying bitch! Brian was furious that his mother would stoop to such lengths to protect her own life.

"It's true, Mother. Please, it wasn't her fault. We should have come to you, but we were afraid," Julie begged.

"It's okay, dear. We understand. We will kill them now. Helen, this isn't your fault. You were just a scared girl," the Elder said.

The triplets were outraged, liars, the both of them. Their father looked heartbroken as he tried to sooth their treacherous mother. Brian changed and motioned for his brothers to follow him. The Venefica were using their magic to try to slow them down, but their Dylia genes made them hard to pin down. They ran away from the coven and never looked back. They would never forget this day as long as they lived. They would have revenge on the entire Venefica coven if it was the last thing they ever did.

ABOUT THE AUTHOR

Shakuita Johnson is a 32-year-old Psychology major. When she isn't going to school or working, she is doing what she loves most. Writing. She started writing in middle school. Starting with poetry. Then short stories in a creative writing course her senior year.

Her love for paranormal and supernatural started with R.L. Stine's Goosebumps books and TV show, Anne Rice's Vampire Chronicles, and Christopher Pike books. She is an avid reader with over 200 books on her bookshelf and 1000 plus on her iPad.

Visit her online and read her poems and one attempt at songwriting on her blog at http://www.dark-indiscretions.com.

You can also find her Facebook Author Page at www.facebook.com/shakuitajohnson.

Or you can find her on her Website at http://www.authorshakuitajohnson.com.

Follow her on Twitter @sljay1184.

To receive up to date info, excerpts, and goodies please sign up for my newsletter http://www.authorshakuitajohnson.com/newsletter

Made in the USA
Monee, IL
11 May 2021